Land Acknowledgement

ʔukʼʷədiid čəɫ ʔuhigʷəd txʷəl tiiɫ ʔa čəɫ ʔal tə swatxʷixʷtxʷəd ʔə tiiɫ puyaləpabš. ʔa ti dxʷʔa ti swatxʷixʷtxʷəd ʔə tiiɫ puyaləpabš ʔəsɫaɫlil tulʼal tudiʔ tuhaʔkʷ. didiʔɫ ʔa həlgʷəʔ ʔal ti sləx̌il. dxʷəsɫaɫlils həlgʷəʔ gʷəl ƛʼuyayus həlgʷəʔ gʷəl ƛʼuƛʼax̌ʷad həlgʷəʔ tiiɫ bədədəʔs gʷəl tix̌dxʷ həlgʷəʔ tiiɫ ʔiišəds həlgʷəʔ gʷəl ƛʼuʔalalus həlgʷəʔ gʷəl ƛʼutxʷəlšucidəb. x̌ʷəla⋯b ʔə tiiɫ tuyəlʼyəlabs.

Blue Cactus Press is located in caləɫali. This land was stolen and colonized by settlers via the signing of the Treaty of Medicine Creek in 1854. Since then, it has not been returned to its rightful and traditional stewards: spuyaləpabš, the Tribe of Indians.

We acknowledge that we benefit from our existence at caləɫali. This acknowledgement is a small step on our path toward true allyship.

Praise for
Moss-Covered Claws

The fears and issues Barnett writes about are issues that people battle with in everyday life, but most importantly, the reader is left with a feeling of contentment and hopefulness.

– Seattle Gay Times

The young author's writing transcends numerous genres, from Queer fiction to fantasy and more. Barnett's works often metaphorically reflect the experiences of LGBT people, as they tend to be seen by society as monsters themselves.

– Tacoma Weekly

The stories in *Moss-Covered Claws* are wildly imaginative, sometimes brutal, sometimes terrifying, always fascinating. But underneath these tales of sea witches and bog monsters and interdimensional gateways and even a creature formed entirely of Benson Bubbler water fountains, lie the fears we all face: cruelty, loneliness, our past deeds, the things we can't control, the secrets we hold.

– Gigi Little, editor of City of Weird

A sharp-fanged debut story collection brimming with real and imagined horrors. These earthy and tangled fables shiver with metaphysical wonders, fierce monsters, courageous heroes, surreal violence, and the clawing anxieties that come with figuring out how to be and stay human in a world where the rules are constantly changing. If you have ever found yourself staring into a dappled forest with your wild heart pounding in your chest, wondering if the shadows at the edges are alive and have claws—this book is for you.

– Valerie Geary, author of *Crooked River*

As a former native of the Pacific Northwest, *Moss-Covered Claws* reignited my awe of nature, taking me on a surreal hike through ancient forests where monsters and humans exist in a wonderland of identity, desire, and vulnerability. This is an awe-inspiring and necessary collection from a writer you'll want to pay attention to.

– Sequoia Nagamatsu, author of *Where We Go When All We Were Is Gone*

If the Northwest offered a stock market for literary start ups, I'd recommend an all-in investment in Jonah Barnett, their superb talent, and growing collection of stories, essays and reviews. Jonah already has that thing so many writers covet: a voice. It is intelligently snarky, insightful and compelling. Hooray for Blue Cactus Press for recognizing a local author who's not afraid to write about home.

> – Bryan Willis, playwright-in-residence, Northwest
> Playwrights Alliance at Seattle Repertory Theatre

With a David Lynchian motif—'things are not what they seem'—Barnett's hallucinatory imagery conjures the horror of living in a world of climate change, fake news, and physical vulnerability. In these stories, alienation and lack of authentic connection are harbingers of violence: humans are pitted against animals, myth against reality, fear against friendship. These tales seem to emerge from the primordial muck and mystery of the unknown and remind us that human survival depends on our ability to turn and face that which creeps in the dark toward us.

> – Heather Momyer, author of *How to
> Swim* and publisher at Arc Pair Press

If Lovecraft lived and worked in the 21st century, if Philip K. Dick were joyfully queer instead of a cishet spouse abuser, if Jeff VanderMeer wrote about the Pacific Northwest rather than the Southern Reach, they may well have pooled their talents to concoct the yarns in Jonah Barnett's *Moss-Covered Claws*. I enjoyed all ten stories immensely and recommend them to anyone who ever sought and then savored the unsettling, supernatural psychodrama of the New Weird.

> – Christian Carvajal, author of *C Is
> for Collection* and *Lightfall*

*M*oss-Covered Claws beautifully digs its way into your mind with a collision of heartbreak and inspiration on every page. Much like a passenger on a train who never wants to reach their destination, each story leaves you craving for more time within Barnett's imagination.

– Jennifer Dean, author of *Bound*
and *I've Been Looking for You*

*W*ritten in vivid and quick-moving prose, this collection of stories from Jonah Barnett packs a visceral punch and asserts a point of view that challenges the way we understand the nature of loneliness and fear, gender and humanity. Our notions are made real, monstrous, ready to do battle. Though you'll tear through the stories, they'll call you back for a true unpacking, layer by mossy layer, as the true monsters are revealed. This is a young writer to watch.

– Averil Dean, author of *Alice Close
Your Eyes* and *The Undoing*

*J*onah Barnett cuts portals into the pea-soup fog of the Pacific Northwest—transporting you places so strange but so familiar you'll have to wonder which side you came in on. With echoes of Lovecraft and Jeff Vandermeer, Barnett calls on old mythologies and builds their own in this uncanny and terrifying debut. Try not to get too lost.

– Sam Greenspan, creator of *Bellwether*,
a podcast of speculative journalism

Jonah Barnett's debut story collection combines the haunted inner lives and nature-horror of Daphne DuMaurier with a kind of Clive Barker-esque fabulism to present a harrowing—but also weirdly beautiful—hike through a grotesque Pacific Northwest. A powerful debut that you'll carry with you into the dark, mossy forests of your dreams.

– Samuel Snoek-Brown, author of *There Is No Other Way to Worship Them*

Moss-Covered Claws is a dazzling menagerie of monsters— monsters that ooze from the mind and clamber from the sea, monsters that strut in Victorian velvet and hunker in interdimensional caves, revelatory monsters that will haunt your imagination and sink their claws into your heart.

– Julia Elliott, author of *The New and Improved Romie Futch*

Jonah Barnett wouldn't be insulted if anyone said their first book was monstrous.

– *Oly Arts News*

Blue Cactus Press | caləɬali

Moss-Covered Claws
By Jonah Barnett

Third Edition

Cover art and illustrations by Sam Breaux
Cover design by Gigi Little
Layout by Knic Pfost and Gigi Little

ISBN: 9781733037563

"Bubbler Man," "Boggy," and "Stripes" were previously published in *Creative Colloquy*.

"The Way Things Were" also appears in *Dispatches from Anarres* from Forest Avenue Press.

"Lowline" appears in *City of Weird* from Forest Avenue Press under the title "Alder Underground."

To the boy from the stage

and the lesbian from space

Contents

Foreword

Once, as a shy city girl, I followed my older friend Gretchen into the woods behind her New Hampshire farmhouse.

She is fun to be with and more daring than me, I wrote in my Cabbage Patch Kid diary on July 1, 1987. *We found a blackberry tree and she grabbed a branch and started to eat.*

I moved to Portland, Oregon, in my twenties—around the age author Jonah Barnett is now—without visiting first. The promise of rainy winters, artisanal coffee, and cozy independent bookstores proved a strong-enough lure. Also, the lush, overgrown mystery. And the gloom.

"Storms always made me feel better, ever since I was little," Jonah Barnett writes in "The Sea Cottage," the sixth story in this collection. "I think it was something to do with being under the covers while it rained. I could always put things into perspective with a storm. Life going to shit? At least I'm inside."

In the Pacific Northwest, you can walk around feeling depressed and anxious and the sky responds, *Yeah, same here. I totally get it.*

By the time I road tripped to Oregon, someone had probably corrected me about blackberry trees. How they're not really a thing. These days, I have a favorite berry patch up the hill from my house, where the canes have grown so wild they punched out a window. I bring bunches of neighborhood kids there in the late summers, providing bowls and buckets and occasional band-aids. Sometimes I stand on the sidewalk and half-expect the hungry brambles to swallow my young charges. *What will I tell their mothers?* I wonder.

The stories in *Moss-Covered Claws*, like the author themself, are entirely of this rugged Northwest landscape, as if the words themselves have been scratched into the paper with thorns or dunked in the ocean for a few months to achieve prime saltiness. Jonah whittles humanity onto the page in every story, while moss and monsters creep out from between the lines. Their stories engage deeply with queerness and gender identity while exploring the risks we take for our best friends—or in spite of them. They have conjured in these pages a heady blend of imagination and heartbreak, the very kind of thing I love to read most.

     Moss-Covered Claws

These stories carve through my heart the way wings cut through rainclouds: buoyant and bursting with the sights, sounds, smells, and mysteries of this region we both claim as home. My publishing house, Forest Avenue Press, had the great fortune of acquiring one of them, which happened to be Jonah's first published story, "Alder Underground." It appeared in 2016's *City of Weird: 30 Otherwordly Portland Tales*, edited by Gigi Little. The book quickly became a regional best-seller. At the time the book released, Jonah was an undergrad at The Evergreen State College, but they were also writing, editing a monster anthology of their own, and making films. They have since added much more to their resume, including creating a literary documentary series called *Wordsmiths*, directing more movies, and earning the role of marketing manager for the Olympia Film Society.

You can feel the influence of filmmaking in *Moss-Covered Claws*. Every encounter with the wild hearts of beasts—human or not, real or imagined—has a cinematic, dystopian quality, as if we have all been wandering around lost in the woods, and here, for a moment, Jonah gives us a clearing, some light, and we see something we've never dared to admit before. Something about what it means to love, or what it means to be scared when your friends aren't.

In this debut collection, monsters are wet-cheeked and made of brass. A gay boy's fairy godmother shape shifts to a less benign being. White pelicans, ghost ships, a seemingly sentient bog, fashionable gorgons, waterlogged books: each of these, Jonah gives us, vivid on the page. The monsters are real to the characters, and therefore improbably but perfectly real to us, the readers. They are our anxieties, our fears, our mistakes and misjudgments, and they all are reminders of how terribly lonely this gray weather can make us feel, even when we're buckled inside a U-Haul together.

"I, for one, have always wanted to be swallowed up by a void," says Sage, one of the characters in "Hole Wall," as she and her friends drive toward the fogged-in Astoria-Megler Bridge. "So, I welcome this journey."

And I hope you welcome this adventure into Jonah's imagination and literary craftsmanship. Settle in and let Jonah's work alarm and inspire you, entertain and bewilder you. You're about to blaze a trail through the undergrowth of the human experience, one monster at a time. You might even find some blackberries.

– Laura Stanfill, publisher of Forest Avenue Press and the founder of Main Street Writers Movement

Content Warning

The following stories include several instances of graphic content that might be upsetting to some. Throughout, you'll find the following themes bubbling to the surface like clumps of peat floating in a grimy bog: blood, gore, violence, body horror, death, self-harm, suicide mention, xenophobia, alcohol, neoliberals, petrified genitalia, and a straight white man or two. Be warned!

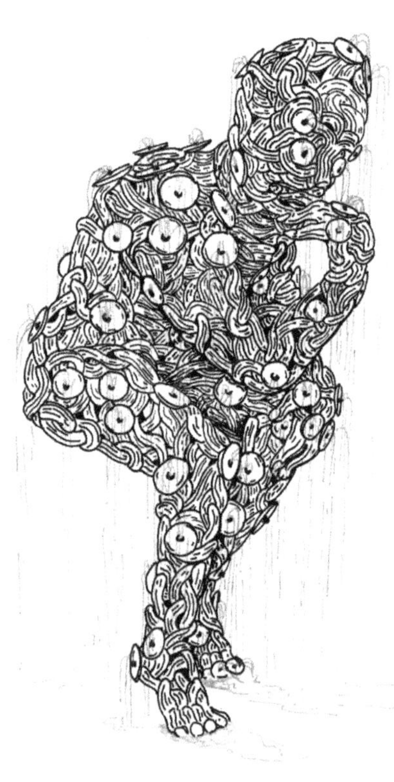

Bubbler Man

The Benson Bubblers are all gone. They have disappeared from every street corner. From Burnside to Madison to Stark to Washington to Alder to Yamhill to Morrison to Hoyt to Salmon to Madison and again to Washington. Everywhere. Zip. Badda boom. Our iconic water fountains have vanished, or so it feels.

The fact of the matter is our Benson Bubblers are not where they should be, but we know exactly where they are. They've all been accounted for in Pioneer Square in the form of a giant, hydraulic man that sits in the center plaza.

We'd call him Bob, but that's a bit old these days.

So we call him Simon.

You can still see all fifty-two Bubblers as they make up Simon's body. He is an eleven-foot-tall man made of oxidized bronze and flowing water. We found him one morning sitting smack-dab in the middle of Portland's living room, and we took pictures with our phones. The rest of us saw these pictures and came looking for Simon.

Simon is so great. He sits there crying, but he isn't really crying—we asked him. That's just the flowing water part of his face. Sometimes he actually cries, but we usually can't tell; it is all fine and dandy. We thought we all might invite Simon over for dinner, but he doesn't seem to fit in any of our houses. And of course, the carpets would get just absolutely soaked. And don't even get us started on how the cat would handle it. He is better suited for outside, but he still asks us what homes are like. We just do not know what to do with our Simon.

When Simon is not crying, he is a delight to have around. Our teacher friends all agree that if Simon were one of their students, they would write, "Simon is a pleasure to have in class" on his report card. When we told Simon this, he started crying for real this time (we could all tell), spouting about how he wasn't "a real human." So, we generally don't mention these sorts of things to Simon anymore.

We decided to build a house around our Simon, right in the plaza. It is not a real house, mind you. It is a tent like those big impressive ones you see at festivals. Simon told us he appreciates the tent. You can only imagine the smile on his twisted face when we came over with dinner, just a little something we all chipped

   Bubbler Man

in for. Simon of course cannot eat real food—he has no digestive system—but he does enjoy when we pour Crystal Light flavor packs into the flowing water that makes up his being. We come by the thousands to see Simon, to sit with him and chat over a nice meal, and to take more pictures with our phones. (#SimonSelfie.) We can tell he enjoys the company.

Simon asks us why we do this, why we never gathered our forces and chased the hideous bronze monster out of town. He knows he is not like us. "Because you are not hideous," we tell him, "and we are just like you."

And Simon cries. And we gather around, and hug him, and get our coats wet.

Boggy

I cannot tell what are dreams and what are memories anymore, and I hope this will not hurt me. I can recall running through grass with my brother, blackberry cobbler in the kitchen, and catching white moths in jars. But I also remember calls in the night, shapes in the water, and a set of cold eyes. I think back on laughing, screaming, nettle stings, sweetness, and a sense of eternal summer, everlasting youth. I rarely recaptured that last feeling later in life, but when I did, it was with my friend Jill.

The two of us set up the tent in the middle of the bog, where the grass was a dry yellow and the dirt was practically sand. She didn't want to pitch it too close to the water because, she said, she didn't want one of us rolling out in the middle of the night and drowning in our sleep. But I think there was another reason. I think Jill was scared, and rightly so. There was something wrong about that water, a murky black that seemed much deeper than the ten feet my brother had told me it was. I couldn't look at it for too long; neither could Jill. It was like avoiding eye contact. I know that's ridiculous. I know the waters in bogs aren't able to sustain life. And yet ...

I told Jill we didn't have to pitch the tent so early—it was only three. She said she wanted to establish a home base early on.

"We need somewhere familiar to return to after each of our numerous exploits!" she said in that deep faux-superhero voice she used all the time. I loved that voice. It was playful and bold all at once, and it made the mundane reality of life almost seem bearable. "D'ya think we should set an alarm system?" she asked, a rascal grin electrifying her face.

I laughed. "Whadda you mean?"

"You know, twine, clanging cans—that sorta stuff. I've always wanted to do it," she said. Jill always felt as if she'd jumped straight from the pages of a Mark Twain novel. I wouldn't have been surprised if I had caught her training frogs. An alarm system didn't catch me off guard either.

"Why would we need an alarm system?" I asked.

She shrugged, wistfully looking up at the sky like she had a secret. "I dunno. Animals? Forest men? Take your pick. We're stranded in the wilderness, Anita. Anything could happen."

Boggy

She winked at me, and I swallowed my feelings. That last part about the wilderness was a bit of a fib, playful make-believe, that we both knew wasn't true. Home base sat in the center of a mini-peninsula surrounded by bog water. Behind us loomed a large hill covered in pines, with my mother's house located just beyond. We were less than half a mile from the comfort of Netflix marathons and roofs, but Jill wanted to make a spectacle of this. She was leaving for college in a few days. This was to be our last official "slumber party," a final farewell to the title before it devolved into just "hanging out" and then later, "catching up." Jill loved slumber parties growing up, and she also loved camping. I came up with the idea of combining the two. Mom didn't know we were out here.

I held up a bucket by the handle—one of two we'd brought.

"Tonight, okay?" I said.

She smiled, sighing, and took the bucket. "Onward, to adventure!" she said.

The bog I lived next to was a blackberry bog, one with vines snaking through the entire peninsula and creeping up the alders and cedars scattered about. We wandered through the sweet August air, trampling through dry grass and trying to shake the melancholy of summer's Sunday off our shoulders. You had to be careful; if you didn't watch yourself, you could walk right into a spider's web. They spun their webs all around the blackberry bushes—large spiders the size of dollar coins that loved to crawl on your face given the chance.

For the majority of the year, the blackberry vines only proved a nuisance for those of us who lived by the forest. In late summer, however, the thorny blossoms pupated into plump berries by the dozen. I spent my childhood picking them from this bog with my family. I remember running around with my brother, buckets in hand, and picking as many berries as we could find. Not many reached it to the bucket, though, and by the end of the day, our mouths would be purple and sticky from juice. We would stay at the bog until the sky turned orange with evening, the crickets in full swing by that point. When we all would get home, our mother would bake our bounty in a berry cobbler—the best part of summer far and wide. But before reaching home, we would have to make our way back through the woods and over the hill. I always hated that part.

Sometimes I dream about those evenings, walking back home with our buckets of berries. It's always one specific dream. It's not a memory: I am three years old and holding my tin bucket. My brother and father are ahead, hacking away at the brush with machetes. We are walking back uphill, surrounded by cedars and Douglas-firs. The evening sky looks colorless behind the forest canopy and I am waiting with my mother who is pulling on her coat. I ask her to pick me up, and when she finally does, I rest my head on her shoulder. I look behind my mother and see a pair of eyes, glowing green things peeking at me from behind a tree. I keep quiet and hug my mother tighter. The eyes begin to rise, and something hisses at me. I scream.

I didn't tell Jill my nightmare about the bog. I'm not sure why; she would've thought it was cool. She always joked that her middle name was "Danger." But I didn't want her to know that part of me was still scared all these years later. This was our last sleepover, but it was also a chance to get over myself, to make peace with my past. I was Jill's coadventurer, not a coward.

Boggy

The weather was warm enough to wear shorts but cool enough to not be called a heat wave. Jill led the way—as she always did. I missed my pants. When I wore pants, I didn't have to worry so much about ticks and stinging nettle. The blackberry bushes themselves could cut up your legs in a matter of minutes. Thorns lined up and down the twisting vines, and even the leaves were sharp. Was it worth it? Absolutely. At the ends of these vines were bushels of blackberries. I held one in my hand, this squishy, juicy thing, then chewed it. I had forgotten what blackberries tasted like. It'd been so long.

Cu-plink, cu-plank, cu-plunk.

The sounds of fruit hitting the bottom of our buckets echoed through the bog. I could feel the sun's rays on my shoulders as I reached up for a cluster of berries, careful not to disturb any large spiders.

"Will the berries go bad if we leave them out overnight?" Jill asked. She stood deep in the center of a berry bush, surrounded on all sides and bleeding slightly from her legs. Standing on the fringes, I could see that her bucket was already half-full.

I shook my head. "They'll be fine. We can cover the buckets at night so animals can't smell them."

"We should've brought a cooler," she said and winked at me.

My heart raced a little faster. "Next time." But there wouldn't be a next time.

We kept picking for another hour, Jill going the extra mile and myself taking extra care not to get scratched or disturb anything. My mouth had turned purple by then—old habits die hard. I looked down at my bucket to see that I hadn't even half-filled it.

Why did it feel as if Jill was ahead of me in everything? Why was I comparing myself to her? I caught myself wondering if I resented Jill. I realized I had lost sight of her.

"Anita! Get over here!" There was a sense of urgency in her voice.

I dropped my bucket, berries spilling all over the ground. I ran toward the noise. I had no idea what kind of trouble Jill was in, but I found myself ready to fight, adrenaline rushing through me. I ran through sticker bushes, my legs getting scratched and torn up as I did so. Where was she?

"Faster, Anita!"

Jill wasn't far away. I could see her shape through some of the bushes ahead of me. I crashed through, thorns sticking to my clothes and ripping as I passed. Jill stood there, bucket in hand, giving me a strange look.

"Whoa," she said. I was bloodier than her. Jill's smirk turned into a laugh.

"Are you okay?" I asked.

She nodded. "Sorry, yeah, I'm fine. You look worse than I do!"

"Then what's wrong?"

Jill blinked at me. "Nothing! Nothing's *wrong*, dude. I just found something." She looked over to the left of me. There, embedded in the blackberry vines and almost melding into the landscape, sat the shell of a car. An old vintage car. Rusted and weathered away. The doors lay on either side of it, having fallen off the hinges ages ago. The windows were devoid of glass, smashed decades before.

"Why is there a car here?" Jill asked.

Boggy

"How should I know?" I said.

"I mean, you live here. You should know the history of this place."

I knew the area had been a mining town a hundred years before, and I knew that the trees on the hill were all second growth. I didn't know much about the bog, though. The car looked as if it hadn't moved for decades. Jill stood on the hood and jumped up and down a few times. I wanted to tell her to get off. To let sleeping ghosts lie and to not disturb this artifact. But I mostly didn't want her to get hurt. The car didn't seem like it belonged here, hidden and dying under the vines. I wondered how long it would take for a car like that to rust into the shell of a memory it had become.

"Where do you think the owners went?" Jill asked.

I didn't respond and looked down at my bloodied legs instead. Warm, red liquid began to creep down from the scratches toward my white socks. I didn't do anything to stop it. I imagined the owners driving the car when it was new. Some happy 1960s nuclear family on their way to a picnic. A mom, a dad, a brother and sister. The kind of family I used to have, sort of. They pick blackberries all day, but when the sun goes down, they find their car's tires stuck in the peat mud. Or the son notices something in the water and inches closer to inspect. The sister screams for him to stop. She runs to get her parents, but it's too late. Maybe the family never returns to the car at all. Or they left it here on purpose. This was a place where you left things.

"Anita?"

I looked up. Jill had stopped jumping. I swallowed.

"How many berries have you picked?" I asked. She looked at me, confused, and then pointed.

"Bucket's almost full," she said. It sat there next to one of the back orange wheels, almost filled to the brim with purple. Jill jumped down from the car. Then she did something terrible: she looked at me. I could see concern on her face, concern I never asked for.

"Are you okay, dude?"

I didn't know what to say. I didn't have any words I was holding back; my mind drew a blank. I stared out for a moment before nodding.

"Yeah, just phased out for a bit," I said.

She laughed, grabbing her bucket. "Well, snap out of it, man! We can't be all mopey during our last sleepover!"

I faked a smile. "You're right."

"We should get back to home base," she said. She put her arm around me and led us back, and I prayed she wouldn't notice my face turning red.

Jill began work on her alarm system that night. Apparently, she had packed the necessary supplies to do so.

"I wasn't kidding when I mentioned doing this," she said.

I tried to muster a level of energy to match hers, but I was tired. I opted to go search for kindling instead. There was a burn ban on, but Jill disregarded it. This was our camping trip, and we were going to get the full experience. I told her I would be back quickly, but I took my time.

I remember, or dream, of standing on the bog's shore with my brother. In the memory, our parents don't know we made it out here all by ourselves. Dad would get angry with us if he found

Boggy

out, because Dad's still around. We are two stupid boys who still think the world is filled with adventure and untapped potential. My brother is trying to scare me by talking about ancient bodies they've found in bogs, perfectly preserved.

"They're always found super jacked-up, like with stab wounds or hung by a rope before their bodies got dumped in," he says.

I stare down at the dark water and peer. I know there's nothing staring back, but on the off-chance there is, I want to scare it. Let it know I am not afraid. My brother isn't helping.

"Then the body stays under for hundreds of years, and the peat in the bog doesn't let bacteria break the flesh down cuz it's so acidic, and—"

"Will you shut up?"

He ignores me. "There's probably a bunch of bodies right here right now. Under the water," he says.

"You're full of shit." I've just started swearing when adults aren't around. Swearing still feels bold and dangerous and not yet oversaturated. "If you're so sure there's a body in there, then why don't you go find one?" I ask.

He looks down at the water, scrunches his face. I think it upsets him more than it does me.

"Screw you," he says.

I'm tired and fed-up with him. I'm not proud of this next part, but I push him into the water. Hard. The dark liquid splashes up into the air. Bits and chunks of peat bob-up to the surface around him. He has to kick to keep his head up; it's an instant drop and the water is deep.

"Dick!" he screams at me between his coughing fits. I laugh. "You suck," he says, and I laugh harder. My brother winces, as if something's not right.

"I just kicked something," he says.

I snort. "Yeah, right."

"I'm serious!" he says.

My eyes drift. There is something floating toward my kicking brother. A log. A very long log. Or an alligator. It looks like one of those floating reptiles you see in documentary footage of the Everglades, except the head is smaller and much farther away from the body.

"I keep kicking something really big, dude," my brother says. The log drifts closer to him. I can see a familiar set of green eyes on its head. It's stalking him.

"Get out," I say.

"What if it's a body?"

I point to the log and shout, "Get out!"

My brother turns; he sees the log. It raises its head out of the water, attached to a stretched serpentine neck and filled with needle-sharp teeth. It hisses. My brother screams. I scream. It lunges, and I am running through the trees.

I never told Jill about this dream. We make things up to escape our realities, but this place wouldn't control me any longer. The sky was a violent orange by the time I got back with the kindling. Jill looked up.

 Boggy

"Dude, check this shit out!" She motioned all around us at her creation. Her alarm system was more intricate than I had imagined. Twine reached out in all directions, boxing us within a ten-foot radius. Empty cans with holes poked into them hung from strings. The surrounding trees and stumps had been dragged into this scheme; Jill had looped twine all around them. We had a clear view of the water—the same spot where I dream of pushing my brother in—but oddly, it felt more secure inside Jill's alarm system. Part of me wondered if she was as scared as I was. Why else would she make this thing?

I nodded. "I see."

Jill chuckled. "Now we'll be extra safe tonight, alert if any monsters come creepin'!" she said. There was playfulness in her voice, but a hint of anxiety, as well.

We managed to make the fire before darkness blanketed the ecosystem. I'd forgotten to bring chocolate, so Jill insisted we use blackberries for our s'mores, instead.

"We can pick more tomorrow," she said, stabbing marshmallows with sticks. I smiled. Jill was always so inventive, much more than I ever was. And even though the idea of blackberries with marshmallows and graham crackers sounded disgusting, I admired her refusal to be set back by anything.

She bumped my shoulder. "Hey." She held a stick with a marshmallow at the end for me. "I told ya to stop bein' moody."

I held my stick over the fire. "Sorry."

She laughed, reaching into her blackberry bucket and popping a berry into her mouth. We sat in silence, the fire cracking and hissing over the sound of distant crickets.

"I can't believe we found a car today," Jill finally said.

"*You* found a car."

"I mean, you're the one that brought me here, right? Nobody else brings me blackberry picking in spooky bogs—or any other adventures we've had," she said.

I snorted. My marshmallow was getting burned, and I blew on it. "Well, there's no one else I'd explore the world with," I said.

Jill giggled again. "Gaaay!"

I laughed back, or at least I pretended to. I watched Jill mush blackberries and melted marshmallows in-between graham crackers and chew them with berry-stained lips, her scratched legs flickering in and out by the fire's light. I swallowed my feelings again. There were other things I never told my best friend.

Something hit the water out in the darkness—a loud crack of a splash less than a hundred feet away. We bolted up.

"What the shit was that?!" Jill asked.

The thing—whatever it was—moved, just barely visible in the moonlight, and sank under the water. I didn't know what to say. Memories mixed-in with dreams filled my mind. I blinked them away and stayed in the present.

"That was a beaver," I said. "They splash their tails on the water when they get scared."

Jill stared out into the darkness, shaking her head. "Pretty big beaver," she said.

We didn't spend the night of our slumber party staying up late talking about boys. I didn't have any boys, and Jill had dated so

Boggy

many that she didn't like talking about them anymore. The two of us slept side by side in the tent in our respective sleeping bags. Despite her unease, Jill fell asleep in a matter of minutes and I was left to dwell on my fictions and childhood memories, and the curves of Jill's body, and the fact that I can't discern reality from imagined scenarios.

I am running through the woods, crying out. I almost stumble over my sneakers at the top of the hill and tumble down through the brush. I'm ripping through the foliage—ferns, nettles, Oregon grape—that cuts my ankles and shins. I burst from the forest and slam my fists on our front door. My brother has fallen in and a monster ate him. I can barely say the words through my choked tears. My mother runs for the hill as my father carries me behind her. I cling to my father's jacket, begging my parents not to go back because I can't lose the rest of my family. My brother isn't there when we come to the bog's shore. My mother is screaming his name, but his body is never found. I tell them about the monster. I don't tell them how he got into the water. I am told that what I saw never happened, that my brother was an adventurous boy who loved catching snakes and scaring birds and making forts who just one day made a mistake and drowned. I am told not to mention monsters, especially to other adults. I am told to never explore again. And after a few years, these are just dreams mixed with memories in order to cope with unsettling natures. Monsters are a figment of my imagination. Monsters are defense mechanis—

Something knocked the bucket over outside. I didn't move. It must've been a raccoon or a possum. That damn beaver. Something real that rummaged around in the nocturnal hours. A hiss. A reptilian throwback sound from long ago that I didn't want to admit was actually happening. I turned over, slowly—oh so slowly—and unzipped the tent door just enough to see through.

Dreams are not memories, and memories are not reality. I held my breath and looked upon what was true.

The bucket moved in the moonlight, the snake-like neck I knew so well protruding from it. I tried not to breathe lest it look up at me. The neck connected to a short lizard body that stood just behind the thread of Jill's alarm system, never setting it off. I could hear its tongue lick against the bucket's bottom as it lapped up the last of the purple fruit. The neck was massive, at least twice as long as the rest of the animal, allowing it to eat up our day's bounty while we slept.

But I wasn't asleep. I was watching my dream scavenge for scraps by the moonlight. My dream was a living thing.

"What the fuck is *that*?"

I looked over to see Jill, her eyes wide with fear and excitement.

Before I could say anything, I heard the bucket drop to the ground with a snarl. When I looked back, there was my monster: the creature I had made up when I was too young to know that monsters didn't exist. It stared at us, that monster, with its unnaturally long neck and slimy skin, and grimaced. I could see the needle teeth, and the lizard snout, and a hint of recognition. I screamed. Jill ran at it with fists clenched. It charged her, and I shut my eyes and screamed and screamed. I felt a crack on the side of my head and everything stopped dead.

I remember silence.

I dream of the next morning, opening my eyes and finding myself lying on the yellow ground. Dried blood cakes my hair,

Boggy

and I smell of grass and campfire. I blink and look around. The ground is covered in dark splotches. It is hard to tell if they are blackberries or flesh. The tent is empty, and our sleeping bags are torn to ribbons, our final slumber party forever finished. I get up. The sky is pink with sunrise, the birds as loud as ever, and the waters are perfectly glassy.

I walk to the edge and look down into the dark abyss. At this time of day—the very beginning—the sunlight hits the water just right and you can see down to the peat floor in honey-golden rays. I peer into the water. It's filled with shapes—shapes that are familiar and yet so remote. There are people down there, so many people, just lying at the bottom as if in slumber. I see loggers from the early 1900s, their flannel stained tea-brown and peeling off in flakes and bits, and Chehalis gatherers from long before when the land was fresh and unraped. The 1960's nuclear family sleeps, too, a mother and father's blonde hair dyed a permanent red as they hold a firm grasp on the picnic basket together. Their children sit patiently side by side. A third child sits with them, my brother, with red, needlelike punctures around his throat. He looks exactly as I remember him, at the bottom of this bog where I left him. Right under me, where I saw her fall in, lies the girl I love, staring out at me from the darkened waters of my dreams.

Acts of Violence

Jaime Craven's head was not soft like a soccer ball, but hard like a small boulder. A jolt of pain surged up Dallas's leg. His toes felt as if they'd been jammed on a table end, but he couldn't show his discomfort. That would be seen as a weakness. Besides, Jaime was the victim of the day. Four other boys gathered around Jaime in the parking lot behind the middle school. The sky, as it did every day, shone down a pointless gray—the only splash of color being the yellow lines of the parking spaces and a dash of blood from Jaime's ears. Wesley Desu barked orders to everyone from afar. As the self-appointed leader of the group, this was his plan after all. His family consisted of devout Catholics who believed birth control to be a sin, hence his being the seventh child in a line of nine. On either side of Jaime stood two other boys, the Donovan twins. The brothers' fists plummeted into Jaime's sides like little missiles. There was never much to say about Ezra and David Donovan. They were both dumb and liked guns.

Dallas walked away from Jaime after kicking him, trying to hide an obvious limp from the others. He walked behind a fourth boy, a dark brooding lad named Kayden Penrose, and patted his shoulder.

"Your turn," he tried to say in a deep tone. Kayden raised an eyebrow, and both boys knew Dallas was faking.

Kayden Penrose, with his dark bangs and confident demeanor, was the most popular kid in the seventh grade. Never mind his awkward braces, ever-cracking voice, or the twelve pinprick hairs on his chin; everyone admired and respected Kayden for his athletic abilities and no-bullshit attitude. It was that attitude that the boys admired the most; Dallas tried to mimic Kayden's composure whenever he could. The older boy always sent a jolt up Dallas's spine whenever they locked eyes—like right now. Dallas broke eye contact. His eyes darted toward the school and widened. He could see a shadowy figure lurking just behind the dumpster. A teacher? Dallas almost spoke up, but when he looked back, the figure was gone. Perhaps he was seeing things. He returned his attention to the boys' victim.

Jaime coughed on the ground and looked up at Dallas; deep down they both knew how easily their roles could have been reversed.

Acts of Violence

Dallas glared at him. "Don't look at me ... you faggot! I'm not interested," Dallas yelled, and it was true. Jaime was too short for Dallas's tastes, a little on the pudgy side, and to be honest, a bit of a bore. It wasn't much of a surprise when Jaime's secret had been revealed; Dallas shared the same admiration for Kayden as Jaime did. The only thing was, Dallas knew how to play the game better. He could hide it.

The problem with Jaime was that he'd gotten too close. Jaime and Kayden had been best friends, calling out the other boys on their shit when they boasted a little too hard, giving Wesley a hard time. The two had similar personalities, identical interests, and a sense of humor only the two of them could fully appreciate. Their friendship had always sparked a jealous fire within Dallas. Except for today. The bond between the two boys came to a close as Kayden stood above Jaime in that cold October parking lot. The Donovan twins held Jaime down. A pause lingered in the air, as if Kayden were having second thoughts. Dallas could see the two share a look, something between "sorry" and "this is necessary."

"Do it, Kayden!" Wesley shouted.

The moment snapped, and Kayden swung his leg back. Blood shot out of Jaime's mouth on impact and he cried into the asphalt. Part of Dallas knew why they were doing this, but another part of him stood outside of time as the others pummeled Jaime. Dallas watched the scene play out as it progressed—what was the point of this, again?

"Fucking gaywad!" David Donovan yelled while he jammed a fist into Jaime's ribs. *Really though, what had Jaime been expecting?* Dallas wondered. Middle school boys never once seemed to be the accepting type; their savage reactions were anything but unexpected. The reason they were beating Jaime to a pulp, the reason Wesley Desu had called the boys over to plot out their strategy to make Jaime's life a living hell, was really Jaime Craven's own fault.

Jaime had told Kayden his truth two days before, and no one could keep a secret in middle school. Common sense. Dallas could not imagine why Jaime had confessed to Kayden—perhaps on a hope that something joyful would come of it, that speaking his feelings out loud would result in a reciprocation and the impossibility of a happy ending (Dallas knew this could never happen in their situation). But the story played out differently, as Kayden was said to only have looked at the ground when Jaime told him. Jaime had confessed everything to Kayden in a dramatic, preteen monologue. The joking around, the late-night conversations, the longing stares in the dark during slumber parties ... Jaime was in love (or what he thought was love). Eventually the confession ended, and a space grew between them. Kayden did not say anything to acknowledge what had been said. Instead, after only a moment, Kayden Penrose had spat onto Jaime's shoe and walked away, Jaime in tears.

But it wasn't Kayden who had revealed the truth.

"Okay. Okay! That's enough," Wesley said in the parking lot. Dallas blinked at the sound of Wesley's tinny voice. The others stopped, looking up at their master. Wesley Desu was the shortest of all of them—the result of some genetic lack of a growth spurt— but he was the boy with the power in the pack. He was the alpha hound—Kayden was the lone wolf, of course. Wesley smirked. "Save some for tomorrow. It's gonna be a long school year," he said.

 Acts of Violence

Dallas joined the others as they stood over Jaime in a circle. The boy looked like a swollen plum. Wesley crouched down to Jaime's bloody face.

"We're gonna get you tomorrow. And the day after that. And the day after *that*. Every day for the rest of your life until you say you're sorry," Wesley said. "You and Kayden aren't a team anymore. He *hates* you now. We *all* do."

Ezra kicked Jaime in the ribs. "*That's* for watching Kayden in his sleep, faggot!"

Jaime looked up at them, at all of them. Dallas could feel Jaime's stare lingering on him, as if he knew. Of course, they both knew; they exchanged these sorts of glances constantly. How easily could it have been Dallas there on the ground? Dallas looked away.

Jaime turned to Kayden. "I'm sorry ... I'm so sorry. I just thought you were really great," he sobbed. Kayden glared, shaking his head. The amount of cruelty in the gesture tugged at even Dallas's heartstrings. Granted, Jaime *was* a faggot, but this was just cruel.

"I really trusted you, dude. I don't know what to say," Kayden said.

"*I* do," Wesley cut in. "You're fucking disgusting, Jaime. You tricked Kayden into thinking you were his friend. Right, Kayden?"

Kayden sighed. "Yeah ... fucking disgusting." Jaime looked down at the ground. Dallas felt for Jaime in that moment. Poor fucker.

"You're more than disgusting. You're a hundred percent *wrong*," Wesley continued. "That nasty stuff goes against millions of years of biology, the natural order. You really wanna go against God that bad?"

"Wesley, shut up. None of that Jesus shit right now," Kayden said.

Wesley held up a finger. "No, *you* shut up. We had a fag in our ranks, and it is *your* fault. Be thankful we're so forgiving."

Kayden's nostril's flared, and everyone tensed. It wasn't like Wesley to challenge Kayden like this.

Wesley turned back to Jaime. "No more Jaime-Kayden power couple shit anymore. Always questioning my plans and decisions, you little fucker. If you tell anyone—your parents, teachers, the supervisors—about today, we'll *kill* you. If anyone asks, you fell off your bike or something. I don't care." He kicked Jaime in the jaw, the Donovans laughed, and Jaime cried out.

"Shut up, gaywad!" David Donovan said.

"Let's go!" Wesley yelled, and the Donovan brothers followed him out to the courtyard.

Kayden stood behind for a moment. Dallas could see a seething mixture of loathing and pity in his eyes as he looked upon Jaime. He turned slowly to join the others. Dallas lingered. Jaime had curled up into the fetal position, crying harder and harder into the asphalt.

"They said you'd be happier once you came out," Jaime cried. "They said you'd be happier!"

Dallas's breathing picked up, faster and faster. That could have been him. That could still be him. He could slip up any day now, thanks to Wesley and the others being on high alert. He turned away from the other boy crumpled on the pavement and ran home in the other direction.

Acts of Violence

Like any twelve-year-old boy, Dallas's imagination ran wild that night. The book he tried to read in bed proved a poor distraction. Christmas lights hung down from the bedroom ceiling like stars and cast the boy and his blankets in a soft glow. Neither literature nor the warmth of his bedroom galaxy could protect Dallas from the dark creepings of his mind. He wondered about all the different ways Wesley and the other boys would destroy him if they found out his similarities with Jaime. The taunting, the exclusion, the beatings. He had seen it first hand that afternoon, and it was getting harder and harder to hide it.

Like the other week, before this Jaime fiasco had taken place. The boys sat on the bleachers during an indoor recess—the outside rain forcing the preteens to take their break in the school gym. The rest of the student body ran around below, second-graders joining fifth- and sixth-graders in games of tag and sprout ball. A circle of girls sat at the bottom row of bleachers talking about who knows what.

Regardless, the girls had the boys' full attention. The subject of each girl's fuckability came up, with each boy listing off which ones in the class they'd rather sleep with. Not that any of them had even kissed a girl at that point. Dallas found himself puzzled at the discussion; they were twelve. Why were they talking about sex anyway?

The topic drifted around the group, boy to boy, before it finally came 'round to Jaime.

"Which one would *you* fuck, Jaime?" Wesley asked. The boys loomed in on the poor boy, an awkward pause if there ever was one.

Jaime glanced at Kayden and swallowed. "Uh … Macy Gibbs," he muttered. The other boys sneered in disgust.

Dallas almost rolled his eyes. "Really? Macy?"

"Y-yeah, she's nice …"

"She's not like, super hot though," one of the Donovan boys said.

Jaime shrugged. "Maybe I like girls for their personality," he said.

"That's fuckin' gay, dude," Kayden laughed. Jaime's eyes grew a little wider but softened as he looked over to Kayden laughing, and they laughed together. The boys turned to Dallas.

"And you?" Wesley asked.

Dallas shrugged, his heart actually pounding. Could he lie successfully? He looked down into the darkness of the bleachers. Something moved below them, and he heard a faint *click, click, click* as he stared off into space.

"Dal!" Wesley said.

Dallas blinked, thought for a moment. "I mean, *are* any of them hot enough to screw?" Jeers turned into weird looks in his direction.

"Whatta you mean?" Ezra Donovan asked. "There're loads of hot girls down there."

"Name one," Dallas challenged him. The others scoffed. Dallas wished this would end quickly.

"Jill's hot," said David.

"Jill? Prepubescent 'I have no boobs' Jill?" Dallas asked.

Acts of Violence

"That's not true. I heard she was wearing a training bra in the locker room," Ezra said.

"No, Aisha's the one with the bra," Kayden said.

Dallas gave out a nervous laugh. "How do you know?"

And the subject on who Dallas wanted to fuck was quickly dropped as the boys took more interest in breasts. Thank god for Aisha, honestly. He looked over at the girls, sorry for them and the world they lived in. The truth was Dallas didn't actually want to fuck anyone, not at his age. Who he wanted to kiss—what type of person he wanted to kiss—on the other hand ... that was a different story.

He had to keep that a secret, but deep down he knew it was pointless. They would find out sooner or later. And then what? Lie in a pool of his own blood and tears in the back parking lot? Get kicked in the head like Jaime? Receive his own customized brooding glare from Kayden? Fuck if that was going to happen. His life was over at this point. He might as well give up now. How long could he really keep up this game?

The Christmas lights flickered on and off in his room, but he gave no notice. Tears welled in his eyes as he lay on his stomach.

He started to cry into his pillow. Liking other boys, in *that* way, was unnatural—Wesley had said it himself. Dallas and Jaime were freaks, abhorrent mistakes in the evolutionary process. Reprehensible perverts abound. Slip up just once, and they would be onto him, just like Jaime. It was inevitable, it was unavoidable, it was his fate.

Unless, of course ...

Dallas's room grew cold as the thought drifted into his mind. A creeping weight settled over him while he mused. Dallas's eyes watered again. How, though? There were his mother's pills—but what kind of pills were they? He could cut his wrists with Dad's razor. But these were things in his parents' bathroom, and they would see him walk though the master bedroom and ask questions. There had to be other ways. He could jump out the window head first. (But what if that didn't complete the job?) Or maybe he could still do the wrists idea. There were knives in the kitchen. Or … or …

Dallas considered his options, each scenario driving more tears out of his eyes like a creek. He grabbed his pillow and cried into it again—the plush object already damp, his body a dead weight. He was useless, just totally useless and a waste of good genetics. All the work his parents had put into raising him would be for nothing now. It was already nothing anyway because of how he turned out. Broken. Worthless. Pathetic. Unloved. He was in for a life of alienation and unhappiness unless he stopped it all tonight. Yes, it was better this way. Better no life at all than a miserable one. Everyone would be happier in the end, or dead. He sniffed a few tears back; he was ready. Dallas pushed himself up from his pillow.

Or tried to.

Click, click, click …

Something slammed his face down onto the pillow, hard. Panic flooded his brain. What was going on? Who was here with him? He could feel chilled fingers holding his head down as he struggled underneath. Reaching behind him, he felt something cold and hard. It felt like a wrist, but a wrist without flesh. Another freezing

     Acts of Violence

hand snatched his own and held it down. Hands held down all his limbs. Dallas squirmed, to no avail.

Something had crawled on top of him while he cried, that was clear. Two more hands pressed down on his shoulders. Whatever was on top of him writhed with life. A deep clicking filled the room. Dallas tried to scream, but found he was voiceless. The bedroom air felt cold. Surely, surely this was the end of his life.

"What's thisss?" a raspy voice asked from above. Dallas could not see his assailant, its freezing hand still pressing his head into the pillow. The other hands held him to the bed no matter how much he tried to thrash, the hard body pinning him down. Other hands felt up his back as if looking for something, in the same sci-entific way a doctor checks for lumps. Dallas felt studied. His lungs gasped for air, and he shook his head in a violent spasm.

"Ah, can't breathe? I forget sometimesss. My apologiesss." The hand gave way for a brief second. Dallas lifted his head, gasping, before the hand came right back down, making sure his nose wasn't covered.

"I did not sssay you could look," the voice said. Clicks followed its statement.

Dallas did not know what to think. He could not see anything in his peripherals, and his previous objective completely left his mind as he tried to understand who or what had broken into his room.

"You're right," the voice said. "I am a *what*."

Then *what* was this? Did Kayden and the others break-in to pull a mean joke on him?

"No," the voice said. "I don't play tricksss."

Was Dallas having a bad dream?

"In a way."

Could the thing read minds?

"Yesss."

Why was it here?

"Because I heard you from far away," it said. The thing continued to produce clicking noises at the end of every sentence it spoke. They reminded Dallas of a cricket, or a beetle.

"I came before beetlesss. Now *listen*," the thing said. It pressed Dallas's head harder into the pillow. "It would be wissse for you to ssstop these thoughtsss before they attract … ssscavengersss."

Dallas hadn't the slightest clue what the intruder was talking about. He had not said anything out loud in his bedroom; he had only cried. Everything else had been in his head.

"Exxxactly," the thing said.

Dallas wondered if the thing was going to kill him, get the job done so he wouldn't have to do it anyway.

"Never," it said. "I do not kill thingsss. But there are thingsss that will kill you if you do not ceassse this mind-screaminnng." Dallas tried to lift his head again. The thing slammed it down once more. "I sssaid no looking!"

He wanted out. Fear began to fade into something else, and the boy found himself wanting the thing to leave so he could get on with his plan.

 Acts of Violence

"You mussstn't! There are thingsss about thisss Universsse that you do not know, that you will never comprehend. Thingsss like me, only worsssse."

Dallas doubted that. What could be worse than a giant beetle that sat on your back?

"I am *nothing* like a beetle! I am one of many unknownsss in the fabric of realitiesss. And there are othersss, very dangerousss othersss, for they feed on anxxxietiesss and fear of the weak. Baphometsss, braxxxens, and banssshees. They will come to your call if you do not ceassse, and they will turn you inssside out and gobble up your greatessst qualitiesss. The thingsss that make you yoursssself and give your life esssssssence."

But I have no good qualities, Dallas thought. And I don't want to be in this universe anyway. The universe doesn't care about people like me; it hates me, and I don't belong in it. I am unnatural and ugly.

The thing erupted in laughter intermingled with clicks and squeals from another time. The bed shook with each great chuckle. The intruder soon composed itself and sighed. Dallas could feel its cold breath on his neck as it whispered.

"I am the ugly one here, make no missstake." He felt *another* hand stroke his face. He could see the tips of dark, pointed exoskeletal fingers brush against his cheek like icicles.

"You are not ssseparate from this Universsse, little one. Think of how the ssstars shine, or galaxxxiesss collapssse. How cowsss ssshit and dogsss pissssss. When eudemons and cacodemons argue for natural order. The way the light of the early morning sssun glimmersss through your window. The rhythm of your breathsss. It isss all part of a unified whole."

Dallas did not follow what the thing was saying. He could hear a sigh from above him. "You cannot leave thisss realm yet, isss what I'm sssaying."

It said nothing for a time. The weight of the thing began taking a toll on Dallas's spine. Parts of it writhed around on top of him, and he imagined a great carapace swaying back and forth atop the bed. He heard the clacking of hard fingers against his Christmas lights, his galaxy.

"Ssstars look nothiiing like thisss, you know."

I am not as important as the stars.

"The vassst beyond isss *jussst* as crucial as you."

Stars won't implode if I die tonight.

"You don't know that! You mussst *hush* or they will hear! They will come! You do not know how this Universsse ssshines the ssstars, conssstellates the conssstellations, or galactiftiesss the galaxxxies. You do not know. That doesss not mean to sssay you are not doing it."

Get off of me.

"Not yettt. I cannot have you tearing holesss. You are nooo thread rider, child, and you belong in thisss Universe. I sssee the outcomesss. Your cesssation of exissstence would spiral into sssomething more. Becaussse you are the Universsse. And ssso isss that sssad boy. Your mother and fffather. And sssisssster. And thisss bed. And that book. The man you will marry. All thingsss."

Including you?

The thing laughed again. "Oh no, I am not part of any Universsse," it said. It giggled to itself at the idea, except Dallas could

Acts of Violence

barely tell they were giggles and not screeches. It whispered into his ear again. "You may not end it all tonight. I will not let yooou," it threatened.

Will my life get better if I stick it out?

"It will take time. It isss a hard reality you live in. Thossse boysss. Ssso cruel."

They will kill me if they find out.

"We both know that isss not the real reassson they are hurting the sssad boy."

The freezing exoskeletal hand covered his eyes. Darkness for a brief moment. An image of Wesley popped into his mind. Like a memory, but something that was not his own.

"I sssee them. I sssee the sssad boy and the mad boy and the tall boy that isssssso confusssed."

The image grew sharp, and Dallas saw Jaime and Kayden talking, standing behind the dumpster after school. He couldn't hear anything though. What the best friends didn't see on the dumpster's other side was Wesley, listening in, creeping around, watching. The scene played out as Dallas had heard, with Jaime clearly spilling his feelings out to Kayden like the moron he was. But something different happened. The story changed before Dallas's eyes. Kayden did not spit at Jaime's feet. He just stood there, staring at that dumb boy. After a moment, he grabbed Jaime and kissed him. Right then and there in the back of the school behind a dumpster inside a stolen memory. Wesley watched from behind his corner as Dallas watched from beyond time.

That ... that didn't happen though, Dallas thought.

"LIESSS."

Jaime pulled back, tears in his eyes. Happy ones. He talked more, probably telling Kayden how happy he was, and Kayden was actually grinning as well. They kissed again, holding each other. Dallas felt a spark of jealousy within. The moment ended as Wesley jumped from behind, shouting, pointing, yelling his little angry head off. Jaime and Kayden stared at Wesley, spooked like two deer in the headlights. That's when Jaime ran off. Wesley caught Kayden's shoulder before he could join Jaime. The short boy screamed at Kayden.

What's going on? Dallas wondered.

"Threatsss, blackmail, betrayal of all sortsss," the thing said.

The memory image vanished as the hand withdrew from his face. Dallas's bedroom had grown colder, as if something had sucked up all the heat. The room was silent.

What did I just see?

"The truttth." Clicks began once more.

Dallas did not know what to say, what with his world being turned upside down and then some.

"Thingsss are not what they ssseem."

But what do I do about my friends?

"Your ussse of that word issssssstrange. They are not ssso acccccepting of thossse unlike them here. But there will be thossse who underssstand in the futurrre, and they will love you for your flawsss. Fellow monssstersss and pervvvertsss."

 Acts of Violence

The clicking increased throughout the bedroom. Dallas's neck had grown numb from the thing's frozen breath. Five of its hands still held him down. His back ached.

Like Jaime? Dallas wondered.

The thing sucked in air, as if contemplating its answer. "You have done the sssad boy a great dissssssservice," it said. "He may never forgive you or the othersss."

The room grew silent, the thing stopping its hisses and clicks. Dallas could still feel it writhing along his back.

"Do what you mussst," the thing finally said, an afterthought.

Dallas swallowed hard. Nightmares weren't real, but this creature certainly was.

What are you? he thought.

The clickings started right back up, the thing giggling once more. "Oh sssweetie," it stroked his cheek again. "I am your fairy godmother."

Click, click, click ...

And a dark shadow swept over the room, and Dallas looked up, alone on his bed.

The next day was different. The previous night transpired over and over in his memory for hours. He watched from afar as day two of Jaime's personal hell commenced. Kayden was nowhere to be found. "You fucking lied to us, faggot!" Ezra Donovan screamed, then kicked Jaime in the gut. His brother David spit on his face for good measure, laughing. Jaime held his stomach, blood coming out from everywhere.

"Like shit you'd wanna fuck Macy Gibbs! More like her *brother!*"

Idiot, Dallas thought. *Why didn't you just stay away?*

"You should have stayed home, fairy. Your boyfriend Kayden can't save you now," Wesley said. Jaime spat out a wad of blood. His face shone a dark purple from the events of yesterday. It would be even darker by nightfall. But Jaime glared at Wesley and said, "Go fuck yourself."

Wesley's face shone a bright red.

"What did you just say to him, faggot?" David yelled. Dallas looked at Jaime. Something had changed with the boy overnight, as if something had come to him, talked to him, given him the courage he so needed today. Dallas looked at Jaime with awe. He did not completely understand why they were supposed to hate people like Jaime and himself so much, or how the boys' approval could be flipped off like a light switch. Jaime would not leave this world though, not yet. He was of the Universe, but then again, Dallas and the other boys were of the Universe as well.

Why would the Universe hurt itself? he wondered.

"Look at all the red dripping from his mouth!" Ezra pointed, and Dallas realized why maybe some parts of the Universe might want to punch other parts in the face.

"Let's finish him off!" cheered Ezra.

"No!" Wesley shouted. The two brothers looked to him like obedient dogs. Wesley turned to Dallas. "Dal's gotta do it. I haven't seen you kick this gay worm once today," he said.

Dallas looked to Wesley, that all-knowing smirk smeared all over his face. He stepped forward toward Jaime. Again, those eyes

     Acts of Violence

pierced through Dallas like a lie detector. They both knew the hypocrisy at play, two parts of the same Universe coming together for the first time ever, understanding one another. Dallas took a deep breath. The Universe was ready for a change. The whole of reality warped around him as he made a new decision.

He exhaled. "Wesley, you're such a little bitch."

"What did you say, you pussy?" Wesley's eyes widened. The Donovan brothers tensed on either side of him. Dallas knew this was a losing battle.

"I said you're a little fucking *BITCH!*" and he walloped Wesley in the nose, breaking it.

A moment passed before what happened sank in. The twins looked on in shock as Wesley held his hands over his face, blood dripping down, the sounds of soft sobs coming from between his fingers. Dallas and Jaime locked eyes, unsure of how this would play out.

"Traitor!" the brothers yelled. And Dallas found himself on the ground next to Jaime, feet and fists pummeling his body. And then something else. A kick in the head that felt different from other kinds of pain. For a brief moment, there wasn't any feeling at all, but a short burst of darkness. Blind confusion. Perhaps it took the brain a few seconds to register that it was being attacked. Shortly after, the pain flooded in, an aching, throbbing pain—a *screaming* pain! That was the moment Dallas realized Jaime's torment.

"Run away!" Dallas yelled. He could hear the shuffling of feet, the beating of his own flesh, Wesley full-on crying. "Run away! Run away! Run away!"

He opened his eyes to see Jaime running into the distance, which was okay: he had done Jaime a greater injustice these past twenty-four hours. He wanted Jaime safe, some part of the Universe that didn't have to feel such terrible pain any longer.

"I'm sorry!" Dallas yelled.

Ezra kicked his mouth. Dallas laughed at his attackers, and before he lost consciousness, he saw something else. A dark shape, some kind of unholy creature, hanging from a streetlamp across the playground, with many arms and an incomprehensible body. The head, whatever shape it was, nodded, and Dallas felt a sense of cold wash over him. He blacked out knowing they would leave him alone after this, and this was not the end of his life.

This was not the end of the Universe.

Acts of Violence

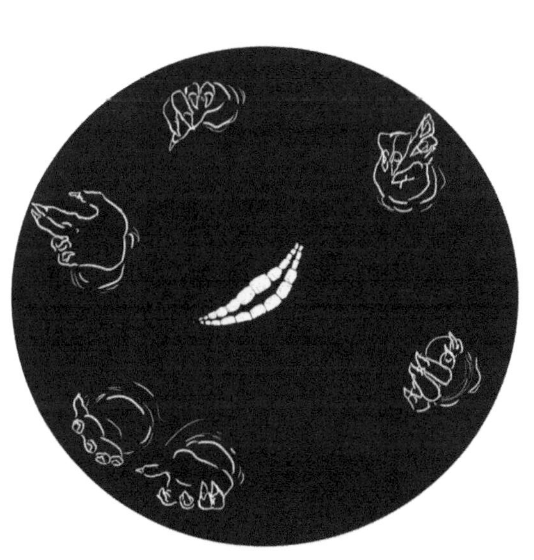

Lowline

8:15 a.m.

We r taking a train down to the City of Roses, or whatever they call it these days. Promised Aisha I'd pay her back for my ticket but we both know I'm full of shit. Will buy her coffee or something as payback.

#PortlandDaycation   #FreeTripForMe
#GonnaBuyAllTheBirdBooks

`8:30 a.m.`

Forgot my journal this morning, so I hope you guys like Tumblr posts. Liveblogging is my passion :-) No but fr I'll make sure to tag everything #PortlandDaycation so you can block this crap if your heart desires. You're welc.

`#PortlandDaycation #SorryNotSorry`

`8:47 a.m.`

No one's posting anything right now. Probs cuz everyone is ASLEEP and only MONSTERS drag their best friends outta bed this early, AISHA. I KNOW YOU'RE READING OVER MY SHOULDER BITCH. Only thing to do rn is just Snapchat clips of trees rushing by.

`#PortlandDaycation`

`10:40 a.m.`

We have arrived! Folks are underwhelmingly...normal at this train station. Expected more of Portland. Was gonna write up a study of hipsters for Nature. (JK!)

`#PortlandDaycation`

`10:51 a.m.`

Soon as we step out of the station Aisha asks, "So, what's first?"

And like, I know coming here was my idea but I didn't make an itinerary or anything. And she's like, "You didn't think this through, did you Danny?"

And I'm like "Girl hush," and pulled up Google Maps. If anyone knows any good foodie spots in Portland plz reblog with suggestions.

#PortlandDaycation

11:32 p.m.

Found the food trucks and gorged ourselves on falafels, praise Britney. Thank you @enbydragon47 for the hot tip! So many crows hopping around the pavement hoping for crumbs. Could not help myself and threw them a few bits of pita.

#PortlandDaycation #TurningIntoACrowLady
#CorvusBrachyrhynchosCuties #AishaIsRollingHerEyes

12:03 p.m.

Things overheard by the food trucks~

Girl 1: Y'know, Alder. It's a street here.

Girl 2: I don't pay attention to the street names. Who pays attention to street names these days?

Girl 1: Okay well, you know that really tall building that looks like Lex Luther's lair?

Girl 2: Ew, I hate Smallville.

Girl 1: Well like, anyway, I was walking by it on the way here…and there were all these trees growing out of the top.

Girl 2: Okay? There's a lot of rooftop gardens here.

Girl 1: No these are like, actual trees. Like cedars.

Girl: 2: Oh shut up!

Girl 1: I'm serious! And I swear those trees weren't there last week.

Girl 2: Bullshit.

I found the weird part of Portland.

#PortlandDaycation

1:08 p.m.

Putzing about n bullshitting through all these little shops. Found this cute hat store on Broadway. Dapper. As. Hell. There are all these $85 bowties I'm currently drooling over. (Why do I have to be so POOR? ;_;) Really surprised at how nice the owners are. I thought people downtown would be more…snooty, I guess.

("It's probably because I'm here," Aisha says while trying on a hat. "You're gonna throw a Black girl out of your store? In the year of our Lord 2015? I think the fuck not." She puckers to herself in the mirror. "Kawaii as hell," she mutters.)

I take it back—there is one old grumpy man in a gray suit that keeps glaring at us.

"Racist old bat. Deal with it," Aisha says.

#PortlandDaycation #What'sHisProblem?

 Lowline

2:05 p.m.

Found a zine on the ground. Talks about "slimy lizard people" and how they're taking over the Pacific Northwest. Feels...vaguely racist :/

#PortlandDaycation #SoInaccurate #LizardsAren'tSlimy #AmphibiansAreSlimy

2:20 p.m.

Discovered a Starbucks in the middle of a big red plaza. There's an event going on in the middle with this bigass tent and some kinda water feature inside. Bought Aisha that coffee I promised. Now sitting on the brick steps people-watching. Folks keep coming out of the tent, soaked to the bone.

"What d'you think is going on in there?" I asked.

"Not anything good," Aisha scrunched her face.

"We could go in."

"We could also not."

Didn't really know what to say after that. Sometimes I can tell my best friend needs help but I don't really know how to do anything helpful. Feels like every time I try to talk about what's going on with her she shuts it down. I was gonna suggest something when she spoke up.

"Didn't we used to have a lot more fun on these kind of adventures?"

Ouch.

"I dunno," I said. "Everything was, like, a lot more fun back in high school when we didn't know how anything worked and we were scared. Now stuff's a little boring."

"Until recently I thought I knew how shit worked. Now I dunno. And everything's still kinda meaningless anyway."

I didn't really know what to do with that, so we're back to just staring up at the tent with all the people. Crows fly all around the square, probably looking for more people to sucker crumbs off of. Aisha just keeps staring ahead, not talking.

I don't think it's just this adventure that's boring...

`#PortlandDaycation`

`3:04 p.m.`

We are not at the plaza anymore.

We're waiting in this big weird lobby. Or at least, I'm waiting around. Aisha is walking all over the place, inspecting everything like some search dog. Just can't stand fucking still! Can you, Aisha? I'm just sitting on this fancy couch, ready to leave.

Back at the plaza, not talking to each other, I started counting the crows flying around. More and more were flocking to this one tree. They just looked like normal crows, the Common American kind I've studied in class, but they were acting strange. Well, strange for crows. There'd gotta've been, like, twenty-five-ish birds hanging out in that tree, and they were all bobbing their heads and cawing down to this one lady on the ground.

Okay, so this lady. Never seen like someone like her before. Or I guess I have, but like in fashion magazines. Big tacky maroon leopard-print jacket with shoulder pads that could poke your eye out. Massive blue shades poking out between a stylish bob. And the shoes? I can't even.

But here's the thing, here's the massively messed up thing that I can't wrap my head around: it all worked. Like the whole outfit just came together and here was this absolute goddess under the tree looking up at the crows. They squawked and cried out at her, and she was making faces back up at them. No one else was paying attention to what was going on. Maybe weird crap like this happens all the time in Portland and they were all used to it. I wasn't though.

I poked Aisha and said "Who is she?" Aisha's eyebrows shot up at the sight of her. The lady cocked her head to the left, and all twenty-five crows did the same. They copied her every move.

"No way," Aisha said.

The woman took off her sunglasses, giving these crows a wicked look. She opened her mouth and—get this—made all these clicking sounds. The crows went absolutely buck wild. They screamed and cawed and flew up in a murmuration, circling around the plaza like a single organism. I looked back at the woman and she was LOOKING RIGHT AT US AND SMILING. I clutched Aisha's arm I was so shook. The lady raised her hand and gave us a little wave, before opening her mouth again and letting out one GIGANTIC, AWFUL SCREECH. Like on command the murder of crows changed course and started flying off in one direction. The woman started walking the same way. We just sat there, blinking.

Again, I'd just like to point out how NO ONE ELSE noticed all of this happening. Did not give one actual shit. They just crowded around the giant tent like an act of literal witchcraft hadn't just occurred on the plaza. Crazy demon bird seductress strolling around downtown with her flock of familiars? Just another Thursday.

"That bitch," I heard Aisha mutter. She stood up and started running for the lady and her flock of crows.

"Hello? Aisha?? Where the fuck are you going?" I called after her. I got up and followed.

#PortlandDaycation

3:16 p.m.

You'd think someone dressed like they walked off the set of Absolutely Fabulous would stick out on a sidewalk, but remember: this is the City of Roses. There were weird hipsters with bowties and beards from 1910 and street performers painted in silver and—Marina and the Diamonds help me—some guy was actually riding around in one of those antique bikes with the bigass wheel in the front. You know the ones. What I'm trying to say is: it was actually pretty fucking hard following Crow Lady down the street. Aisha never seemed to lose track, though. We trailed the lady from a block behind on the crowded sidewalk. I accidentally bumped into someone. I looked up to see this young businessman glaring at me, a sexy gay otter if I ever saw one. He only mumbled when I apologized and gave me this angry look—but it was kinda hot, not gonna lie. There was something there. A connection, y'know? I wish I got his number, but I didn't really have time.

 Lowline

"Aisha, this is stupid," I said, almost JOGGING alongside her while she simply walked at her super weird pace with her super long legs. "Maybe she's just a freaky-deaky lady that likes annoying crows."

"Hm," is all I got back.

"Is it cuz she's hot? Listen hon, I know it's been a dry spell for you lately but chasing after the first hot mom you see isn't how you spend a daycation."

Aisha snorted a laugh. "That sounds like a great daycation to me. Is that why you think I'm following her?"

"Isn't it?"

Nothing after that. Aisha just kept trudging on. That's the thing about my best friend: when she gets something in her head she's not gonna let it go. I hate her for that.

We turned a corner and had to stop. Or at least I did. A block away, among all these other tall buildings, jutted out this giant black and blue tower that, well, towered over the rest. That wasn't the weirdest part though. At the top of this tower sprouted—and I shit thee not—these giant evergreen trees. Just some bigass sequoias on the top of this hella high building. The murmuration of crows swarmed around, squawking at each other. I looked back down to see Aisha twenty feet ahead. The entrance doors of the building began to close, the Crow Lady just slipping through. I ran to catch up with Aisha. Lining the pavement were two parallel rows of decorative metallic sculptures—trees, with solar panels for leaves. As we went through the doors I caught the name "Arborealis Botanicals" printed over a leaf symbol on the frosted glass sides.

And that's where we are right now. Still nothing. We entered the building and turned a corner to find this empty lobby with the Crow Lady nowhere in sight. There's a fountain, and some nice art, and a T.V., but no Crow Lady. I'm not really helping out because I don't really wanna find that woman, and this couch is comfy. There are no doors anywhere in this lobby, except for the ones we came in. Aisha's still looking around trying to find something that would explain where the woman went. I'm watching the little flatscreen in here. Tbh, really just wanna go home at this point.

`#PortlandDaycation`

`3:20 p.m.`

Things this lobby doesn't have:

- other doors

- people

- eerie elevator music

- elevators, now that I'm thinking about it

Things this lobby DOES have:

- marble floors

- walls made of wood

- annoying LED lights that suck out my soul

- painting of a minotaur

- another painting of a giant pyramid floating over Portland

- pedestal with a bust of a horned woman

Lowline

- huge fountain with a pissing cherub, the kind you throw pennies in at the mall

`#PortlandDaycation`

`3:25 p.m.`

"At Arborealis Botanicals, we know inner beauty…is a thing of nature. The natural world holds a variety of answers to questions weighing on us today. Biomimicry meets design in our luxurious, affordable personal care brands—all sourced from naturally sustainable materials. We keep you looking your best, so you can take on the world."

–the commercial playing on the screen on repeat

`#PortlandDaycation`

`3:32 p.m.`

Aisha was all huffing and puffing and getting all mad about losing the Crow Lady.

"I knew she went in here, and then she's like…gone," she said.

"No shit, Sherlock."

She threw me a dirty look then rolled her eyes. "I checked everywhere from here to the door. Maybe there's a secret door or something. Unless…" She was looking over at the fountain.

I snorted. "Aisha we're not in some spy movie. There're no secret doors. Let's just get back to our little trip and have more falafels. This is dumb."

"Y'know what's dumb?" Aisha poked my chest. "Bringing me down here for this lame-ass trip and ignoring all the obviously weird shit that's going on around us, pretending that everything's okay."

I opened my mouth to tell her to eat shit, but the sound of the sliding doors stopped me. We both froze at the sound of footsteps, louder and louder on the marble tile. In about five seconds whoever it was would turn the corner and find us in the lobby.

"What's our alibi?" I whispered.

"Ssh!" Aisha grabbed me and hid us behind the horned lady bust. The steps rounded the corner, and someone entered the room. I could feel Aisha flinch when she saw who it was, so I just had to sneak a peek myself. And oh my God, here's the wacky part: it was hat-store guy! The old wrinkly racist one in the gray suit. We watched as he approached the fountain. I was about to make a comment but Aisha clamped her hand over my mouth. I almost bit her right there I was so mad. The old man stepped in front of the fountain and looked down. I figured he was contemplating all his past mistakes, or whatever old people do when you catch them staring off into water. But then he did something else, kinda batshit. We watched as this man jumped forward, diving into the pool with a splash, completely submerged.

We waited a good minute before Aisha said: "What in the actual fuck?"

#PortlandDaycation

3:46 p.m.

We have transcended the WEIRD element and have gone straight to the realm of HOLY SHIT. Having a rough time believing

 Lowline

anything that's gone down. Also...phone still works. HALLELU-JAH. THANK YOU, BEYONCÉ.

So back in the lobby we stood in front of the fountain wondering what the shit had just happened.

"Okay we should like, seriously go now, right?" I said.

"She's down there," Aisha said back. Lord all-fuckin'-mighty.

"Big whoop. So's that wrinkly guy. Let's just chalk this one up to 'Huh that was weird let's never talk about it again' and go home. We don't even have to stay in Portland," I said.

She turned to me and shrugged her shoulders. "Listen, you can scam if you want and play tourist or whatever. But I need to know what's going on. You can leave or stay, I don't care."

I crossed my arms. I'd had it up to here with her. "Why are you being like this?" I asked.

Aisha, my stupid fucking best friend who I don't even know is my best friend anymore at this point, shook her head, and cannon-balled into the water. I yelped out as the water hit me.

"Aisha! You fucking bitch!" I cried. But like the old guy, she never resurfaced. I winced, paced back and forth as I tried to make up my mind.

I really should just leave her, I thought. Serves her right for thinking everything is boring, including me. I dunno what's up with her. I'm a fucking delight.

But then probably the worst thing that could have happened...happened. The doors slid open again. I heard more footsteps coming toward me. Clack-clack-clack down those goddamn marble floors again. Probably another weirdo who likes jumping into fountains and never coming back up. Something told me if I got caught, these freaks wouldn't exactly let me go.

"Halsey save me," I muttered, and dove into the pool.

There really wasn't a bottom. I just kept going down, down, down. Everything became darker the further I dove. Eventually I could make out this big, gaping hole (ha ha), and felt myself getting dragged in. After a huge WOOSH I plummeted down through the pit into what felt like a sort of tunnel. I tried to scream but again, I was underwater.

And then, light! I did get to really scream as I was flung into the air and dropped down into another body of water, much larger—and darker—than the fountain. I hit the surface with a slap and started to thrash as I fought for air. Aisha was doing the exact same thing five feet from me—look at where this led us, idiot—and we coughed while trying to tread water.

This stream of water kept pouring down on us, and this rank stench of rotten plants hit my nose as I looked around. We were under some sorta waterfall, in the middle of a huge pool of black water with a shore off in the distance. I could make out this little patch of land, a small island, much closer to us. Tall, dead grass and a few sparse yellow-leafed trees sprouted up from the island.

Aisha grabbed my shoulder. "Something just touched my leg," she said.

Ew.

I started swimming toward the island, with Aisha following me. Something dark rushed past my peripherals under the surface. I tried to not think about it. Disassociate and ask questions later, y'know? We were in some kinda bog, I guess. The island had no

 Lowline

natural beach or anything, with the land just cutting off straight down at the water, so we had to hoist ourselves up. I collapsed onto the dry grass and turned over onto my back. Bright light, BLINDING light, streamed down on us. Over our heads hung this huge rusty metal tube spewing out water into the bog like some waterfall. That's what must have shot us out. I looked around, and it hit me how HUGE this place was. On the opposite shore I could make out a small forest with yellow and orange shrubs that stretched on forever, bordered by two massive steel walls on either side reaching up into the light. But the weirdest thing, sprouting up from the yellowed forest, were these three giant pillars.

We heard clanging from over our heads. Something big was coming down the tube. It cannonballed down into the water. Aisha and I both scrambled up and into the tall dead grass. A head surfaced, it was the hot otter from the street! The young businessman, hair slicked back and suit soaked to the bone. My dick twitched at that.

"I know that guy, kinda. Maybe he'd help us," I started getting up, but Aisha yanked me back down.

"Stop being an idiot," she whispered. The man swam away from us, toward the shore with all the trees. He dragged himself up, straightening out his suit jacket like it wasn't fucking ruined, and walked off.

Aisha hasn't said anything else while I type this. There's a third wall behind us and it feels like we're in some big metal box. Or a terrarium. Nothing is making any damn sense. The only way off our little island is to swim to the other shore, but there are...weird shapes in the water.

Where are we??

Still haven't left yet. Aisha is freaked out by the things in the water. She says she saw one while I was peeing.

"This weird fish came up to the edge and looked at me. This gross slimy thing with feathery gills."

I crossed my arms. "Oookay, now you wanna talk like nothing happened up there?"

She did this big dramatic sigh and buried her face in her hands like I was the annoying one.

"Danny, we don't have time for this. We can talk when we're out of here. Let's just put that stuff away and focus on finding that lady."

"You mean escaping," I said.

She did this big heavy sigh again. Bitch. "If we find the lady, she probably knows the way out. Right?"

"I mean, I guess. But she seems kinda…pure fucking evil? Maybe?"

"I'll handle her when the time comes," she put her hands on my shoulders and gave me this really serious look. "I need your help right now. Use that big science brain of yours. We need to figure out where the hell we are and how to get across this water without freaking out those giant fish."

She keeps calling them fish but they sound more like tadpoles. I keep getting reminded of axolotls or something by her description. But okay, reality check: amphibians don't get that large—except for like those giant salamanders in China. Really regret not taking that herpetology class last quarter :/ Anyway, I rolled my eyes and agreed. She's right.

Okay, scientific method shit. Time to put my (incoming, probs useless!!) Bachelors in Science to the test. This place might be... some kinda underground garden or artificial biosphere? Weirder shit's happened in the world of science. Still wondering about those pillars on the other side. If we're really underground, maybe those pillars are our ticket up and outta here.

#NoMorePortlandDaycation

4:12 p.m.

Crossed the bog. Fucking disaster. I figured we just had to be slow about swimming across so we wouldn't disturb the tadpoles. (HELLO?? WHY ARE THERE GIANT TADPOLES??) We eased ourselves into the water. I led the way. I think we made it like, halfway across before I heard some thrashing behind me. The water was already a bit choppy from the makeshift tube-waterfall, but then I heard Aisha scream. I looked behind to see a SWARM of those creatures writhing around Aisha, Lana del Rey have mercy! I panicked and yelled at her to just keep going—couldn't exactly help her in my situation—and swam the rest of the way as she kept yelling out. I scrambled to shore and held out my hand to her, she was almost there. She took my hand and there were all these little nips and scratches on her arms. Aisha screamed again, twisting around and dropping onto the ground. As she jerked her ankle out of the water, one of the eel-like critters came out with it, jaws clenched around her.

"GET IT OFF!" Aisha yelled. It was dark brown with black splotches down its back, with the set of feathery gills she'd described earlier. Four little legs were also starting to sprout from its body. Like I guessed: bigass tadpole.

"STOP LOOKING AT IT AND PULL IT OFF!" she kept yelling at me. There wasn't a stick anywhere, and I started mad scrambling through the leaves trying to find one.

"What are you going?!" she screamed.

"I'm looking for a stick!"

"Just kick it!" I ran back and she was taking her own advice, hitting the thing with her own free foot. She leaned down and screamed into the tadpole's face, digging her fingernails into its eyes. It let go, and she kicked it back into the water. It swayed back and forth before swimming off.

"Fucking hell," she inspected her ankle. A perfect black ring had formed around her skin. Little needle punctures.

"Oooh girl that looks bad," I said.

"No shit," she looked up and glared at me. "Big help back there, Danny. Real big help."

But like, what was I supposed to do??

4:35 p.m.

Went out to explore a lil while Aisha tends to her wounds. Took off in the direction of those three massive pillars. Maybe the hot otter is there. He could help us, if I can find him. (And maybe he could fuck me behind one of the pillars...KIDDING, kinda.)

This place has got to be some sorta man-made biosphere, like that one disaster in Arizona. Maybe we've discovered some kinda secret ecology experiment, courtesy of Arborealis Botanicals. I

Lowline

gotta say, if that's the case, they're doing a shit job. The ground's super soft with layers of rotting leaves and forest garbage (smells like it too, tbh), and the trees (alders?) are all malnourished as fuck and twisted under this harsh light. That light in question? If I look up and squint super hard I can make out that it's coming from hundreds of little symmetrical lights that line this biosphere's ceiling. This is like, a very huge and shittily-made greenhouse. Everything dying in here.

Also, just an aside I've noticed...there are hardly any bugs?? There should be way more. If anything should be thriving in what's essentially a massive compost pile it should be bugs and worms. What gives?

Aisha's caught up with me.

4:44 p.m.

Reached the three pillars. No sign of my otter, though. (UGH! <3) These pillars are HUGE. AS. FUCK. Remind me of the redwoods in Northern Cali. Except they're made of some kinda metal. Looking up, I can see a big, dark square opening in the ceiling that these pillars reach up through into forever. Where do they go? Fuck if I know. Wrapped around these pillars are...wires of some kind. They loop around each pillar in loose coils and swing from structure to structure like vines, some draping down to the ground as well. The—wires? coils? fiber-optic cables?—look like they're creeping up the pillars like ivy. The whole thing looks more organic than technological. (Haha I sound like my professors jfc.)

4:48 p.m.

We stood at the base of the nearest pillar, still trying to get over how massive it was.

"D'you think we could climb it?" I asked.

Aisha rubbed her eyes for a sec and then walked around, tugging at the lower cables.

"Shouldn't be too hard," she said. She then took a big sigh and held tight onto one of the cables, like she was trying to keep balance.

"What's up?" I asked.

She ignored me. "Look at that," she walked to the base and pointed to a little square opening in the pillar, around the size of a laptop. She placed her head inside. "It's sucking up air, like a vacuum." She picked up a handful of soggy leaves and threw them in. A whirring noise started up and we watches the leaves get sucked up into the pillar. The sound traveled out of earshot.

"It's a chute," she said. "Not really big though."

Gotta keep looking :/

4:52 p.m.

Found a sliding door on one of the other pillars! No way to get in tho, not even an elevator button. The Arborealis Botanicals logo is engraved on the door's surface.

BUT...that means there's some way to get up...we just don't have the key, or something.

Me: Okay, don't freak, but I have...a theory.

Aisha: Kinda too late to not freak at this point.

Me: I think we're in a sorta man-made biosphere. Like they designed this place.

Aisha: I'm getting that vibe, yeah.

Me: We should be taking pictures! We could blow this place's cover. Be whistleblowers!

Aisha: Go ahead.

Me: Girl, doesn't any of this excite you? This is the adventure we were talking about.

Aisha: Listen. I'm tired. And dirty. And I can't feel my legs, or fingers.

Me: What?

Aisha: Nothing. It's just...maybe you were right, about going home. This was a mistake. This whole day actually was a mistake.

Me: You think hanging out with me was a mistake?

Aisha: No! I mean, probably not. I don't fucking know. Danny, I just wanna go home.

Me: You're the one who wanted to follow the Crow Lady.

Aisha: I said this was a mistake, didn't I?

Me: What's with your obsession with her anyway?

Aisha: Come on. Let's just find a way out.

Are any of y'all even fucking reading this? HELLOOO. HELP US.

God. We shouldn't be here.

No one should ever be here.

The two of us made our way through the forest, Aisha going a little slower than usual. The ground was squishy and slushy with mud and rotten leaves. Aisha had a rough time with it, starting to limp from the bite on her ankle. I can tell she's trying to ignore it. If I mentioned anything she'd probably just shoot me down like she always does. The heat under these lights is godawful. It's a literal miracle anything's been able to grow under this harsh shit. After a bit, Aisha yelped and pointed to something over to the left.

This person was just laying down on the ground. Which, y'know, maybe it was just one of those crawling weirdos taking a nap. We rushed over to him and turned him on his back—and gave out a big ol' SCREAM. This guy was dead as hell. Miley Cyrus forgive me but I peed a little. His hipster clothing was all torn up and absolutely soiled, and the smell of rotting leaves was totally taken over by the ABSOLUTE FUCKING STENCH of rotting flesh. This dude looked like he'd been there for weeks, and maggots writhed around the tears in his flannel.

Anyway I fucking puked.

That's when a noise came from some bushes not far off. I was still retching when Aisha grabbed my wrist and dragged/limped with me behind the nearest tree.

Just in time, cuz like a millisecond later...THIS DINOSAUR walked out from the shrubs.

Or at least, it looked like a dinosaur.

Okay, scientist-hat time. I'm not nuts. Like this is literally what I saw. I'm not making this up.

The animal walked up on all fours and then STOOD UP LIKE A PERSON when it got to the body. It had this big crest running down from its neck to its tail. Its arms and neck were way, waaaaay longer than any human's. Patterns on the skin were a dark muddy brown with black spots and an orange underbelly—like the tadpoles from before. This thing, this motherfucking creepy crawly slimy thing, started sniffing the air, making a clicking noise. If I hadn't just pissed myself two minutes earlier I would've for sure just then cuz RIHANNA IT WAS HUNTING US. This thing looked like a lizard-man. No, fuck that—a NEWT-man. Like I know newts don't get THAT big but honestly what HAS made any scientific sense today?

This bigass newt, that really shouldn't have existed tbh, loomed over the dead hipster and started sniffing round. IT LAPPED AT MY VOMIT FOR A SECOND before starting to claw into the man's shirt. Eventually the cheap rotten Forever21 clothing ripped off, and...

Uuuugggghhhh. Okay.

And a SPEW OF LITTLE WRIGGLY GROSS-ASS MAGGOTS POURED OUT FROM THE DEAD HIPSTER'S RIBCAGE. THE NEWT-MAN OPENED ITS GODDAMN MOUTH AND STARTED SCOOPING UP THE MAGGOTS LIKE DIPPIN DOTS. WE WATCHED AS THIS THING JUST KEPT AT IT FOR MINUTES. OM NOM NOM MOTHERFUCKERS. AISHA HAD TO SQUEEZE MY HAND SO HARD BECAUSE SHE KNEW I WAS DOING EVERYTHING I COULD TO NOT SCREAM TO MY

LORD AND SAVIOR HILARY ERHARD DUFF TO BEAM US OFF THIS PLANET AND UP TO SAFETY AND AWAY FROM THESE SLIMY FREAKS!!!!

When it had its FUCKING FILL of the MAGGOTS farmed from HUMAN REMAINS, the newt-man stood up and dragged the body away, holding onto the head with a single clawed hand.

So anyway that was five minutes ago and if you're reading this COULD YOU PLEASE FUCKING GET SOMEBODY AND SEND THEM DOWN HERE SO WE CAN LEAVE.

K thanks.

6:10 p.m.

SCRAMBLED back to the pillars and immediately started climbing the cables. Not today, Satan! We're already pretty far up—fear has a funny way of making you go real fast. We keep having to stop and catch our breaths every few minutes—or at least, Aisha does.

6:49 p.m.

Have reached the ceiling, taking a break beneath the big square opening the pillars reach up through. Can't see anything but dark when I look up. When I look down...well we don't talk about that. Shit, we're high. I can see the whole biosphere up from here. Most of it's just those dying alder trees, but on one edge I can make out the bog with the big tube and island. On the other side I can make out all these little figures running around. Are they people? Are they newt creatures? Is one of them my hot otter? I don't wanna

Lowline

find out! I don't care anymore!! Aisha needs to hurry up and catch her damn breath.

Bordering the square opening are the same lights that are scattered all across the ceiling. It's so hot, and bright, and miserable. The lights are all honeycomb-shaped. Most of the cables up here connect to the ceiling, but some keep goin' on up into the darkness.

6:53 p.m.

Aisha can't move. She's just clinging onto one of the cables like an asshole and not letting go and staring at me while making these noises.

6:54 p.m.

Me: Aisha, we need to fucking haul ass.

Aisha: Mistake...This was a mistake.

Me: Yes no fucking shit but we don't have time for that.

Aisha: She knew we'd follow.

Me: That's great sweetie, but now we have to follow our guts and climb outta here.

Aisha: Danny...I'm sorry.

Me: That's fine. I'm sorry, too. I don't really know what for but I'm sure we can figure it out when we get out of this, okay? But we need to GO GIRL.

6:56 p.m.

This girl is just not fucking moving. She's not even talking anymore. The beings from the other side are making their way toward the pillars. Oooh my god. Tried shaking her out of it and THAT didn't fucking work. Now she's looking all over the place, reacting to shit that's not there. Is this bitch hallucinating?? Her fingers are TURNING BLUE and her leg is TOTALLY PURPLE. Why didn't I notice before?? I should've said something about that limp! Okay, enough of this liveblogging shit. Gotta put the phone away and haul my best friend up through a fucking hole in the ceiling. Again, if you're reading this: SEND. HELP.

6:59 p.m.

SHIT. Fucking shit. Tried to get Aisha to move. She started making her way toward me, struggling, and I held an arm out to help her but then she just started fucking screaming at nothing and breathing harder and harder and her eyes got all wide and I think she was trying to yell something at me but she lost her grip and

Shit.

7:12 p.m.

Can't go back down. Just up. They're at the bottom, inspecting Aisha's body. I'm sorry, Aisha. Some of them are def not humans. Can't cry yet.

Don't fucking cry.

7:26 p.m.

There is a crow perched up here. Why is there a fucking crow up here?? It's cawing at me. I can see a tiny red light coming from its eyes.

Shit it's a camera. There are cameras in its eyes.

Fucking snitch crow.

7:31 p.m.

Shit shit shit fuck shit this shouldn't be a thing I hate this place I hate biospheres I hate huge mystery buildings I hate the stupid fucking City of stupid Roses and Aisha's dead and fUUUUCCCCKKKKKK.

7:32 p.m.

Calm the fuck down.

7:45 p.m.

Passed through the opening. No lights up here, obvi. The farther I climb the dimmer it gets.

Hold up. I hear something. A song. Muffled but...elevator music? And something else, right on the other side of this wall...

"At Arborealis Botanicals, we know inner beauty...is a thing of nature."

You're fucking kidding me.

8:11 p.m.

Almost at the top. Can't see Aisha down there anymore. I think they dragged her body away. Some of the newts have left but some are climbing up. They're a lot faster than I am. Stop looking down.

Keep going keep going keep fucking going.

8:19 p.m.

If Britney could get through 2007, I can get through evil newt-men.

8:25 p.m.

Top.

8:25 p.m.

There's a trapdoor.

8:26 p.m.

Okay.

8:37 p.m.

On the roof of the building. The pillars keep going up, pointing into the sky. Remember the bigass sequoias on the top of the build-ing? Surprise, bitch! Bet you thought you saw the last of them. This isn't a roof garden, though. The pillars have all these panels around them, artificial branches stemming out and supporting

 Lowline

solar panels in the shapes of evergreen trees. Crows perch from the branches of these fake-ass trees. They're all hella quiet, and looking at me.

There're bones scattered all over.

A door with the leaf symbol sits at the base of this pillar, just like the one at the bottom. It's opening.

8:51 p.m.

Okay, for real. Hasn't ANYONE been reading this?? Can't literally ANYBODY fucking help and send a helicopter or something? PLEASE??

I'm up in one of the pillar-trees. It's rough cuz all the crows are up here with me, cawing at the creatures below to let them know I'm here. Little pissant snitches.

As soon as the door started opening I was like "Fuck THAT" and started to climb one of the trees. Without the cables up here to help me I used a chute like the one down below to help me get a foothold and reach one of the branches. I got about twenty feet up before the crows started cawing and dive-bombing me. Now I'm stuck between two solar panels on a metal branch. There are about six newt-men at the base, chirping at me and clawing at the metal. More newts are coming out the trapdoor. The crows keep screeching and circling around the building.

The door in the pillar slides open, and there's that goddamn Crow Lady walking out. Two more people follow her, wearing robes. The man in the gray suit and...my otter. The two men have blue vertical lines painted down their faces.

The otter points up at me and says: "That's the one."

The woman nods. "Why don't you come down?" she calls up.

No-fucking-thank-you. I'm staying up here. (HELICOPTER?? ANYONE??) The newt-men keep clawing up at me and clicking away like it's going to change my mind. Their glossy eyes stare into mine as they open their toothless mouths and taste the air with their purple tongues. Is that how they tasted Aisha?

"If you don't come down, we'll have to come up there and get you," she says.

A whirring noise starts up and the chute below us starts spewing out a pile of chunks and bones and flesh. One of the chunks is a human skull. The crows cry out and swoop down, stripping clean the pile that I'm pretty sure used to be my friend.

"I'll give you to the count of three!" says the Crow Lady. The newt-men are crawling over each other, one newt over the other, over the next, making a newt-tower at the base of the tree. Crow Lady nudges my otter.

"One!" The young man starts crawling up the pile, up toward me. I can see the animalistic want in his eyes. Up until an hour ago, I would've loved that. I still kinda love that—what the fuck is wrong with me? Horny at my hour of death. Look at that.

"Two!" He's almost at the top, he's gonna take me down and they're going to kill me and use me as a maggot farm or whatever. Can I survive jumping off this building? Would it be at all possible for Mariah Carey to come swooping down with that helicopter? He's standing right infront of me, his arms out like we're going to embrace. Crows are circling all around, spewing hate calls. For the first time, I don't want to be in the arms of a strong man. Aisha, you were right. I'm not sure if Portland was such a good idea.

"Three."

#PortlandDaycation

U HAUL

Hole Wall

Emily owned too much stuff, and it became apparent as we loaded the U-Haul that she wouldn't part with any of it. It had been a puzzle fitting it all in, but we had succeeded in real-life Tetris and were on our way to Astoria. We drove parallel to the sea, separated only by a jagged line of rocks running between ocean and asphalt. Choppy, gray waters crashed against the rocks in impressive displays. A bright fog permeated the landscape as flocks of seabirds littered the white abyss like flies. Rain shouted against the windshield.

"I really should've thought of this sooner." Emily drove the U-Haul through the weather like it was nothing. "Cuz, like, my uncle's always complained about never having enough help at the hotel, and I get to live on a beach, guys!" She laughed at the thought of her new life two hours south and into the wilderness, away from everyone she loved, helping her uncle's business while living in a cottage by the sea.

"It's the dream, honestly," Sage said in the back. The truck did not have back seats, but there was a crevice behind the front seats just big enough to fit my best friend and some extra piles of clutter. Sage's legs and arms spread out over the junk, making herself comfortable via manspreading. I could barely make out their voices amongst the clunky vehicle and screaming rain. I watched the scene outside. Avian swarms populated the air, a contortion of gulls, cormorants, and the looming silhouettes of pelicans. Of all three, the pelicans were the most graceful. The great creatures soared through the air as rightful royalty of the salty skies, almost prehistoric in their presence and always an awe to witness. Hundreds of seabirds writhed through the white mist as we drove past, but the pelicans were the only ones who spiraled down to dive into the sea with a form of grace that none of the other flocks could muster. One flew with the vehicle for a brief moment, then descended into the water after spotting something.

"How're the birds lookin', Kate?" Emily asked.

I turned to her and faked a smile. "Majestic, as always," I said. Emily laughed, and I turned around to meet Sage's gaze. She knew when I was faking. The U-Haul turned a rocky corner, the weight of the truck almost threatening to swing us into the icy waters.

Hole Wall

"There's the bridge!" And Emily was right. Out of the white appeared the beginnings of a road above sea. The rain began to retreat, and as we turned onto the Astoria-Megler Bridge, more of the looming white confronted us, still only penetrated by the hundred black-feathered denizens.

"S'foggy as shit," Emily anxiously chuckled. "Makes me kinda nervous."

Sage leaned in from behind. "I for one have always wanted to be swallowed up by a void. So, I welcome this journey," she said.

That was probably another call for help disguised by depression-set humor, but instead of acknowledgement, I said, "Shut up, Sage."

My best friend whined a little and slumped back on her junk pile. We had not passed a single car the entire time—the bridge just a straight line with a bright void enveloping us on all sides—and yet the skies grew darker with birds.

"Where the fuck *is* everyone?" Emily asked. Neither of us responded, and Emily kept driving into the fog. The U-Haul continued bumping down the road over the sea for some minutes, cutting straight through the misty white. Emily's things rattled and clanged in the back.

"Water," Emily muttered. Her breathing began to grow louder, filling the entire truck, and she swallowed. "Water everywhere."

"I mean, it's the mouth of the Columbia, my guy," Sage said. "Shocker."

Emily sucked in air and began tapping the steering wheel in a nervous beat. Her forehead shone with sweat.

"You're not scared of bridges, are you?" I asked. She shook her head. The U-Haul swerved as she did so, a few birds screaming as they flew out of the way.

Emily began breathing in and out very fast. "I don't know what's wrong," she said, "I just want to get off this fucking bridge!"

I hovered my hand over the steering wheel. I was not ready to die in the icy waters because of one of Emily's numerous freakouts.

"What do you need us to do?" I asked.

"Shut up."

"Anxiety attack?" Sage said.

"I said *shut up!*" Emily slammed a foot on the gas, and the truck ripped through the milky void. Seabirds cried all around us.

"Slow down!" I yelled.

"Do *not* kill us!" Sage screamed.

"Emily, slow the fuck down!"

And in mere seconds, through the fog, it came: an eight-foot blur of ivory. A collision with the windshield. Screams from all of us. Streaks of red blood and white feathers on the windows. A screech to a halt. The vehicle skidded sideways on the road and a thunderous crash rained down from behind—undoubtedly Emily's things toppling over. The sounds of heavy breathing over the distress calls of outside birds, the settling of clutter, and the angry sea.

Calm.

We looked at one another, hearts pounding and our brains still processing.

Hole Wall

"Did you just hit a flipping bird?" Sage asked.

Emily blinked, a few tears in her eyes. She looked down. "Sorry," she said.

Sage and I looked at one another. Whenever shit hit the fan, I usually looked to her for guidance. She nodded, and I opened my door.

The air outside was a ghastly cold. We piled out of the U-Haul and stared down the road. From behind the truck a trail of blood ran on the wet asphalt. At the end lay a white mass of feathers and beak in the center of a pool of maroon. Its chest moved up and down, almost spasming. That is how we knew it was still alive.

We crept forward slowly. Emily stayed back with the U-Haul, her hands covering her face. I wish I could say I showed bravery that day, but I hid behind Sage for the most part. The other seabirds, as numerous as they had been, had disappeared into the fog. Nothing made a sound on that bridge. We walked closer, careful not to step in the blood and a rapid wheeze began to grow. Breathing.

"It's still alive," I whispered.

Sage wrinkled her nose at me. "Well no flipping *duh.*"

"What kind of bird do you think it is?" I said. "An albatross? Do you think it's an albatross?"

Sage shook her head. "I don't think those come up this far north, really," she said. She ventured further toward the body. I wanted her to stop, turn around and get in the truck with me and Emily and never talk about this again. The white seemed to close around me. The light steeped in a soundless air.

"Let's go back," I reached a hand out.

"Is it still alive?" Emily asked. Both her and the truck were obscured in the milky mist.

"Yeah!" Sage called back.

"Sage, please, I want to get in the truck," I said. The light around us grew intense, and I wanted to say something. I wanted to comment on the brightness, but I knew I'd only sound foolish, so instead: "Sage, please!"

"Oh fuck! Oh *fuck!*" I could hear a muffled sob from the U-Haul. "I'm sorry I'm so sorry I just don't do well in confined spaces and this is really hard for me and I need to get off this bridge and—"

"It's a pelican!" Sage called. She crouched near the creature; I could not see it clearly from where I stood. The brightness of the fog seemed to die down. "Get over here, you wuss," she said to me. "I think we can help it."

I kept standing there stupidly. I did not want to walk any further into the glaring abyss toward Sage, but I could hear Emily sobbing behind me and I wasn't ready to console anyone. I stepped forward, walking around the feathers.

A white pelican lay in its own pool of blood, clearly distressed and still leaking liquids. Part of its upper beak dangled from the rest of its bill, still connected by a few strings of flesh, and its left wing was twisted in an ungodly shape, bone sticking out. It made a gurgling sound as I approached.

"Oh my god," I muttered.

Sage sighed. "We banged her up pretty bad, but we just need to get her to a vet or some animal rescue service. Emily! Can you look up 'animal rescue' on your phone?"

 Hole Wall

"I ... why?" Emily's voice called back. "It's just going to die, right?"

"Not if we can save her. Get over here!" Sage yelled.

"Guys, can we just go?" Emily called.

"She's right," I said. "Maybe somebody else will find it."

"Not you, too!" Sage said. She looked back at the poor creature. It continued to gurgle in agony. I could see its eyes pitifully blinking up at her. "These guys are, like, super flipping rare in Washington," Sage said.

"I've seen pelicans before," I said.

"No, *white* pelicans. Climate change is pushing them north," she said.

"Guys!" Emily again.

"Get the flip over here!" yelled Sage. The pelican snorted, and it shivered with unease. I could hear Emily's footsteps as they approached. Sage stroked the pelican's head; it did not move away. "It's all right," Sage said. The mangled bird jerked its head toward Emily as she appeared from the fog, hands around her shoulders.

Emily's face lost color when she saw her handiwork. "It's in pain!" she cried.

"Well, yeah. But we can still take her somewhere and get her fixed up," Sage said.

"Look at its fucking bill!" Emily said.

"They 3D-print prosthetic bills for rescue birds these days."

The pelican began to gurgle again, clearly suffering.

"It's okay," Sage said, "Em, I'm gonna use a few of your towels. Sorry." She started for the U-Haul.

"D-don't do that! No! It's just gonna die. I *hit* it, Sage!" Emily yelled.

Sage ran off. "And find an animal rescue!" she called from the fog. We were left, the two of us, with that pile of blood and feathers and guilt. The pelican squawked in misery.

"O Christ!" Emily cried. "Kate, what do you think about this? What did you do at the dorm when there was an emergency?"

I thought a moment. "There was one student when I was an RA," I said. "But she just cut herself. It wasn't like ..."

I looked down at the poor wheezing animal, in horrible agony with no idea why. My gaze drifted out to the fog. The mist began to grow thick once more, slowly creeping its way toward us, and I crossed my arms in protection. The sliding door of the U-Haul roared open, and from somewhere out there in the land of mist and snow, we could hear Sage rummaging though Emily's clutter.

Emily snorted. "This is stupid. This is so fucking stupid. It's obviously going to die!"

I sighed and looked out to the water, the fog growing brighter again. "This is just a bump," I said. "Maybe this'll be over sooner if we help Sage get the bird to a rescue." A crack came from behind me, followed by an inhuman scream.

Emily was stepping on the pelican's back, focusing all her pressure on its spine, tears in her eyes. The bird screamed the unholiest of cries.

"What the fuck are you doing?!" I screamed.

Hole Wall

"I'm putting it out of its misery!" Emily cried.

The white pelican shrieked, blood surging from its mouth as its bones splintered within, under Emily's foot.

"You're making it worse!" I yelled. I had never seen an animal cry actual tears, but I could have sworn the godforsaken bird's eyes had gone wet. It looked up at me in complete screaming agony. I wanted to cry myself.

"Help me!" Emily said.

"What's going on? What are you doing?" Sage called from the mist. The white pelican was red at this point, its suffering too intense to watch. I ran to the bird. I kicked it in the head. It screamed louder and blood flew amongst the asphalt as I kicked it again.

"Do it!" Emily yelled, "*Do it!*"

The pelican, head on the ground, gave out one final pained gasp. Ruined, mangled, and terrorized, it looked up at me—just for a second, the most innocent pain in its eyes. I winced, and my foot slammed down upon its head. A splashing of organs extended from beneath my shoe, and the gurgling stopped.

With my own foot, I killed the pelican. Emily and I looked at each other. An unmistakable mixture of disgust and shame linked us together.

"How's it going?" Sage called. The pelican lay still, now a gory mess. Emily shook her head. Silence rang through.

"It's dead," I shouted.

Nothing came from the mist after that, and the moment felt like eons.

Sage finally sighed from afar. "Uh … *well* then."

I could not look away from the blood, the piles of strewn out flesh upon the road. The pelican's remains lay frozen, but something moved inside its body among the red. I peered closer. Something small, and white, and wriggling. Emily grabbed my shoulder before running back to the truck. I had no choice but to follow, leaving the pelican to a permanent rest. The milky void gave way to Sage sitting at the end of the U-Haul, towels in hand, and a disappointed frown on her face. She did not look up as we came near.

"We should go," Emily said, opening the driver-side door. I stood in front of my best friend biting my nails.

"It just died?" Sage asked.

I swallowed. How could I lie to someone I love, to admit to something so horrifyingly wrong?

"Yeah. I guess it did," I said.

"What does *that* nonsense mean?" Sage said.

"We really need to go, Sage."

"I wanna see the bird!"

"Sage! Get in the fucking truck!" I yelled.

She shut up, her mouth tight. I could see her fighting internally, wanting to argue and go back to the pelican, only to find out what we had done—what monstrosities we'd committed—and denounce me from her life and never speak to me again. But I knew Sage; even an outburst like this was rare. She opened her mouth to say something.

"*SAGE!*" I screamed. I walked to the truck door and opened it.

Hole Wall

Sage looked back to the ground. "Fine," and she climbed in the back.

Emily started up the U-Haul and we drove away from that awful scene alone on that wide, wide sea of white. We did not speak, Sage's lack of words somehow being the loudest of all, even over the constant rattles and screams from Emily's belongings.

I looked out the window. The U-Haul began to climb up as the Astoria-Megler Bridge rose out of the sea and into the air. Higher and higher, as tall as a skyscraper, the creation towered over the seaside town like a great iron beast. I could see the town of Astoria appear from the fog as we flew over. While the majority of downtown had been built near the shore, the densely packed houses of the sea folk sat on a sloped hill of evergreen trees that reached up into the mist. Victorian and decrepit in nature, the decaying houses stacked over one another as if they would spill over into the sea.

From the top of the bridge, I could see the entire port, where the Columbia River met the Pacific Ocean. I peered out over the water. Amongst the scattering of dingy fishing boats, a great shape loomed in the distant miasma. Something large and skeletal—like an ancient ship. I blinked, and the vessel disappeared back into the fog.

The bridge looped down into the industrial center near the harbor, and as we drove to the depths of land, I could make out the ancient and cracked architecture of the storm-worn buildings. They threatened to free themselves from the shackles of their foundations with one more gust of wind and crush the traffic and docks below.

Seabirds swarmed over the sky once more like a single organism. Emily watched them at a red light and swallowed, and I understood.

"Think I'm going mad," she muttered to herself. The writhing avian conglomeration served as nothing but persecutors—their eyes ever watching, their very forms consistent reminders of the ghastly crime we had committed. Thankfully, the light turned green and Emily sped the U-Haul into the heart of downtown. She parked the massive thing behind a decrepit coffee shop. The vehicle hissed and groaned as it turned off while the cargo clanked and settled to a still in the back.

Sage sighed. "This isn't a cottage," she said. The statement held venom in her voice.

Emily tapped away at her phone, ignoring the source of conflict in the back. Seconds passed; we stared at our driver as nothing continued to happen.

"Are we getting coffee?" I asked.

Emily cleared her throat. "My uncle's gonna be here in, like, twenty minutes with the keys. It's his cottage. You guys are welcome to hang here if you want and meet him," she said.

"Are we welcome to take the truck for a spin and kill another bird?" Sage asked.

"I had a *panic attack*, Sage!" Emily yelled.

Sage crossed her arms and snorted. I knew sitting in the café would only get increasingly awkward as Sage continued to glare.

"Why don't Sage and I go look around while you deal with your uncle?" I asked. Emily seemed relieved at the idea, and Sage didn't say a word. We left Emily at the coffee shop, making our way

Hole Wall

downtown, walking fast. Sage kept her hands in her pockets with her head down. I didn't know what to say. I was a bit afraid to say *anything*, to be honest. I had never seen Sage this angry before. Apparently pissed-off Sage just clammed up and didn't acknowledge anyone.

The fog had finally burned off, and the swarm of seabirds continued watching me from the skies. We passed an arcade, colorful blinking lights illuminated from within, while depictions of *Pac-Man* ghosts and *Frogger* plastered the windows.

"Hey, an arcade," I said. "Wanna go in?"

"No." Sage walked right past the doors.

I ran to catch up. "Well, what do you wanna do?"

We stood at a crosswalk. Past the crumbling buildings on the right loomed the dark hill with stacked houses, while beyond the left's architecture glowered the mouth of the Columbia. The bridge hung over us like a structure of guilt. The crosswalk turned green and as we walked, a screaming seagull flew over me. I cried out and ducked as it flew off to join the rest of its flock. Sage laughed at the scene, but it lacked any kindness. It was a mean laugh, something that told me I got what I deserved. I glared at her.

"What?" she said defensively. I walked back toward the sea. Now we were both angry. We walked in a mutual silence. The town gave way to a landscape of wooden planks and crusty shacks the closer we got to the water; the constant cries of seabirds and crashing waves intermingling with something deeper, sinister. The waterlogged docks sprawled out right under the looming Astoria-Megler Bridge.

I felt like a fly looking up into a spider web, with the bridge's numerous spokes and trusses poking every which way like an industrial skeleton, doubtlessly a physical manifestation of my unspeakable sin. A gust of wind stirred from behind and whistled through the bridge's bones, a haunting call from the sea itself, like a mixture of groans and whistles.

"Spooky," Sage said.

I looked upon the rotting sea. The fog still latched itself to the opposite landmass, and the bridge plunged itself into that whiteness, shining bright on the other side. There was a deeper sound, too. A rumble echoed throughout the port. I saw the shape again in the mist—that ancient vessel from another time.

"Do you see that?" I pointed.

Sage squinted. "What?"

"That! That pirate ship out on the water."

We stood there, me pointing at the ship and Sage trying to follow, but the damn thing began to turn back. As it pivoted, I saw its true nature, as if sliced down the center from bow to stern. Half a ship. Half a nightmare. It wandered back into the fog after a few seconds.

"Didn't you see that?!"

"Don't see nothin', man," she said.

"It was there, though. Really!"

"Uh-huh ..."

Hole Wall

The bridge's whistling evolved into something else as we walked on. Less of a call and more of a deep vibration we could feel in our chests.

"You hear that, too, right?" Sage said.

The rumbling increased, louder and more dreadful by the second. And then a second noise. Roars. Barking. Hundreds upon hundreds of barks overlapping one another. We turned a corner to find a gap in the boardwalk, and there writhed the source of that unholy sound.

A raft of sea lions squirmed about in the choppy waters underneath. Their great bellows echoed along the coastline. Only Sage and I were witness to the wriggling ball of organic mass in the witch-oil water. There were over fifty blubbering beasts. They cried out in all directions, scrambling over one another in a chaotic dash up the scraggly rocks that led to the shore. Beyond these slime-covered rocks lay a parking lot protected by a chain-link fence. Some of the dominant sea lions forced their weight against it as they snapped at their aquatic brethren down below.

I watched from our eldritch deck as a solitary pinniped—the only quiet one—swam below and shot a glance back from the blue-green waves. It had a haunted, cautious look—as if it knew, as if it had swum under the bridge when it happened.

"He must not like us," Sage observed. I watched as the creature ducked its head under the surface as if to escape my presence.

The raft's calls and barks grew louder, and the animals upon the rocks began to bash their muscular, blubbery bodies against the fence barrier. The others screamed from the water, and the bashers screamed back, the second instance of inhuman cries that day. A roar of dominance and pain rang out, and they threw themselves against the chain-link border. Blood began to fly up into the air with each impact and rain down on the creatures on the lower rocks. Bits of flesh rubbed off raw as they continued to hit the fence.

The sea lions screamed, oh how they screamed, slimy things writhing about upon the slimy sea. With a final thrust, the chain-link came crashing down onto the asphalt.

"Holy butts!" Sage yelled. We could only watch as the lead marine mammals made a mad dash to swarm the parking lot with the others scrambling up from behind.

One of the larger sea lions climbed up on the hood of a car, its hulking weight tipping the trunk into the air. The creature let out a mighty bellow and proceeded to bash its head into the windshield over and over, until the red glass shattered into shards. Others approached the vehicle from the side. As a team, they pushed the car over, throwing the original animal off with it and crushing its skull as the vehicle's frame landed. The animals climbed over the car, crying victoriously, while the rest of the sea lions flooded the streets and attacked other cars, benches, and trashcans in a similar fashion.

I looked over to Sage, who was as silent as myself. "Let's, uh …" she said. "Oh, uh … I don't know, man. Uh …"

Another sound of glass shattering. Some of the animals broke into a clothing store. They mauled the front-window mannequins with their canine teeth, tearing fabric and plastic as if it were flesh. Other sea lions poured out, away from the streets and onto the boardwalk itself. The pinnipeds began directing their screaming at us—at me—and hobbled their way forward quickly.

Hole Wall

"Nah! I'm out! I'm *out!*" Sage yelled. We headed back the way we came, outrunning the creatures. Their cries rang throughout the town, overpowering the seabird calls from before. A black bird, a cormorant, swung down and attacked my head, scratching at my scalp and tearing at my hair. I screamed. Sage swiped it away and grabbed my hand. Seabirds continued to rain down upon us as the sea lions gained footing.

We made it to the coffee shop. Emily was just walking out, coffee in one hand and keys in the other.

"Hey, guys!" she said. "Got the keys." She looked at us. We were panting, and my hair was a ratted tangle. She looked up to the sky. "What's that sound?" she asked. Above the boardwalk swarmed a gathering of seabirds twice the size of before, threading through the air and creating the illusion of a blackened hurricane over the town of Astoria. Crashes and barks echoed through the streets.

"We need to fucking leave," I said.

"Did you two do something?"

A scream behind us. We turned to see the colony of sea lions down the road huffing their way up.

"Are those ... seals?" Emily asked.

We grabbed Emily and pushed her toward the U-Haul. "Get in the truck! Get in the truck! Get in the truck!" We piled in.

"Hold the fuck up!" Emily nervously laughed in the driver's seat. "What the shit is going on?"

A sea lion slammed its head on my door window. Drops of fresh blood splattered over the dried pelican blood on the glass. The creature looked into my eyes, the same knowing creature as before. The glass fogged up as it screamed at me with its haunted eyes.

"Emily, drive!" I said. Emily stared at the beast. Her coffee had spilled onto her lap. The sea lion bellowed.

"Kate said to freaking drive!" Sage yelled. Emily fumbled with her keys, dropping them on the truck floor.

"Emily!" I screamed. The sea lion bashed its head on the door again, the glass cracking into spider webs as it continued to do so. Emily put her hands over her head, hyperventilating. The creature looked at me through the cracked window, shards of broken glass lodged in its eyes. The damned thing roared.

"Emily, you *need* to drive!" I screamed.

"I can't! I can't I can't I can't! This is *so much!*" Emily said.

"Now is *not* the time, my guy!" Sage yelled.

Tears streamed down Emily's face. "I can't control my anxiety, you guys!"

The U-Haul shook as more sea lions slammed against it. More of Emily's clutter came crashing down in the back. Something dark slammed against the hood; the cormorant had followed me. It spread its wings in a threatening gesture and hissed at us. It pecked at the glass.

Emily cried out.

"Get the heck up, you big baby," Sage said. She grabbed Emily's collar and pulled her to the back after an awkward shuffle, the truck rattling the whole time. "Kate, can you drive?" Sage asked.

Hole Wall

I stared at the cormorant hammering its beak into the windshield. Its head smashed through, and I screamed as the bird snapped at me. To the right the sea lion's gaping, screaming mouth stretched outside the glass.

"Kate, get in the flipping driver's seat!" Sage yelled. Emily cried next to her.

I stared out past the creatures into the distance toward the sea. The white fog had completely rolled back in, almost blinding at this point, and the deep rumbles began anew. I thought I could see something moving, drifting in that bright abyss. That half-ship! It was a huge shadow in the void, far liker Death than he, the air still cold with its flesh—

"*Kate!*"

I did not respond as Sage shook my shoulders. I could not respond. None of this was really happening, surely. The sea beasts and birds screamed outside.

"Y'all are so flipping useless!" Sage said. I could see her from the corner of my eye climbing in next to me. I could hear Emily's soft sobs in the back, the shifting of clutter, the rattling of the truck as skin met metal. The sea lion screamed again, and glass from the door fell into my lap as it hit the vehicle's side.

Something snapped deep within and I cried out. I grabbed the nearest box and rummaged through it.

"What are you *doing*?!" Sage yelled.

I held up a letter opener and shouted back at the sea lion. The stubborn thing crashed away the last of the glass with one final blow, and I jammed my hand into its wide mouth. The letter opener met the soft flesh of the animal's mouth roof. The sea lion's glass-cut eyes widened as I felt the instrument cut deep into its brain.

"Katie, what the *fuck!*"

I heard the U-Haul start up, and the cormorant, its head stuck through the windshield, screamed as the wipers hit against its neck. It glared at me—such hatred in its gored eyes—as we drove. There were screeches of crushed marine mammals and awkward bumps as Sage ran them over. I turned to the cormorant. I glared right back.

"Don't!" Sage screamed.

I took a paperweight from Emily's office supplies. I crashed it into the cormorant's skull. Brain matter splattered the dashboard. I twisted the fucking bird's head until it snapped off, and I howled as I threw it out the window. Tears streamed down Sage's cheeks as she drove.

As I drifted out of reality, I heard the calm whirr of the truck engine as we sped away from the coffee shop, from Astoria—a whirr that lulled me to unconsciousness before I could glance out the blood-stained window again. I once more saw that half-ship, so *wrong* in that fog. The world darkened.

I woke up to a water-stained ceiling. I thought I had died in my sleep at first. Stacks of cardboard boxes towered over me. I was laying on Emily's futon—the same futon we had helped her heave into the U-Haul earlier that morning, a hundred miles away. I sat up to find myself in a room smaller than a studio apartment, a fridge and kitchen sink right in my face, and the walls covered from top to bottom in hideous wood paneling. This must have been the cottage. Sage kicked the front door open while holding a micro-wave with a lamp on top.

     Hole Wall

"Hey there, sleepyhead," she smiled. She casually plopped the armful of things next to the fridge. I held my skull. A headache was starting to form.

"What happened?" I asked. Sage walked back to the door. Misty white leaked in from outside and silhouetted her against the brightness.

"Come help us move stuff," she said.

I hauled myself up and stood in the doorway. Dried blood caked my arms. Underneath a white sky gray waves rolled, leading into a beach of black, sandy pebbles and a dirt road at the end of which sat the cottage. Emily's new abode was, essentially, a sea shack. Sage and Emily heaved boxes from the bloody U-Haul.

"Sup!" Emily yelled over the waves.

I blinked, amazed at the casualness in their voices and bewildered at the suspicious amount of denial. "What ... what are we doing?" I asked.

"We're, uh ... We're moving in," Emily said. She passed me and disappeared inside. "Are you gonna help or what?" she called.

"Help me with the table, my guy!" Sage called. I walked over to the open truck. "Cool. Okay yeah, get that side of it. Sweetness. Okay: one, two, three ... Heave!"

We carried the dining table into the cottage.

"Just set it over there, guys," Emily said as she ran back to the truck. We placed the table in an empty corner. I grabbed Sage's shoulder.

"What the fuck is going on?" I asked.

Sage gave me a puzzled look. "We're moving Emily's shit in?" she said and slinked her shoulder away from me. Sage didn't like to be touched.

I stammered. "But ... but ... those seals, and the fucking pelican from before. That black bird! Shouldn't we, like, bolt? They might come out from the sea. We shouldn't *be* here!" I said.

Sage snorted as if chuckling to herself. Another unkind laugh at my expense.

"Seals?" she said. She walked outside, leaving me alone amongst the city of cardboard.

The cottage really was a shack. The seventies wood paneling reminded me of stale wafer crackers, the warped, carpeted floor brought to mind the sea. The water stains upon the ceiling sprouted zoological horrors beyond human comprehension. This was really where my friend was going to live, out in this haunted coastal town, until the end of her days—either that or until something big swished the cottage out to sea ... a tsunami or something.

At least I wasn't living here. I was just staying for the night. If, of course, the night was survivable. The thought of staying anywhere near Astoria filled me with dread. I fully expected the haunted sea lion pod to surface from the waves, their awkward flippers squirming up the pebbled shore as they swarmed the cottage as a singular army. The waves themselves, the very Astorian sea, served as a horrific reminder of the day's events. That miserable seabird. Blood upon white. Maroon on the asphalt. Crusted splatters of avian and pinniped blood stared at me from the U-Haul's surface. I glanced at it frequently as I helped Sage and Emily move belongings from the truck to the building. That and the blood on myself acted as

Hole Wall

the only proof of the terrors that had transpired, no matter how much care the others took to neglect the recent past.

The bright skies had turned to black by the time we finished moving, and Emily's cardboard cityscape had developed into an empire. We pushed a few boxes off the futon and set up Emily's old portable television with a built in VHS player. Emily grabbed a bottle of gin from a nearby box.

"You guys are welcome to get drunk with me if you'd like," she said. Sage cheered, and I tried to smile.

"I think we all deserve a drink after today's events," I said.

Emily was already pouring alcohol into three cups. "I know, right?" she said, "Moving is always such an exhausting process."

My smile held still as I watched Emily mix the gin with Sprite. Sage popped a Disney movie into the television.

"I haven't seen this one in years," she said.

"No," I cut in, "I meant … hitting the pelican. The stampede downtown."

Emily chuckled, handing a cup to Sage. "I think the last time I watched this all the way through I was nine," she said. They laughed together, settling down to watch the movie. Green FBI warnings from the past flitted onto the screen.

"You guys—" I said.

"Ssh! It's starting," Sage said. Old discolored images faded in. I looked down at my cup of gin. Something swam around at the bottom. I rubbed my eyes and lookied again, but I saw nothing. The movie began with some animated boy holding a pig in a medieval village. Sage and Emily sighed at the nostalgia. I had never seen such a film before. Minutes passed. I was in agony and wanted to scream at my friends. I grew increasingly anxious over the fact that I *did not* want to spend another minute by the dark sea outside. Sage and Emily stayed silent, glued to the screen. A frame skipped in the animation. And then another frame.

"What's wrong with the TV?" I asked.

"It's old," Emily said. More frames began to skip, and the entire video grew choppy.

"Guys," I said, reaching for the VHS slot.

"Don't touch it!" Sage yelled.

Static crawled up the image. The character's eyes grew white. Animated blood poured from every orifice on their drawn faces. The images kept skipping. A deep groan emanated from the TV's speakers. On the screen, the pig's neck elongated, and its skin turned gray while its feet turned into flippers. The animated sea lion screamed at the boy and clamped its jaw around his throat. The boy screeched as the creature tore out flesh from his neck, pixels of red anatomy covering the screen, and red physical liquid began seeping from the VHS slot. The boy's screams transformed into guttural avian cries as his mouth sprouted from his face to form a yellow bill. The sea lion roared again, looming over the bloodied bird-boy, and the image gave in to static. We sat there in silence as the VCR slot oozed blood onto the warped floor.

"What did you *do*?" Sage yelled.

"Christ, you ruined it, Kate. Thanks a lot," Emily said.

"I ... uh—but—" I didn't have any words. I took a deep breath. "I really think we should go."

Hole Wall

"Stop! Just stop," Emily yelled. "You already ruined today enough as it is."

Sage glared at me in silence, shaking her head. Ostracized, I looked down in submission. In my cup, yet again, something swam underneath the liquid in a circle. I peered in. A small, fat wriggling thing, the color of fog. It jumped out at me, and I shrieked as it flew past and hit the wall.

"Jesus fucking god!" I yelled.

"Kate, *shut up!*" Emily said. The white thing skittered down the wall and into an empty socket, a square plastic fixture with a single hole in the center. A hole in the wall.

"Something just crawled into there!" I pointed. Emily cocked her head to the side and got up. She crouched down to inspect, tapping the plastic a few times.

"Hey! I think this is for an internet connection," she said.

"I bet we could find that movie on Netflix!" Sage said. She furrowed her brow in contemplation. "But we would need a router."

"My aunt gave me a router, actually! It's in one of these boxes!" Emily said.

Sage's face lit up. "Well get it, boi!" she cheered.

Emily laughed, beginning to dig in the boxes around her. Cardboard towers toppled over in her frantic, animalistic search.

"There is something *alive* inside that hole!" I cried.

Sage groaned. "Well, you probably scared it, and it's just afraid," she said. She hopped over the fallen boxes and crouched down by the hole, spying in with one eye. "I mean, it seems cozy in there," she said. She tapped the plastic covering in the same way Emily had. Something squealed from within as a response. Sage put her hands up to her face in delight. "That was so cute!" she said.

I watched her from the futon, unwilling to get any closer to where that thing was—that hole. I tried to swallow down my anxiety. My lips wet and throat cold.

"Sage," I said, "get away from that hole."

But Sage laughed at the panicked look on my face and shook her head. "It's a flippin' bug, my man," she said. She looked around the room. "I need a glass and a sheet of paper," she said.

Emily continued to ransack her boxes, knocking everything over as she went. She tore into the cardboard, chaotic and hungry like a raving beast. Openings and taped slits were ignored as the thing that was once Emily physically began tearing the cardboard into shreds in its mad search.

"Router!" the mad thing said. "Router!"

"Hey!" Sage shouted. The mad thing turned to her, a demonic look in its eyes not unlike the cormorant's. I could see red on the end of its fingernails. Drool dripped down Emily's chin. Sage and the Emily-creature stared at one another, the contest broken as Sage smiled.

"Do you have a glass?" she asked. The mad thing snarled and hunched over as it swatted boxes to either side in its search. Sage ducked just in time as a box crashed into the wall behind her. The quick sound of broken glass filled the room as it thumped to the floor. Sage rummaged through the box, filled with shards and wads of uselessly protective paper, until she pulled an untouched glass from its contents.

Hole Wall

"Thanks, man!" she said.

The mad thing responded with a guttural mutter as it resumed its search for a router. I watched the creature as it tore through its own belongings as if in a junkyard. The shack was quickly starting to resemble one, anyway. The mad thing still looked like Emily, in a way, but I knew it was something else. I think Sage knew too, but she didn't say anything as she tapped the plastic casing around the hole once again, glass and paper at hand.

"Hey little guy, yoo-hoo! I just want to help you get back to your home outside," she said.

I stood up on the futon. "Sage, I don't think that *came* from outside."

"I told you to *shut up!*" the mad thing yelled. It stopped its search to look me straight in the eye from across the room, its hatred pouring into my retinas.

I glared back at it. "*You* shut the fuck up, Emily," I said.

The mad thing laughed and threw a box near my head for amusement, barely missing me.

I turned back to Sage. "Sage," I whispered, "I want to leave."

But Sage waved me off. "Then help me capture this critter. It's not coming out," she said.

I hesitated. "Sage ..."

She looked up at me, completely serious. "Why do you hate animals so much?"

"I don't, I just—"

"Here, hold the cup and paper while I try to lure it out," she said and held up a finger between us. "It was this big, yeah? Maybe it just needs a friend. God knows I do," she said.

More crashes from the cardboard boxes clanged around the cottage. I tried to remember where the U-Haul keys were. Had Emily left them on the counter? Were they near the futon? Had they been buried under the freshly trashed piles of the mad thing's destruction?

"I think this'll work," Sage said, holding her finger in front of the hole.

"Sage, this makes no sense," I said.

I saw a hint of recognition, of sanity, in her eyes and my best friend smiled at me. "Does anything?" she said. Sage turned back to the wall hole and stuck the tip of her finger in. "C'mmmon," she said, "c'mon little guy. Take this here bait."

"Router! Router!" the mad thing screamed in the background.

The thing in the wall squealed again, and Sage's eyes lit up, the sanity gone. "I *found* ya!" she cried. The squeal gave way to a deeper roar, and Sage yelped out as her finger was pulled into the wall up to the knuckle. "Aw shit!" she cried.

"Sage!" I screamed and pulled on her hand.

"Stop! Stooop! Ow!" Sage yelled and pushed me away. I could hear a squishing and slithering from the other side of the wall. Over the sounds of the mad thing's tantrum, the rumbling from before began to start up again. It was coming from outside.

Hole Wall

"Oh man, I can *feel* it!" Sage said. She looked at me and smiled a grin of insanity. The silence between us sank like music in my heart. She laughed a kindless laugh. "It's so *warm*, Kate," she said.

The rumble increased, and the ugly walls began to shake. The warped floors swayed to and fro under our feet.

"Router!" the mad thing yelled, blood up to its arms. Sage and I held onto her stiff right arm, straight and tight, as something pulled on it from the other side. I pulled once more, and the thing briefly gave way. I saw the flesh of Sage's finger, skinless and hot red as if burned by a torch. Sage screamed in laughter and pain, then screamed louder than the damn bird from that morning. Her cry broke my heart as it popped my eardrums.

"What did you do on the bridge?!" Sage yelled. I could barely hear her over the outside roar, the crashing of clutter, the foundations coming undone, the cries of "Router!" and my own screams. Tears poured from my eyes as I shook my head.

"*Liar!*" my best friend screamed. The warping floors knocked me to my knees, and I scrambled for the front door. "*Kate! Don't leave!*" Sage cried out.

I looked back at her—there was that hatred again. It was the same hatred I saw in the eyes of the gulls and the sea lions and the cormorant, and now in my best friend.

"*Fine then. Go fuck yourself, Kate. You always run away. You always fucking run away and leave me to—*"

Something dragged Sage's entire arm into the wall. Her head slammed against the wooden paneling and a crunch came from inside the wall. My best friend wailed, tears mixed with blood streaming down her face. Sage screamed as it pulled her farther in.

The mad thing that was once Emily sat in the center of its trash kingdom as it screamed "Router! Router! Router!" and the cottage shook all around.

Sage screeched and pulled her arm back. Completely skinless, the muscles and veins mangled beyond all comprehension. She looked up at me.

"You need to help me, Kate."

Her arm jerked back into the wall, and she wailed again, looking at me and reaching out with her free hand.

I shook my head. Everything and everyone screamed all at once. I shut my eyes and swung the door open. I ran through, ignoring the screams behind me—the screams of my loved ones.

"You're a fucking coward, Kate."

I slammed the door.

Silence. Nothing.

I opened my eyes to see a blue evening, the horned moon up above. Waves crashed against a pebbled beach and a slight wind blew through the night. Not a mist or cloud in the air. I stood up and could not feel my limbs. I was so light, almost drifting though the moonlit porch.

No light came from the cottage, not a sound or a tremble. I looked back through the window. Moonlight shone on an empty carpeted floor inside, the wood-paneled walls bearing witness to an empty room. On one wall was a small hole with a plastic covering. I stared through it and into the room, fully aware that I was not alone. I buried my face in my hands and cried. I cried so much.

Hole Wall

I walked toward the blood-stained U-Haul. I had never found the keys. Something stood on the truck's hood: a pelican, covered in blood, half its beak hanging off its head. We stared into each other's eyes by that coastal moonlight. This pelican did not hate me, like all the others.

I wiped away my tears. "I'm sorry," I said.

The pelican blinked and spread its wings out to either side of the truck. I watched as it jumped off the hood and ran across the sand. With a few wingbeats the bird soared out over the sea, twisting into a corkscrew and submerging itself in moonlight. I sat on the bloody hood and waited.

The rumbling began anew, and on the waters of the Columbian estuary I saw that unholy half-ship. The sailors aboard jeered and snarled at me as it sailed toward me. Their heads were not heads at all, but clumps of kelp that hung loose down and across their chests. Two of the sailors wore skinny jeans and hoodies, and I could tell these were the ones who had once been my friends.

I slinked down the hood and waded into the waters with open arms. The sailors cheered, and I welcomed them with acceptance, a sadder and wiser woman.

The Sea Cottage

Storms always made me feel better, ever since I was little. I think it was something to do with being under the covers while it rained. I could always put things into perspective with a storm. Life going to shit? At least I'm inside.

But I wasn't under a blanket that day. The rain whipped and stung my face as I ran. I was miles away from home; I'd never stopped. The longer I ran, the further I could distance myself from the seaside town. I had only lived there for two years at that point, but I was beginning to think of it as home. That was all gone now.

I needed something to get my mind off what happened. Maybe that's what they call a runner's high. It felt good either way, at least emotionally. I loved storms more than ever in that moment. My feet hit the wet sand with violent slaps, and the crashing of the waves drowned out my crying.

I slowed down and stared at them for a second, panting. Screamed right at the goddamn Pacific Ocean. I was supposed to get away from this kinda stuff out here. I wanted to make it all leave me the fuck alone.

Sharp, black rocks pierced the sea like slivers on skin. They rose out of the water farther on and compiled themselves into large mounds and cliffs. A few seabirds circled above. The rocks sat grotesque and jagged in their forms, and they almost created an alcove from where I stood. I noticed a few of the seabirds nesting atop the tallest rocks. Patches of grass and creeping ferns had managed to grow near their peaks. Maybe there was somewhere I could just sit and cry. Running from everything had admittedly taken a lot of out me, and I realized how much my legs ached. I made my way toward the sea rocks.

They were massive, towering things—as tall as two-story buildings, dark forms against the blue-gray sky. The rain had died down a bit. I pulled my bag closer for comfort. I wished I had packed a beanie or something before I left. The seabirds above cried out to one another, mostly cormorants and seagulls. I noticed a larger creature among the rest, a great white pelican that stood away from the others. It looked me in the eye from up above, and I gasped when I realized it was missing the upper part of its beak. I put my head down and hurriedly walked deeper into the rock formations.

     The Sea Cottage

I knew the birds were above, watching me, so I tried to look neither up nor down. Something about these animals unnerved me. I kept on, trying to get away from them, but there were birds above me at every turn, every rock. I tried to distract myself as I walked. I glanced at the sides of the rocks to find walls of sea life covering them. Tan barnacles, black mussels, and large swaths of green anemones clumped tightly together. I shuddered to look at their formless, circular bodies drooping down toward the sand, waiting for the tide to come in and relieve their tentacles of gravity.

The tide. I looked down to see a shallow depth of water covering my shoes. Spinning around, I realized walls of living sea rock surrounded me on every side. I could hear the smacking and crackling of the wall creatures intermingled with the calls of the birds.

"Which way did I come in?" I asked myself. I looked up at the birds, who stared straight back.

"Which way did I come in?!" I yelled at them. They screamed back as if laughing, and one by one they flew-off and away from me. I swallowed. Tried to stay calm. I hurried along, each step sloshing through the cold saltwater that was collecting at my feet.

The smacking and gurgling sounds of the anemones and mollusks seemed to grow louder. Air excitedly released as they anticipated their return to the ocean.

No! That's not true. They don't have minds for things like that. But I couldn't shake the feeling that I was wrong as I walked along. This way? That way? How did I get here? Why had I kept my head down for so long? I turned the corner of yet another formation when I saw it. I screamed.

It wasn't always like this though. You know this. You remember when the sky was white and the seagulls didn't cry out at you like murder victims. You are inside at work. The bookstore. You try to keep yourself busy with tidying up the shelves, but today you've given up and read at the counter. No one's in at the moment, so you figure it's fine.

The tiny bell above the door chimes, and someone walks in. Your book will have to wait.

"Hello," you say in your customer service voice, but your cheery demeanor is cut short. This isn't your average customer.

He's an old seaman with a scarred face and a thick, wrinkled neck that probably hurts to the touch like sandpaper. An old brown coat hangs down from his shoulders to his knees. Like the jaw of a humpback, it looks to be encrusted with sea salt, and a number of barnacles litter the fabric. An old shitty sailor's hat covers his bald head. He looks as if he could snap you in half if you said the wrong thing. And yet, despite all these qualities, he does not seem unkind. He smiles at you with squinted eyes the color of galaxies.

"Good morning," he says in return. He looks around the bookstore, as quaint and humble as himself. You can tell he likes books.

"Can I help you with something?" you ask.

He raises his eyebrows. "Yes!" he says. "I'm wondering if you have any ledgers. You used to keep them back here in the day."

You don't know if you carry "ledgers," if the store has ever carried ledgers, but you know better than to correct him.

"We haven't carried ... uh, ledgers in a while, but let me see if I can find something in the back."

"Splendid. I'll be in the stacks if you need me." He makes his way toward the nautical section but turns back. "What was your name?"

"Jaime."

 The Sea Cottage

You smile, trying not to be too uncomfortable by his vague statements, and walk to the back. This town has the strangest characters.

A dark shape floated in the water, trapped with me in this cold hell. It gently swayed as the tide came in. The stench hit me soon after that.

It was a round, furry thing—a dead seal. Or sea lion. Whatever. I covered my face and stepped forward. I don't know why. My panic subsided momentarily as I crept closer. The poor thing had been dead for a while and probably died from unnatural means. I could see shards of glass protruding out of a rotten eye. Past the wet fur, part of the animal's body had been ripped open. I winced as I noticed several rib bones jutting out of the black, rotting meat. Bits of muscle still clung to the bones, and I could see the color.

Red.

Just like earlier.

Just like death.

Just like—

This animal died here, and I was going to go with it if I didn't find a way out soon. I looked into its cloudy, mangled eye and I could see myself reflected in the broken glass. My heartbeat picked up and my body started to sweat. Adrenaline seeped into my system, screaming, "Run run run run run!" but I didn't do anything. I didn't do anything at all. I just stood there as water splashed onto my shins and the body bobbed on the surface up and down up and down like a buoy and I knew in my heart that this could be me soon and that I would die—my blood would spill—my flesh would blacken. Run run run run run!

Jonah Barnett

"Fuck. No. *Fuck no!*" I yelled. I kicked the carcass, bits of dark flesh flying off and splashing into the water. I ran.

Wall crackles and pops picked up volume all around me. I turned corner after corner, lost in a labyrinth of sea creatures and rock. Stupid green fucking anemones clicking away in celebration. Of the water. Of my death. I grimaced and clawed at the nearest batch of the green creatures in frustration.

"Leave me alone!" I cried. The pain stung as I scraped a few of the creatures off the wall. I tore into the wall of life in a frenzy, screaming and swearing as the water came up to my knees. Prying off the barnacles, mussels, green anemones, flecks of red kelp— *red! Goddamn red*—a blue starfish.

I stopped. My hands began to bleed from the sharper creatures, but I didn't look at the red creeping down my fingers. I only stared at the blue starfish. Something about it ... I don't know. I felt calm, peace.

I can't describe how vibrant it looked in contrast with the dulled colors around it. The plain creatures, the darkened sky storm, the gray saltwater at my legs. The sea star almost shone in this drab nightmare of mine. I looked down and realized what I had done. Several damaged anemones floated alongside me. I covered my face in shame.

"No ... No, please."

Lightning flashed across the sky. I looked up. There was another blue starfish. And another. And one more. They almost formed a trail along the rocks. I stepped forward in a daze.

"I ... I can't."

The Sea Cottage

Thunder boomed through the air and the rain began anew. I walked, leaning on the wall of ocean life for support to ground me. I followed the stars through the rain, small cerulean shapes with twisted arms and crude, raised textures. The rain pattered all around me and into the small waves at my waist.

Logically, I knew I might die, but my energy had been sapped from running. The stars trailed up one of the rocks, which was slanted upward, so it wasn't so impossible to climb. I dug my nails into the barnacles and seaweed that encrusted the rocks. The skin underneath split and bled, but I hoisted myself up. The inanimate creatures under me snapped and crackled louder as I kept climbing.

I looked down. The water lapped below, higher than before. I kept on. For a time, the rocks flattened out and I could walk upright once again. I noticed small pools of marine life scattered about this clearing. I peered closer. A source of light poured out from these pools. The blue starfish. Yellow kelp. Small purple and gray swimming fish. They were all glowing with bioluminescence! I spotted my old friends the anemones clustered underneath the surface of these pools. Their green, dead tentacles came to life under the water in hues of red.

Red.

I continued, following the star trail. I was beginning to feel as though it was time to give up. To just sit in the pouring rain with my bag over my head and maybe wait for low tide once more. But as I looked back, I could see the waves almost following me, taunting me. The water lapped at where I had walked mere minutes before. I tried to ignore this.

I found more rocks to climb, and as I proceeded to higher ground, I wondered if there was an end to all of this. Waves washed over the tide pools now below me. It wouldn't be much longer until the waves caught up. I quickened my pace and squeezed through a slight uphill opening between the rocks, the stars still my guide. I saw something.

High up, nestled between the rocks and gasping sea life, stood a shack. Or a cottage. Some kind of small building. A neglected space constructed of stones. No one stone shared any similarities with the others, as if each rock had been collected from a different edge of the world. At the front I could see a heavy door and a few windows. The blue sea stars led to this structure, intermingling with the other sea creatures that swarmed the entire building. The cottage looked to be over a century old, an undiscovered fossil long since abandoned and never violated by human eyes. Until today.

The door swung open.

An old woman as ancient as the cottage itself stood in the doorway. Her clothes were tattered and browned with age. Something about her struck me as familiar. I realized she was glaring at me.

"Who do you think *you* are?" she called.

Thunder rang again, and I heard the waves roar behind us. The opening was beginning to fill with water coming up toward me. I ran toward the woman.

"The water!" I cried. "It's following me."

She looked behind me, unimpressed. "It always does that. Don't think yourself so special." The sea creatures clicked and sizzled louder than ever.

 The Sea Cottage

"Are you a marine station? Or something?"

"Hah! As if," she said. She stepped back, beginning to close the cottage's large, antique door. "You can swim, right?"

Another wave crash. I stepped forward, pushing the door.

"Please, I'm soaking wet," I said.

She pushed back. "You're trespassing. Please leave." The water pushed through the opening with one final wave. Saltwater lapped at my feet.

"Miss ..."

"What?" she snapped.

I hesitated, looking behind her into the room. Something about her home seemed unnatural. Wrong. Part of me wished to follow her advice and leave.

But I remembered the seal.

"I don't want to die!" I said.

She stopped and seemed to think this over. Another wave spouted water through the opening. I yelled out.

"Fine!" she said and hurried me inside. The roars of the ocean overwhelmed our ears. The woman struggled to close the heavy door. It slammed shut and all noise stopped, as if never there.

I caught my breath, dripping water onto the floor. I looked up to see her glaring at me again. She stared into my eyes with her own, the color of stars. I could see sand encrusted into each crease of her ragged face. Her frizzed crimson hair was tied-up in a bun, with a few salty bangs hanging down either side of her head.

"You shouldn't have come here," she said.

Something hit the door with a loud bang. I flinched at the sound. "What was that?"

"What do you think?" She walked-off into another room. I ran to one of the windows; the water halfway up its frame. I could see the anemones and starfish underwater outside. The creatures glowed in the same way they had in the tide pools. The sea was alive with light, and the water-level kept crawling over the house in the storm.

"What kind of a place is this!" I yelled.

"What sort of establishment is this?" the seaman says at the counter.

You had managed to find a single blue journal in the back. It was in an old box at the top of a shelf. The pages are long-yellowed, and you can't fathom it's less than forty years old. But that's not why the old man is cross with you.

"I'm sorry sir," you say, "but we simply cannot accept these diamonds as a form of payment." You gesture to the pile of little red rocks that he's scattered all over the counter.

"They're rubies!" he says.

"Still, I can only take cash or cards."

"You lot accepted my payment last time I was here. I bought six boxes of ledgers with my currency!"

You look down again at the rubies, eyes widened. They never trained you for this. You think about what a nice customer service horror story this will make on social media.

 The Sea Cottage

"Please, Jaime, dear boy," the old man says. "It's to make someone happy. It's my old wife, you see? She's so miserable these days. Like a wee little clam. She gets like this when she can't write."

You didn't ask to hear his life story. "Can't she write on her computer?"

"Her what?"

You sigh. He looks genuinely upset, and he smells of sea salt. The sooner you can get him on his way, the sooner you can get on with reading your novel.

"Fine. You see that building?" You point across the street. "That's the pawnshop. I have no idea if they can even remotely do anything with rubies, but that's probably your best shot. Come back when you have payment."

"What large sums will I be required to exchange for this book?" he asks.

"$19.95 ... Plus tax."

He nods and sweeps the rubies back into his hands and down into his pockets.

"I'll be back before the day's over, Jaime," he says.

"You better hurry. They close in twenty minutes. Quick! Quick!" you yell, a bit facetiously. The man's eyes widen, and he rushes out of the shop. You chuckle to yourself, knowing full well that the pawnshop doesn't close until 8:00 p.m. Weird old man. You open your book, trying to get back into the chapter you were at.

Outside. A horn. An impact. An old man's cry.

You drop the book.

Schools of fish swam by the cottage's glass, glowing in the murky waters. The bioluminescent light poured into the house's living room. To the right was an archway that led to a small kitchen. I could hear familiar pops and crackles. The inside walls and ceilings were completely covered with the same forms of animal life that swarmed the rocks outside. I winced, wishing I could be rid of the anemones once and for all.

My host had seemingly retreated into another room, so I was left to entertain myself. Bookshelves made from driftwood lined the walls, the occasional sea star clinging to one of their volumes with titles like *Pelagic Spells* and *Mastering the Language of Ammonites*. One shelf housed a goldfish bowl with a small jellyfish inside. In the center of the room sat two ancient, waterlogged chairs surrounding a lone fire pit. The pit itself boasted a purple flame.

The woman walked back into the room. We both jumped at the sight of one another. She let out a sigh.

"No one ever makes it up here," she said, sitting down in one of the chairs.

I followed suit. "Do I trouble you?" I asked.

She snorted. "No," she said and reached into her pocket. Rubies. She flung them into the fire, and it flashed brighter for a moment. I noticed then that the fire appeared to be fueled only by a small pile of red stones. The familiar gems made my palms sweat, that awful red color glaring at me.

"You do annoy me, though. I'm not in the mood to entertain guests. I haven't needed to entertain any soul for a matter of ..." she glanced at me, "... years."

      The Sea Cottage

I looked around the room, noticing a number of the wall-anemones and mussels that had creeped onto her shelves. "Clearly."

She didn't say anything in return. We let the moments pass as we sat in the gloom of the fire and outside glow.

I motioned to the underwater scene outside. "What is that out there?"

"Well, the ocean, I gather."

"But how are we alive right now? What's keeping this building airtight? This place is unreal," I said.

She shrugged. "It's fine."

"Do you live here alone?"

"Apparently," she scowled as she said this. "My husband has lived with me for most of my life, but he's been gone for over a day now."

I blinked. "That's only a day, though. Where do you think he went off to?"

"The town." She looked right into my eyes as she said this. Something came over me as she stared with her starry eyes. "You wouldn't happen to know anything about that, would you?"

I swallowed. "No."

She looked away, cutting-off whatever dreadful feeling had taken ahold of me. "That's enough questions for now," she stood up. "You're welcome to stay here, although don't expect me to be much of a host. You've come at an awful time."

She began walking to the other room but turned back. "I can feel him, you know. I can feel him gone, and I can feel you lying."

I was left to wonder why I had not told the truth. I sauntered over to one of the shelves and chose a book about fortune-telling with seaweed.

She's a witch, right? A sea witch? a little voice asked within me. *She knows. She must know. Why she hasn't killed me yet is anyone's guess.*

I turned the pages, trying to distract myself. *Maybe she wants me to say it, to admit to doing it ... then she'll murder me.*

I glanced outside at the glowing sea life. My eyes widened as a giant spotted eel with a hideous round face swam past. I walked to the window to see a number of larger creatures swimming outside, all aglow in the water. The cottage was completely submerged. *Then again, where would I even run?*

I returned to the book, but I must have fallen asleep because the next thing I remember is waking up in the dark. The glow from the outside creatures had died down but the purple fire stayed strong. The clinging things on the walls did not make a sound. I tried to go back to sleep in my chair, to no avail. From outside came distant calls. I realized they were whale songs. They were impossible to sleep through. I gave up and placed the book back onto the shelf, looking elsewhere amongst the books for something to keep me occupied.

The majority of the books on the bottom shelves turned out to be waterlogged to the point of rot. I opened one of the drier volumes to find a great deal of handwriting and sketches. These must have been the witch's diaries—or perhaps spell books. Several photographs had fallen to the floor as soon as I opened the diary. I bent over to pick them up.

The photographs in question were old, tattered, and brown—not unlike most things in the cottage. They appeared to be vintage. A

     The Sea Cottage

stoic-looking woman looked straight into the camera without the hint of a smile. I looked closer. It was the woman, the witch, in the portrait. She looked the exact same age as she had hours before, and yet these photos couldn't have been younger than a hundred years old.

I turned to the next photograph: the same witch posed with another woman in a veil. The second woman was, if anything, striking and sent shivers down my spine. On the back of the photograph, a handwritten message:

> *Dearest friend, so lovely to see you two this time of year as always. Please accept these prints I had Irving whip up in one of his little labs. Your everlasting companion, Florence Ellon. 1906.*

I flipped to the last photo. The witch stood with a man in this portrait. Again, the mood was solemn, but they were close together as if they were intimate, perhaps husband and wife. Something about the man struck me as familiar. Weathered face. Broad shoulders. Something wild about the eyes—

The seaman.

The whale songs outside grew louder. My heart raced. It really was him. I was right. I was absolutely right. She and he were together and now there was proof and she was going to kill me in the night because of my sins and I deserved it! I would die if I did not escape!

I ran to the door and tried to pry it open. The outside glow brightened and illuminated the whole room. I couldn't escape! Of course! I heard another great call—screeching this time. I looked out the window.

An entire pod of whales swam above the sea cottage, their underbellies aglow from the bioluminescence beneath. Their songs no longer sounded beautiful but distasteful, twisted. Their calls screamed in my ears, and I screamed right back.

"I didn't mean to! I didn't know!"

The door to the other room swung open. The witch had come to take my life! She peered at me in the bright light. She called to me, but I could not hear over the whale songs—a piercing barrage of calls that filled the room and made my ears bleed.

I shook my head. "No! Stay away! Please don't touch me!"

But she stepped closer. Closer and closer. We were confined in this little damned space under the sea and I was to die here by the hands of the witch to the sounds of her whale familiars and no one even knew where I was and I realized I should have never left and I was dumb I was so so dumb I should have just accepted those rubies and that would have been it but now I was going to die and it was all my fault and—

I fell to the floor.

You remember that day. It's the whole reason for everything. You think back on how things could have been different. How you could have prevented it.

You rush out the bookstore toward the sound. A car has swerved off the street and into a light post—it's one of those antique fixtures that makes the town seem "quaint." Between the car and the light post, the old man is pinned in place. His upper half is sprawled out over the hood, and his legs are mangled underneath. You can see bone sticking out. Blood pours from his mouth. He's breathing.

The Sea Cottage

"Hello? Sir?" you cry. You check on the driver as well. The person behind the wheel is unconscious. The seaman wheezes and holds a hand out. He looks at you for help, his starry eyes pleading for a savior.

You pull your phone out. Your hands are shaking. As you look down, you see it. Blood pools beneath him, mingling with the rubies scattered on the asphalt. Blood. So much red, red blood. It reminds you of a time long ago. Your own blood splattered on the concrete as those boys kicked you senseless. You remember curling into a ball and sobbing. You remember the pain. You remember wanting to die.

You drop the phone in the blood. His blood. He is wheezing. Remember when you wheezed? Remember when you cried out and no one helped you at first? When you got the chance, you just ran and ran and ran and changed schools and never went back.

You scramble for your phone. You're trying to wipe the blood off the screen, but the more you smear off, the murkier the glass gets. Breathe. Breathe. Stop breathing so hard and help!

You look up at the man. "I ... I just have to ... Hold on—"

But you slip! Like an idiot you slip and fall back into the blood. Red! It's just so fucking red, and it's all over you. Your throat begins to tighten. Kicked in the face because of that boy. The faces of your abusers flash through your mind. The face of the man looks at you for help, and you realize you're crying. People are starting to gather at the scene. They can see you cry.

"I'm sorry, I just ..." and the rest of your words are lost to sobs. A moment passes, and you're running. Get away. Get away get away get away! The others can help him. You just need to leave.

Seagulls cry out at you from above: "Coward! Coward coward coward!"

You must get out of there! You push your way back into the book-store, blood smearing on the door handles. You grab your book and the blue journal and whatever else you can find on the counter it doesn't matter and stuff it into your bag and flee. No one notices you as you run past, down the lane and into the mist.

But the seaman knows. He watches you as you run, and the stars go out from his eyes.

"Coward!"

The smell of cooking filled my senses. I opened my eyes. The sea creatures on the ceiling clicked and popped at me, and I could see the room was awash in sunlight. A cushion had been placed underneath my head with a blanket thrown over. The clanging of cooking came from the kitchen.

Why am I not dead?

I looked at the door. I could see the rocks outside the window. The tide was low once again. I could escape! I grabbed my bag.

"Are you awake?" someone called from the kitchen. "I'm making breakfast."

I didn't say anything back. I could imagine the witch cooking something sinister up in her cauldron, her preparation for my death.

"You might as well eat before you leave," she called.

I clutched my bag closely. If I left, she would just bring me back, wouldn't she? I knew in my heart this was undoubtedly a trap but walked toward the kitchen anyway. I found her standing over a rusted stove with a purple flame. She poked and prodded a sizzling pan with an antique spatula. Her salty hair was tied in an old

The Sea Cottage

ribbon, and I noticed an array of barnacles on the apron she wore. The small beige things opened and caught whatever flecks of food and grease flew out from the pan.

She looked up. "Good morning, dear." She motioned toward the dining table behind her. "Why don't you take a seat?"

I shook my head. "I'd rather stand."

"Suit yourself. Hungry?"

Whatever sat in the pan smelled wonderful, and my stomach grumbled. I'd neglected to bring any snacks in my bag the day before.

"What is it?" I asked.

"Seagull egg omelets with kelp. Not as odd as it sounds."

"It *does* sound awful," I said.

She tipped the omelet onto a plate and set it on the table, then returned to the stove. I crept forward. It looked to be a regular omelet with flecks of kelp embedded for flavor. I hesitated.

"I didn't poison it, if that's what you're thinking," she said without turning.

Reluctantly I sat at the table. Perhaps my hunger got the better of me. I looked around the room, the décor of which seemed to be salvaged from various sea wreckage. Ship ropes decorated the walls above a submarine sink; small familiar blue starfish clung to their threads.

"You don't have to wait for me; *you're* the one who fainted last night. You need your strength," she said.

"I'd rather be polite," I said.

She shrugged. "Fine." We sat in silence for a few moments.

"How did you find me?" she asked.

I picked at my omelet with a Victorian fork. "I got lost."

"Lost people don't wash up on my doorstep. You were looking for something."

"Well, I wasn't looking for you, if that's what you're implying."

She turned and gave me a dirty look, galaxy eyes glaring at me. "I don't have to keep you alive, you know."

I looked down, swallowed. "Sorry. I … I don't know what I was—what I *am*—looking for."

She sighed and flipped her omelet onto a plate. I saw her wave her hand over the stove, and the purple flame flashed away. We sat facing one another.

She stared at me. I stared back. Neither of us touched our food.

"You were there," she said.

I looked down. "I wanted to go away. Just for a little bit. To get my mind off things," I said.

"To run away."

"Yes. How did you know?"

"The seagulls told me."

"Of course they did."

"You'd better eat."

I did as she said. She looked off as I ate. I wondered if this was going to be my last meal. I glanced up to see her nodding, her eyes

The Sea Cottage

closed. She opened them to look at me, and something immensely sad shone inside them. Dying galaxies.

"I know I am going to die alone in this house. I do. But it hasn't settled in yet. Not completely," she said. She rubbed her arms as if to keep the sadness away. "I didn't want to come here, you know. It was his idea. He said we could live off the sea, and we followed the stars scattered across the sands. The birds screamed secrets, and the waves whispered things only we could hear. He taught me how to listen. And now I'm stuck here, and he's ..." she stopped.

She composed herself after a moment and continued. "Something happens, or doesn't happen, and you come to some sort of terrible realization within the comfort of your own home. And all of a sudden, it's not your home anymore, is it? It's a prison."

I stopped eating. Stared at the floor. "I ... can't run away from this," I said.

She smiled. "No."

I dropped my fork. My breathing picked up again. I blinked. Once. Twice. My eyes widened, and saltwater sprang-up underneath. Tears. I broke down crying in front of the old woman. I cried at the kitchen table onto my omelet and I couldn't seem to stop myself.

"I didn't mean to. I really didn't. I just couldn't. There was so, so much blood! And I tried to help but I just—I dunno. And people crowded around and the seagulls were screaming and I just wanted to die but I don't think I actually want to die but I don't know how to *stop* this. I don't know how to make this go away. I couldn't help. I didn't help. I just ... I just ..." and my tears once again took over.

She stared at me from across the table. I might have seen pity in her eyes. I may have seen hatred. Perhaps it was a mixture of the two.

I gasped amidst my sobs. "And the color. Red! It follows me everywhere I go. It … cuts! It cuts into my mind and oozes its way in until it's all I can fucking see, even when my eyes are closed. It is loud. It is pain! It is every person that has ever hurt me and every person I have failed!" I cried.

Thunder clapped above our heads and rain poured outside once more. I wanted to be under a blanket. The witch's cold, starry eyes stared at me, lips pressed together and fingers digging into the table's antique wood. I could see something in her, like a great purple fire rising up from within. I feared for my damned life at that moment, but I realized I deserved whatever she did. I deserved it all.

"Please, just do what you will," I said. "I accept my cowardice." I shut my eyes.

The rain outside died down, and nothing happened. I waited, but no harm came to me. I opened my eyes to see the old woman, calm. Now she was crying softly.

"You did nothing wrong," she whispered. I cried harder.

I stood in the doorway hours later. I reached into my bag before she saw me off.

"I think he wanted you to have this." I handed her the blue journal. Her hands took the book and smoothed it over as if it were alive. The galaxies looked up at me.

"You must focus on this. Not red, but blue," she said.

I stared out into the sky. Seagulls flew where whales once swam. They screamed secrets.

"How do I focus on blue when there is so much red inside?" I asked.

She shook her head. "It will never fully go away. You will have to make peace with this, and I will as well. I have been here for so long, and now I am alone. I suppose we all transpire to sea foam in the end."

I looked into her eyes. The constellations shone vibrant within, but I knew they would never be as bright as before.

"I'm sorry," I said.

She smiled. "Thank you."

There aren't ways to make this immediately better, only to cope in the meanwhile. Slowly healing until you don't notice how far you have come until long afterward. You walk away from the stone cottage, never looking back. Golden light from afternoon sun shines down on your face, but it doesn't warm you.

Never look back as you walk—perhaps you would turn to salt or sea foam. Follow the blue sea stars home, away from all this. The sea life that covers the rocks sing you farewell, good riddance, whatever. Seagulls scream goodbye.

Storms arise throughout this process of healing. The red violence springs forth again, bubbling up in your mind—but the blue soothes it over, at least for a moment.

You make your way out of the rocks and stand in front of the Pacific—this great blue thing that swallows all in the end. You exhale. It won't be like this forever, but it will never be the same either. It starts raining.

Stripes

1 Missed Call, 1:25 a.m.

Sylvia Zou, 1:26 a.m.: Are you asleep? This isn't anything scary but could you call me?

Sylvia Zou, 2:34am: Okay possibly scary. Not about us but I'm freaking out right now. I feel really bad, and I think your phone is down and… fuck. I'd really love your help right now Megan. I know you hate it when people are touchy feely, but you help me a lot sometimes

2 Missed Calls, 2:39 a.m.

Megan's room lit up in blue light, and her eyes crept open at her vibrating phone. Her girlfriend's face stared out at her from the bright screen.

No. No no no no. God! she thought. Maybe she could just let it go, pretend to have slept through it, and finally get a full night's rest. She had to set boundaries—that's what her therapist told her. Sylvia was taking up too much space. And honestly this was getting ridic—

The phone stopped. The room settled into darkness. Megan happily sighed. Crisis averted. Sylvia could handle this herself. She was a fully grown adult—almost. She could imagine Syl alone in her nest of a dorm room, with all those disgusting candy wrappers and crinkled chip bags and messy clothes and beer cans and wrangled blankets crying herself to sleep, and …

Ugh.

She picked up the phone and groaned at the time.

1 Missed Call: Sylvia Zou.

Heavy breathing picked up when she called back and, as expected, crying.

"Hello? Syl?" Megan said. "Why did you call?"

"Could, could you come over?" Sylvia sobbed on the other line.

Megan winced. "Why?"

 Stripes

"I just ... I need you right now. Please," she said. She started crying again. Megan sat in the dark as she waited for the girl to calm down. "I think I had another dream. I dunno. I'm just kinda freaked out, and I want you to be here."

"Syl, it's three in the morning, and—"

"*Please*, Meg," she cried.

Megan rubbed her eyes. Her mind could not function at this hour.

"Listen ... go back to sleep, okay? It was just a bad dream. You're fine."

"But I don't think I am!"

Megan gritted her teeth. She had been told about this, how relationships required a fair deal of sacrifice and compromise, but she had this feeling that she had struck a crap deal with this first one.

"Please just go to bed. I'll see you tomorrow if you need to." That was the "compromise" element talking.

Silence on the other end for a moment.

Then: "What time?"

"I dunno. Breakfast. Text me."

"You promise?"

"Y—yeah?"

"Okay."

Megan closed her eyes, rolling back her head. Something popped in her neck. "Great. Now go to sleep."

"You promise I'm okay?"

"Sure, Syl."

"I love you."

Megan hung up and slid back onto her pillow, staring at the ceiling. She should have let it go.

```
Sylvia Zou, 7:02 a.m.: Martin Way Diner at 9?
Megan Gibbs, 8:23 a.m.: Yeah. See you there
Sylvia Zou, 9:05 a.m.: Here
Sylvia Zou, 9:18 a.m.: Hey, are we still
meeting?
```

Sylvia tried to distract herself with her notebook, scribbling away in one of the diner booths. Megan was coming. She said she was coming. She wouldn't stand-up Sylvia like that. She glanced up. No Megan, but plenty of people surrounded her in the diner. Plenty of people probably wondering about the loner weirdo sitting alone.

She returned to her book. Its pages turned black with pen scratches and marks. Perhaps drawing her nightmares would help her process them. The figure of a woman appeared on her paper—a nightmare incarnate. Ink started to stain her fingers as she sketched. The woman stood tall, with a long flowing dress that covered her legs and stretched on past the paper's edge. A pattern of tar-colored stripes covered her arms and face, and two sinister horns jutted out from the woman's head. Black wisps of darkness seemed to rise from her very being. Blood dripped from her mouth as the woman snarled. Something about that face. Something outside her dorm window. In the trees. In the darkness. Staring in at her.

          Stripes

Sylvia squeezed her eyes shut. The early-morning noises of clanging and cooking echoed throughout the establishment, and the smell of burned coffee and deep-fried corn syrup helped calm her nerves.

"Is that from your dreams?"

Megan sat across from Sylvia. Her fears melted.

"Hi!" She sighed and smiled. She looked down at her sketches and quickly shut it. "They're just doodles."

"Can I see?"

Sylvia hesitated but handed the notebook to Megan. She quickly thumbed through the pages.

Sylvia squirmed in the silence. "Sorry about last night," she said.

"It's fine." Megan didn't look up. "I guess I'm just unused to being so … available, I guess."

"I mean, I'm your first girlfriend, right?"

"You're my first *anything*."

Sylvia's heart fluttered. Megan handed the book back to Sylvia.

"It's okay. Your style's messy for my taste, and the proportions are a bit off. No one's arms are that long," she said. Sylvia felt her smile drop. Megan shrugged. "Sorry. I'm more of a realist. Fantasy's not really my thing."

Sylvia smiled. "I know. Opposites attract, right?"

"Sure."

An outdated waitress arrived with glasses of water and took their orders. Sylvia tried to smile as the stranger stood before them, but something within her tightened and threatened to burst. She ordered waffles with a side of eggs. Megan passed, only wringing whatever sat inside Sylvia's chest further. Sylvia sighed with relief as the waitress disappeared behind the kitchen's swinging doors.

"You're not hungry?" she asked.

"I actually have to bounce. I just wanted to … check in on you, I guess," Megan said. "You feeling okay?"

"I …" Sylvia trailed off. "Yeah. Just … very vivid dreams. I keep dreaming about being, um …"

"What?"

"Being … tortured, really," Sylvia admitted. She looked around the room and spoke in a lower voice. "I know it sounds dumb, but it's like I can feel what's being done to me, and I can hear her voice as if she's in the room with …" she noticed the weird look Megan was giving her. "Anyway, they're just dreams."

"Sylvia, you know dreams aren't real, right?"

"Yeah, of course."

"Good. You're probably just stressed."

"Maybe. Yes. You're right. It's gotta be the midterms coming up."

"Next time we hang out, we should study together. That sounds nice, right?"

The waitress returned with Sylvia's plate. Smells of waffle and egg wafted toward Sylvia. She stared off into space, not knowing what to say.

"Syl?"

     Stripes

"Yeah! That sounds great. Thanks, Megan." She smiled again.

Megan smiled back. "Glad you're feeling better."

"I ... yeah."

Megan got up and kissed Sylvia on the head. Sylvia stared down at her breakfast as Megan walked off. She wasn't so hungry anymore.

Thursday.

Sylvia Zou, 4:45 a.m.: I had another dream. It seemed really real. I don't think I can go back to sleep. Are you there? Can we talk?

Friday.

1 Missed Call, 2:10 a.m.

Sylvia Zou, 2:12 a.m.: Dreamed again. Really hurt everywhere.

Megan Gibbs, 2:14 a.m.: Your probably fine. Go back to sleep. Ill come over tomorrow

Sylvia Zou, 2:14 a.m.: Ok

Saturday.

3 Missed Calls, 2:56 a.m.

Sylvia Zou, 3:01 a.m.: Fuck fuck please help me I think I'm having another attack or something I don't know

Sylvia Zou, 3:02 a.m.: You're probably asleep now aren't you?

Sylvia Zou, 3:04 a.m.: I'm sorry

Sunday.

Sylvia Zou, 1:22 a.m.: Hey sorry I don't wanna keep dragging you into my dumb freakouts but I dunno maybe I shouldn't be so freaked out about whether I annoy you with this kinda stuff. Trying to be calm.

Sylvia Zou, 1:29 a.m.: I think I'll be alright

Sylvia set her phone down after sending the last text and stared at it. She was so annoying, but she couldn't stop herself. One message back—or anything—that's all she wanted. Some confirmation that Megan had read it and acknowledged she cared about Sylvia. Her heart beat, adrenaline pumping. Late nights were not good for anxious minds. She buried her head into her pillow and groaned.

I should forget Megan, a tiny voice in her head whispered. She breathed in sharply. No! Don't be like that. Every relationship has their ups and downs.

When was the last time there was an "up"?

Stop it!

She pushed the phone off the bed and flipped over, facing her dorm window that looked out into the trees. The campus had been built at the edge of an old-growth forest. She could look up and see the outlines of dark cedars against a night-blue sky.

No dreams had come yet, but she was terrified to fall asleep. Why didn't Megan care more? Maybe she was right; maybe Sylvia was overreacting. She stared out into the cedar branches and sighed.

Something moved within the trees.

Sunday.

1 Missed Call, 2:32 a.m.

 Stripes

Megan marched through the dormitory doors. The disgusting stale scent of the dorms flooded her nose and she winced. It was almost sour. She could hear wails coming from a few floors up and echoing through the building thanks to its cold, concrete architecture. Megan rushed up the stairs.

A small crowd had formed in the floor's common room. Megan forced her way into the center, saying she was Syl's girlfriend and asking if they could all move out of the way. She came upon Sylvia on a couch, covered in blankets that were not her own. Sylvia shook violently, shutting her eyes as the RA sat next to her and bandaged one of her arms. She held the other arm close to her, its open wounds smearing blood into her nightshirt.

"Don't do that, please," the RA winced.

Sylvia put her arm down, and tears streamed down her face. "I thought I was getting better … I really thought I was getting better, but then she came back. She … cuts me. And bites me. She hurts me whenever I sleep. Sometimes I can't see what she's doing, but I can still feel it."

"It's … okay," the RA said.

"It's not, though!" Sylvia said.

Sylvia looked up and noticed Megan. Little red scratches covered Sylvia's face.

"Megan!" she cried. "Why are you here?"

The RA looked up, relieved. "Hey, are you the one I called?"

Megan sighed loudly. "Yes." She turned to Sylvia. "Why am I your emergency contact?"

Sylvia looked down, her faced reddening. "Shit. I'm ... I'm sorry. I forgot I did that. My parents are out of state, and—"

"Can I speak with you for a minute?" the RA asked.

Megan nodded.

The RA asked one of the students to tend to Sylvia and took Megan aside. "So ... your girlfriend claims she was attacked by someone, but I can't find any signs of entry. None of the girls on her floor fit her description either."

"Is she making it up?" Megan asked.

"I wouldn't put it like that," the RA said.

They looked back over at Sylvia. Megan reddened at the sight of her sobbing in front of these people. This was so embarrassing.

"Dispatch is on their way. They'll probably want to search Sylvia's room and ask her some questions about her attacker."

"Who attacked her?"

"She said it was a woman with horns and a striped face?"

Megan put her face in her hands. She sighed once more. "Oh god."

Stripes

"You don't know anything about this, do you?"

"Yeah, it's this character she doodles all the time. It's stupid."

"It's not stupid to her. I don't think she's well, Megan."

"Well what am I supposed to do about it?"

Sunday Afternoon.

Sylvia awoke the next day to find herself in a familiar bed. Megan's sheets. Clangs, rattles, and sizzles came from the kitchen. The walls surrounding her were adorned with Megan's model sketches—charcoal drawings showcasing various poses of the human body. Syl remembered her own sketches and reddened. Megan was right about her drawing style; she just wished it didn't sting as much. At least it was safe here. The thing from last night wouldn't ...

She rubbed her eyes and stared into the ugly, popcorned ceiling above her. Like the rest of the room, it had been painted beige. She buried her face into the pillows and breathed in Megan's scent; she didn't know if she liked it or not.

No, of course she did. *Of course* she liked it.

Megan stepped into the bedroom with a bowl of soup, wafts of steam rising from its center.

"You made me soup?" Syl asked.

Megan shrugged. "Don't get too excited. It's Campbell's."

Sylvia tried to smile. She lifted her spoon to find four prongs at the end instead.

"Oh, sorry." Megan left the room, and Sylvia placed the fork on the nightstand beside the bed. Megan held a spoon up as she reentered. "Here."

It plopped in with a splash. "Thanks."

Megan sat as Sylvia cautioned a bite, blowing on her spoon. She took a gulp before Megan spoke up.

"Feeling better?" she asked.

"Not yet," Sylvia said.

Megan smiled uncomfortably. Sylvia's body grew tense as Megan watched her eat.

"You gave us all a fright last night."

"I didn't mean to."

"I know, it's just ... I guess it's certainly one way to get my attention."

Sylvia put the spoon down. "What?"

"I mean, I'll admit I've been a bit distant lately, but cutting yourself?" Megan laughed. "That's a bit dramatic, don't you think?"

Sylvia was speechless. She placed the soup on the nightstand and got up. "I don't have to be here."

"Actually, yes, you do." Megan stopped her. "You can't leave, Syl."

"Yes, I can."

Megan seemed hesitant, as if trying to find the right thing to say.

"What's wrong with you?" Sylvia asked.

 Stripes

"You're … you're under twenty-four-hour supervision," Megan said. "I promised I would keep an eye on you."

Sylvia's eyes narrowed. "I'm fine."

"Look at yourself. Look at your fucking arms. You're not fine, Sylvia."

Sylvia sighed and slumped back onto her pillow. She felt Megan's lips kiss her cheek. She cried.

"She's hunting me, Meg," she sobbed. "She's hunting me, and I don't know why."

Megan wrapped her arms around Sylvia, kissing her face as she cried. "You need to stop, Sylvia. She isn't real. Please, stop. Just stop."

Sunday Night.

Sylvia lay in bed next to Megan, who was fast asleep. She felt weird next to this person, this woman she called her girlfriend. The feeling of Megan's body next to her own repulsed Sylvia, and she pressed her arm into herself to keep away from Megan.

I was crazy about you, she thought. It made her sad. She wanted to roll over and away from Megan, but she was forced to lay on her back because of her injured arms. She stared at the ceiling once more. *Hopefully for the last time.*

It sunk in as she thought that. This wasn't healthy for her. She thought of what she had become in this relationship—a strange anxious version of her former self just *waiting* for that one text message to assure her she was loved. She looked over at Megan and remembered how it had first felt to date her. The excitement, the joy, the elation of having found someone new. Something squeezed inside her, and her chest actually physically hurt.

Goodbye, Megan.

She turned back to the ceiling, trying not to cry again. She was sick of crying at this point. The lump in her throat would not go away. But up on the ceiling, she noticed something. A black swirl. A few bugs? No, it grew larger than that.

Smoke. Black smoke. Just like in her dreams.

The darkness swirled larger on the ceiling as Sylvia tried to shake Megan awake. She didn't move, and Syl found herself pinned to the bed, frozen, as she watched. Her breathing grew shorter. Her heartbeat picked up. The storm of darkness drifted down to the side of her bed and began to dissipate, revealing something underneath. A pair of sharp eyes first. And horns. And stripes.

And that smile.

Sylvia screamed.

Megan woke with a startle. "What the fuck, Syl?" She reached over to flip on the lamp. She turned to see the light hit something that had lived in the dark its entire life.

A horned woman sat atop Sylvia Zou and pinned her down with a pair of strong, striped arms. A pattern the color of night scoured over the woman's sickly white skin. Her horns sprouted from a bird's nest of hair, tearing at the pillows as the woman bent over to bite Syl. Black smoke whirled around the two as they struggled.

Sylvia freed a hand and punched at the beast. The horned woman tore into Syl's flesh with its claws. Rip went the bandages. Rip went the soft skin. The claws tore through day-old wounds,

Stripes

reopening scabs that had just begun to heal. Syl squirmed and attempted to throw her attacker off, but the monster only laughed and pinned down her free hand yet again. It tore a gash into Sylvia's shoulder.

"Help me!" she cried.

But Megan only screamed. Sylvia watched as Megan jumped back from the chaos and only looked in horror instead of pity. Her blood poured onto the sheets and she reached out with a red hand.

"Megan ..."

Megan hesitated and reluctantly reached for Syl's hand. The monster looked over and snarled. It swiped its claws at Megan. She screamed and fled the room. Sylvia watched as Megan abandoned her, left her to face the evil that had followed her into this home. Something cracked from within as her worst fears confirmed themselves. She was alone.

Laughter filled the room. Sylvia looked back up at the creature on top of her. She wasn't entirely alone. The demon looked down at her and grimaced, then wrapped its claws around her throat. She punched it in the eye. It roared into her face.

"Why are you here?!" Syl cried out.

The horned woman laughed, cocked its head to the side, and grinned, sharp rows of teeth gleaming behind its lips. "I am the Baphomet. I am here because you called. The anxieties of one's subconscious cry out to me like owls in the night. I am not one to neglect."

The demon leaned toward Syl, holding a hand up with long, curled fingers. Sylvia could see the black patterns up close now.

The chaotic stripes seamlessly integrated with the rest of the monster's skin. Sylvia looked into the monster's eyes; they were not much different than her own.

"Of course, we only ran into each other by chance. College dormitories are *so* ridden with the stress of young people. But then I heard you, Sylvia Zou, the worst of them all. The paranoia, the self-loathing one develops when they depend on another for so much. She never loved you, Sylvia. Not like I love you, delicious girl."

Claws stroked Sylvia's temple, and the horned woman licked her opposite cheek. Sylvia reached out to the bedside table. Anything to hit the horned woman with—anything!

The Baphomet whispered in her ear. "I think you came along at the right time. What a feast you've been, darling one. I really needed you, and I think it's safe to say that you needed me. I'm sorry to say it has to end. It's been a good run, but it's all ruined. We can no longer say it was 'just a nightmare' anymore, right? She knows now, you needy little brat. She'll believe you. What an awful, awful thing to be heard." The creature grinned.

Sylvia's fingers brushed over Megan's phone, the lamp, her empty soup bowl, artist pens, the fork—

The fork.

"Are you ready? I don't know if I'll be gentle, but I will try my best. I can't say I won't miss you. It's been so lonely lately. I adored our time together, Sylvia. Close your eyes. I will be done soon. One ... two ... thr—"

Another rip.

     Stripes

The horned woman's eyes widened. It stopped, still. The room rang silent until a faint gasp escaped the demon's lips with a mouthful of dark blood. The Baphomet looked into Sylvia's eyes once more. Sylvia looked right back.

Black smoke rose from below the demon, enveloping, spinning, twirling around the thing's entire body. The end of the utensil sticking out from its chest. The horned woman screamed. A loud burst of air erupted from the cloud and it imploded, leaving nothing behind but a single bloody fork on the bedroom covers.

"I don't need *anyone*," Sylvia said.

```
Monday.

3 Missed Calls, 11:19 a.m.

Megan Gibbs, 11:21 a.m.: Where are you?? Can we
talk?

Sylvia Zou, 11:27 a.m.: Hey, I went back to my
dorm. I'm feeling a lot better. Thanks.

Megan Gibbs, 11:28 a.m.: You need to come back.
Please. I told your RA I'd take care of you.
And I think I had one of those dreams you were
talking about…

Megan Gibbs, 11:35 a.m.: Sylvia this isn't funny
I don't remember what happened I just woke up
on the kitchen floor with a bruise and you were
gone. The bedroom is covered in blood.

Megan Gibbs, 1:12 p.m.: Please. Talk to me. What
happened?

Megan Gibbs, 1:44 p.m.: Syl??
```

Warmonger

Hammeg shut the front door behind her, escaping the shouts and jeers of the small crowd that had once again gathered at her doorstep. She sighed at the sight of her home, adorned with silk rugs and pillows imported from the capital. Her assistant, Estod, tended the fire in her cottage living room. It was the only fireplace in Amlota, but hadn't she earned it? She was the village Matriarch, after all. It was a thankless job. She sat down before the hearth, hoping to warm her old bones. The ruckus continued outside.

"Difficulties?" Estod pulled the pillow Hammeg rested on. The old woman groaned as she sat forward, waiting for Estod to finish fluffing her pillow.

"Nothing new. Just chased into my home once again, like the village dog. They think they know better," Hammeg cleared the phlegm from her throat. "As if my role isn't hard enough. As if I'm not the one who must *make* these difficult decisions."

"And you've made your decision?"

"Of course, girl. We must fight. Our way of life is at stake. You heard that General. These are dangerous times."

Estod murmured in agreement, digging her fingers into Hammeg's knotted shoulders. Spirits bless Estod. Her assistant was not like the shouters outside; she was one of the few young ones who still maintained sense. Why couldn't the others be like Estod? They called for Hammeg to come out every night, shouting horrible things, throwing a waste of roots and tubers at her stone house.

"Shame on the Matriarch! Rubbish Mother!" they shouted.

Others, mostly older folk, tried their best to shame the crowds into leaving her be. Honestly, both factions caused her one headache. She held her head.

"Why do they have such anger?"

Estod stopped, thought for a moment. "They are afraid, Mother. They see their futures slip from their grasp like sand. The water, the taxes, and now this."

"The future's always uncertain," Hammeg scoffed. "I remember being your age, I really do. But you get used to it. We didn't have it easy, either. You've yet to develop backbones, that's really the root of all this."

A large bulb flew through the open window and landed on the carpet, the word "COWARD" carved into it.

Hammeg yelped. "Get that, will you? Off the carpet! Off the carpet! This was a gift from the Tsarina, produce might stain it!"

Estod scooped up the offending bulb, setting it with the rest of the Matriarch's food stores. "Fear comes through in many ways, Mother. Perhaps this is their fight for a better life."

"They don't have to be so rude about it!"

Her assistant hummed—whether or not it was in agreement or disapproval, Hammeg could not tell. "They have a duty, and they're shirking it. I've done my part. We all know it. You saw those soldiers; you saw those beasts they brought! This is war!" the old woman said.

"You must rest." Estod pulled an elaborate blanket over the Matriarch.

"It's not fair. Can't they see this hurts me as well? These two weeks have been the worst of my life. Someone *spat* at me in the streets today."

"We must forgive and move forward. Not everything is set in stone."

"*This* is!"

"Rest. Reflect." Estod left Hammeg to drift on her nice pillows. The old woman could hear the assistant clearing away the crowd in her calming, authoritative voice that Hammeg never seemed to have.

Hah, please. Don't be jealous of a girl! Hammeg thought. Estod knew the younger folks who screamed at Hammeg's door. Of course the assistant had easy control over them. Real leadership was hereditary; just like the Tsarina, just like herself. Amlota had a proud lineage of Matriarchs, with only one Patriarch in its history—Hammeg's disgrace of a grandfather. It had been Hammeg's mother who taught her right from wrong. She missed her mother at that moment: the great Matriarch who had led Amlota and the neighboring villages into stability as the Fifth Province of the Nation. Unity. Justice. Respectability. These were the elements of leadership her mother had taught her. The shouters outside would understand with time. The old woman stared into the fire and drifted into a slumber, the protests of the new generation lulling her to sleep.

A half-month before she became the most hated woman of Amlota, possibly the entire Fifth Province, Hammeg was happy. Amlota sat in the center of a vast prairie of cultivated mounds, with larger hills forming a natural barrier between them and the rest of the Nation. Mist steamed from the surrounding mounds at the break of dawn and it delighted Hammeg to see the workers in these early mornings harvesting the edible bulbs and roots that allowed the village to thrive. Nothing could be heard but the calls of birds and the gentle trickle of the stream that ran through the heart of Amlota.

Soon though, the rumblings of the village market would rise up and drown out these sounds. This is what excited Hammeg the most. The market sat in the heart of the village square. She loved visiting the vendors in the late mornings and walking amongst her citizens—"the people of the hills," as others called them. The Matriarch would peruse the village's Nation-renowned produce

Warmonger

and goods, making idle chat with the stand owners. She would impart knowledge onto the younger workers who would politely smile as she talked to them and listened to her with gratefulness. The shopkeepers told her the most wonderful stories, as well. Hammeg's heart always fluttered when they tossed extra goodies into her basket with a wink, kissed her on the cheek, and told her how much she was loved. This was her village. Her family.

But that morning, the ground rumbled slowly and from far away. The trumpet of some great creature, perhaps several, echoed throughout the lumpy land. The hustle and bustle of the market came to a halt, and the villagers stopped and looked upon the hills.

Sharp decorated ivory. Swinging trunks. Followed by two massive gray bodies. The forms of two hairless mammoths descended from the hills hauling an ornate carriage behind. Soldiers riding macrauchenia—a kind of trunked llama—flanked either side of the procession. This was a war cavalry, straight from the heart of the Nation's capital.

The frozen market watched as the beasts of burden approached. A few villagers turned to Hammeg, fear in their eyes, in search of guidance.

"What do we do?" a woman asked. But Hammeg only stood there with her little market basket, the elephantry only approaching closer. The Tsarina had sent them, no doubt. But her Holiness had never sent more than a simple messenger before, often discreetly to Hammeg's doorstep. Something must have been brewing beyond the mountains.

"Mother Hammeg," the woman grabbed the Matriarch's shoulder. Hammeg flinched at the touch. "Mother Hammeg what do we do?"

Hammeg swallowed. This wasn't normal.

"We'll talk. That's what we always do. We will talk." She walked toward the mounted fortress of stomps and groans before the woman could ask anything else. The calls of mammoths rang over the village.

Hammeg's eyes opened. Mammoth calls again. The cavalry had returned. Exactly two weeks, just like the man said. She could see blue sky through the cottage window. Another night passed and yet the nightmare persisted. At least it would be over soon, the soldiers would march off with their new recruits and perhaps she would stop receiving death threats when walking down the street.

Death threats. In her own village. She let that sink in for a moment.

The early morning damp chilled her to the bone. Was Estod back from the market yet? She needed tea. The Matriarch was useless without her morning brew.

As if she'd heard, Estod walked in with two full baskets. For the past two weeks Hammeg had been sending her assistant in her place. Estod carried a bouquet of white orchids in the crook of her arm as well.

"Oh, how delightful!" Hammeg exclaimed. She took them from Estod's arms, leaving the produce baskets for Estod to handle. The young woman grunted as she set the baskets down.

"Those are from Alcomer. I saw him at his flower stand today."

Hammeg scrunched her face. Alcomer served as a councilmember, as well. The old woman placed the flowers in a clay pot and stroked her face in thought.

Warmonger

"The village is expecting you to make a public comment this evening for the ceremony," Estod said as she put away the produce.

Hammeg cocked her head. "What ceremony?"

The question stopped Estod in her tracks. The girl turned to face the Matriarch. "The farewell ceremony … where we're expected to send off the young villagers. Our soldiers for the Tsarina's war. Don't you remember?"

Hammeg squeezed her eyes and shook her head, as if the thought were a distraction. "Oh, no. Yes. That. I'll get to that."

"Are you not comfortable with sending them off anymore?"

"No, that's fine, it's just … There's something more important I need right now." Hammeg held her forehead, as if dizzy.

"Should I make your usual tea?" Estod asked.

Hammeg turned to the young girl. Estod was nice, but she didn't understand Hammeg sometimes. It was that generational divide. She needed allies. Today of all days, she needed her friends.

"No. Well, yes. A strong brew. Two, actually. And I need you to make a fresh batch of scones."

Estod was brilliant at baked goods. The Matriarch allowed Estod to use bits of ground tubers from Hammeg's personal patch of mounds, using up a fine butter Hammeg saved for special occasions. It was a special occasion, wasn't it? Hammeg had been through enough stress as it was and needed her people around her before sending off the soldiers later that night. She had called a council meeting. Why hadn't she thought of this sooner? Everything had been so stressful that they had missed the last one without even noticing! It was madness.

The first councilmember to arrive was Alcomer.

"Morning, Mother," he smiled a little too wide, which Hammeg ignored. He always did that.

"You must be overwhelmed. Today's the day," he said.

"Yes, I heard the war animals."

"Did you like my orchids? I thought they might help. I can't imagine this is easy. And yet look at you, sticking to your morals. Such strong leadership in the face of adversity and civil unrest."

The Matriarch smiled at the councilmember. In reality, Hammeg loathed Alcomer. Couldn't stand the gossiping little man. He presented himself as a youthful character, but his true age was beginning to show in the form of crow's feet around the eyes. In the thirty-nine years she had reigned, he had never taken a partner, always hiding behind walls, channeling his energy into pointless chit-chatter and flattery toward her alone. At least it made council discussions easier.

"Come in, Alcomer. Estod's making scones."

The slim man squealed in delight, and let himself in. The other three councilmembers soon followed and Hammeg's home was bustling with activity. They all gasped in delight at the sight of fresh scones and sat around the room enjoying the fire's warmth.

It hadn't always been like this. Traditionally, council meetings had been held at the village square in view of the public, but the public had all but stopped attending around ten years ago, and Hammeg thought a cozy environment would result in sparkling conversation. Her house had been the setting for these meetings since the last decade. Over time these meetings had evolved from

 Warmonger

boring hearings to delightful dinners. It was easier to talk policy in a living room.

"You always have the best treats," said Memmion between bites. Hammeg smiled. She liked Memmion best, the only other woman on the council. She liked to think they were close friends.

"It certainly helps distract from what's happening," Walan raised his eyebrows. The old man was a pessimist at heart, and Hammeg always kept a careful eye on him. Something told her he would rather be Amlota's leader, instead. But the one Amlotan Patriarch had been enough of a disaster. Walan should have known better than to covet something that could not be.

"Oh please, do we have to talk about that?" Alcomer rolled his eyes, ripping up a scone in his lap and eating the baked good piece by piece. He never wanted to talk about anything serious, which Hammeg was just fine with.

The last councilmember, Rokogai, coughed and sat forward. "It's a pressing issue. The majority of villagers are still upset. We don't want this leading to any riots," he said. Little beads of sweat lined his forehead. The Matriarch could never tell if Rokogai was either constantly anxious or actually concerned about what was happening. There was a good chance he didn't know himself.

"You give them too much credit, Rokogai. This is just youthful rebellion, it'll do them good to go and serve. Better than them staying here and dozing off on the mounds," Walan said.

Memmion bit her lower lip. "But think about it. Their youth being taken away like this. It breaks my heart. Of course they're angry, we never had to deal with anything like that at our age." The woman seemed at the point of tears, but that was how she always sounded.

Alcomer rolled his eyes and shook his head. "Oh, you do so much, Mother Hammeg. I can't imagine it's easy to stand your ground like this."

Hammeg swallowed down her last bite of scone, clearing her throat. "The younger generation, they break my heart. Where has their love for the village gone? For their Nation? The enemy threatens our very way of life and all they can think about is …" She sighed, laying an open hand on her lap. Memmion grabbed hold, soothing her.

"Of course," Memmion said. "I didn't even *think* about what you must be going through. They're young. They'll be okay. We must obey the Tsarina's orders."

"So relieved to have a woman on the throne," Alcomer interjected. Rokogai sighed loudly, his knee bouncing up and down to a nauseating vibration. Hammeg looked around the room. These were her allies. A knot formed in her stomach at this thought, but perhaps that was all the baked goods.

"Those kids only think of themselves," old Walan muttered, biting into his scone. Crumbs littered his shirt and tumbled onto the floor.

"Except Estod!" Memmion chimed in as the assistant entered the cottage. Estod stood between the council and the fireplace with her hands folded. One by one they ceased licking their fingers and turned their attention to her.

"Wonderful scones, girl," Walan remarked.

"Thank you, sir. Council, we have a public remark this afternoon. Shall I let them in?"

Warmonger

The council looked at her for a long moment. Estod looked at every one of them, returning their stares.

Alcomer spoke up. "A *what?*"

"A member of the public. They are waiting outside to speak with you, the Amlotan council. I'll get them now."

Hammeg's heart raced as the other four looked to her for guidance, just like the woman at the market. A public comment? She couldn't remember the last time they had *had* a public comment. How did they even know there was a council meeting?

A young boy, around Estod's age, was led into the hearth. He held a scroll in his hands. Estod nodded to him and stepped aside.

"Betson?" Alcomer said.

"Do you know this boy?" Rokogai asked.

"Yes, he's one of my flower boys at the market. Why aren't you manning the stand, Betson? It's your shift today."

"I got my shift covered. This is more important," Betson said.

"Not more important than my flowers!" Alcomer said. Estod raised her hand, and the room quieted down. Hammeg felt another pang of jealousy at that.

"Please, let's let our public member speak his concerns," Estod said. Attention shifted toward the boy in the room. In reality, he was a young man, but Hammeg couldn't think of him as anything other than a boy. He just looked so young. His hands were shaking; he was nervous.

"Well, come on now!" Walan said.

"Hello council," Betson began. He held up his paper. "I have with me a list of signatures, over 500, that we are presenting to Mother Hammeg today. I am glad to see the Amlotan Council here as well."

"Signatures for *what*?" Alcomer crossed his arms.

"We, the citizens of Amlota demand that Mother Hammeg take a stand against the capital's draft for soldiers. We have not been given sufficient information regarding this war, and we do not wish to engage in pointless bloodshed," the fabric underneath the boy's arms grew damper by the minute. "Furthermore, we advocate for the secession of Amlota and all the neighboring villages in the Fifth Province."

A chuckle traveled around the room. The councilmembers looked at one another with a knowing grin. Alcomer put his hand over his mouth.

Estod stepped forward. "I would encourage the council to remain civil and just during this hearing. Betson is a citizen and deserves respect when heard," she said.

Walan continued to chuckle. "But what he says is such a stretch. You see how we cannot simply secede from the Nation just because we disagree with a little draft, right?" He turned to the other councilmembers. "Am I the only one thinking this?"

"No, you're right," Rokogai sighed. He pinched the bridge of his nose, as if it hurt him to explain things. "Listen, it's not that simple. Defying the draft alone would be an act of treason, let alone secession. The Nation brings us unity and protection from neighboring countries."

"What neighboring countries? Besides the capitol, the nearby villages are the only other settlements we have ever been in contact with," Estod said.

"Countries that threaten our way of life!" Walan said.

"The world isn't as small as you may have been led to believe, sweet one," Memmion chimed in. "Think of the backlash we would get from defying the Tsarina's orders. The military would wipe us out."

"The military is already wiping us out with their weapons factory beyond the hills. Why do you think our water makes us sick now? Why are over half of our bulbs and roots taxed to the Tsarina's city? Why do we just keep sitting here as our world dies?" Estod said.

"'Over half'? Surely the tax isn't *that* much. I only paid a mound's worth of bulbs last year," Alcomer muttered.

"Shut *up* you wealthy rat!" Estod yelled.

The room was silent. Hammeg could feel her breath growing shorter, her face getting redder. She had never seen Estod this enraged. It was horrific. It was embarrassing. In front of her own council!

"Estod, I think it would be best if you made some tea," she said.

Her assistant looked around the room, disgust on her face. "You don't care, do you? You really don't care about your own people."

"We certainly care," Rokogai said. "But there are rules in place. Things are already set in motion."

"I believe we care a bit more than you, young girl," Walan coughed. "Why haven't you spoken up about these issues before?

Why haven't you run for council? This all just seems a bit ... childish, and rude."

Estod glared at the old man, and the rest of the council. "So, is that the consensus?"

"All in favor of continuing with the draft tonight?" Walan asked, again to Hammeg's annoyance. That was *her* job to ask. Everyone raised their hands, nonetheless. Estod's mouth hardened. She looked over to Betson and nodded. They shared a look of understanding, but what it concerned Hammeg could not fathom.

Memmion made a tsk-ing noise. "It's a shame about the water, dear, it really is. I heard about your mother's death and I sympathize. It's heartbreaking. But these are complex issues. We cannot simply secede and lose the great benefits the capitol provides us."

"I had a great idea about that, by the way!" Alcomer raised a finger. "I have heard talk of large seeds with water inside from the south. A trader referred to them as 'coconuts.' Might it be possible for us to import these seeds and sell them for a low price? The proceeds could go toward improving our local economy."

Hammeg shook her head. This was all too much for her. "We will come back to that topic later. However, I do have a speech to make tonight. I will need my rest. I adjourn this meeting. Thank you all for attending and lifting my spirits, and to others"—she looked over at Estod and Betson—"for addressing their concerns. I assure you, this is a very difficult time for all of us. I do hear you. I am learning. I am listening."

The meeting ended, and Hammeg could not feel but as if she had thrown a failed party. Her spirits were even lower now. She glared at Estod from across the room as her assistant gathered the dishes.

Warmonger

"That was quite a moment you had back there," she said. She watched as Estod set the dishes down, preparing to clean them. Assistants were not supposed to make political comments. They were there to serve and clean.

"You're really going to send all those people off to a war that not even you understand?" Estod asked.

Hammeg scoffed. "You sound like my grandfather, before Mother overthrew him."

"Your grandfather was a good man who opposed the annexation and fought for Amlota's independence—"

"He was a *man*!" Hammeg exclaimed. "Always thinking they know better. Everyone doubts the woman in the room. Even us! Woman to woman, you still look down on me as a leader. In our matriarchal society."

"Your gender has nothing to do with it."

"Gender has *everything* to do with it! I've seen the side-glances. The always double questioning my policies. Fighting damned Walan every step of the way to get anything done! *You* try being in my shoes for a day, girl!"

"Be in your civilians' shoes! Our water is poisoned. Every root we dig up, taxed away. And now the capital has asked us to die for their own selfish reasons and you've simply opened the door for them!"

Hammeg glared out the window. The mounds' grass blowing in the afternoon wind. Mound after mound after mound, as far as the eye could see. The capital would take all of it if they did not cooperate, and yet here Hammeg was, being talked down to by a young girl who thought she knew better.

"There are things about the world which you don't understand, girl," Hammeg sighed.

Estod shook her head; she seemed tired, too. "Apparently not."

The kettle went off, screaming into the quiet cottage. Estod moved over to take the shouting thing from the fire. "Are you ready for your tea?"

"Might as well, a rotten day," Hammeg said. She watched as her assistant poured the tea and let it steep. The Matriarch inhaled the steam.

"Smells different," she said.

"It's a new batch. You'll like it."

The Matriarch scrunched her face. "You know how I feel about surprises, given today's events."

Estod gave her an unhappy grin. Hammeg inspected the tea, not exactly in the mood for a new flavor. Nevertheless, she persisted, and found the new flavor enjoyable.

"At least the scones were good," she muttered.

"Excellent," said Estod, and she went off to clean the dishes. Hammeg looked out the window again, the cries of mammoths softly heard in the distance. Why couldn't things go back to normal already? Couldn't that happen? She missed normal. She slipped down further in her seat and fell to a rest. Sleep overcame her as she wished for the negativity to evaporate.

That day, two weeks ago, the entire market watched as Hammeg approached the war elephantry. The capital had doubtlessly sent the soldiers to intimidate the entire village. But there she was: a little old lady against the armed forces. She found she was not

Warmonger

scared, for even the smallest person could make a big difference. But she was no small person; she was the Matriarch.

The procession stopped a few hundred feet from the village, with one of the mammoths awkwardly perched atop a mound. A lone General galloped his way toward Hammeg on a decorated macrauchenia. She winced at the sight of the creature—like an elephant had bedded a deer. The General dismounted and stood her down with his golden armor and spiked helmet. Typical men, asserting their self-ordained dominance. The mammoths didn't help.

"Where may I find the leader of Amlota?" he asked.

"She's right here," Hammeg said. She felt silly with her basket, but that couldn't be helped. She gripped the handle in confidence.

The General looked her up and down, pursing his lips. "Right." He looked up and addressed the market crowd. "I have an announcement from the Grand Tsarina herself." Hammeg's ears perked up. At least another woman had sent her this messenger; whatever he repeated was bound to have *some* sense.

"We find ourselves on the brink of war, on the eve of this autumn. The oversea enemy is growing in number, and the very livelihood of the Nation is threatened. The Tsarina demands every able-bodied citizen between the ages of sixteen and thirty report for duty in a fortnight. The Tsarina brings a message of unity and camaraderie. Only together can we defeat this great enemy!"

The market folk were silent. People looked to one another, some nodding, some shaking their heads. But most importantly, people looked to Mother Hammeg.

The Matriarch took a deep breath. This was certainly troubling. She opened her mouth to speak.

"What country are we fighting?" someone asked.

The General blinked, caught off guard. "The details are not as important as our need for unity."

"Yes, they are!" another yelled out.

"Why is the cutoff at thirty, anyway?"

"Where are we even going?"

"Do we get mammoths, too?"

"Silence!" the General shouted. A hush swept over the marketplace. Hammeg looked at the faces of her people. Many of the younger ones seemed ... impassioned, angry. Older villagers, but not all, stared up at the war parade, sadness on their faces.

She raised her head high. "This is a very big ask, for all of us. I think not only of the young citizens that must fight. I think of us at home, who must send them off. It is a heartbreaking, but noble, cause." She turned to the General. "And of course, Amlota will aid this conflict. We have always prided ourselves on being on the side of justice. I trust the Tsarina. She is a dear friend of mine. I trust the Nation." She smiled out to the crowd. "We are all stronger when we fight together."

Her people looked at her, some nodding, some still with that sadness on their faces. Hammeg looked to them, saddened as well. Upset but all-knowing. This was for the best.

A rock hit her face.

The sting took seconds to fully register, and as she drew her fingers from her face, she saw blood on them. Hammeg gasped.

       Warmonger

"To hell with that!" a boy cried.

"I'm not dying for no reason!"

"Easy for you to say, old hag!"

"How dare you insult the Matriarch like that? How dare you resort to violence?" a vendor cried. More and more chimed in, talking over one another like a cascade of screams. The entire market exploded in arguments.

"Mother Hammeg is right. We must support the Nation!"

"Easy for you to say, you're forty."

"Why don't you go fight in that stupid war?"

"We don't even fight countries; we all know we just invade them!"

"Those are my children!"

"They're my children, too! War requires sacrifice!"

"What have the other villages said?"

"Secession! Secession! They've poisoned our waters for too long!"

"How dare you, Hammeg? How *dare* you?!"

"Go back to the capital and shove that spiky helmet up your ass!"

"I refuse to fight for no reason!"

The villagers bickered and fought, shoving one another. A punch was thrown. Hammeg turned to the General to see him remounting his macrauchenia. He shrugged at her.

"Two weeks," he said, and rode back to the elephantry. The crowd formed into a mob, some screaming obscenities at her, some coming to her defense. Another rock flew past her head, and another. Hammeg threw her hands over herself, dropping the basket. They followed as she fled to her hut and screamed at her door until their voices were hoarse. So began her public shame.

The Matriarch woke to the sound of a man screaming. Many people screaming. Not much had changed in two weeks. The sky beyond the cottage's window was dark with an orange haze. Sunset? No. The orange flickered too much. Glowed too bright. Fire. And smoke.

Fire!

These weren't the regular shouts and jeers she had come to know. These were screams. Screeches. Yells. People in pain! Hammeg tried to get up but something held her down. Rope! Tied around her ankles and wrists. The enemy! Impossible! That was overseas, never the Nation! How did they get here?

They were right! The Tsarina and the General had been right. War had come straight to the Nation, for whatever reason. Those who had opposed her decision would most definitely feel foolish right about now—but that could wait. Safety! She had to get to safety before it was too late.

She tried to wriggle free but the knots proved too tight. Estod! Where was Estod? She screamed and thrashed about, rolling onto the floor. The impact proved more painful than she would have liked! Hammeg cried out in agony. Something had physically snapped from within as she fell.

"Estod!"

The bellowing of mammoths echoed through the air as if in reply. The war procession! They had members of the royal army here to protect them. The drafted soldiers would get their first taste of battle right here at home! Screaming! And the sound of

Warmonger

… fighting! Yes, she could hear fighting! Oh, why couldn't she see anything? Who had tied her? What member of the enemy had come to kidnap the Matriarch? She screamed. For Alcomer, for Memmion, for Estod, the woman at the market, anyone! But of course, they'd never come; she was held captive in her house. She hoped they were safe. She hoped they were all safe and away from this madness.

A wall of her cottage toppled over and she cried out at the sight of a great leathery leg. A mammoth had stepped backwards onto her home.

"Here! I'm in here!" she yelled. The mammoth charged forward and away from the building, and at last she could see. She lay horrified.

Villagers fighting. Soldiers fighting. Homes up in flames. Archers on macrauchenia. Swords and spears clanging against one another. The mammoths standing tall, sweeping fighters away with their mighty trunks; it was all too horrific. Someone grunted, and a decorated man fell in front of her home with a spear sticking out of his back. The General, his blood oozing into the cottage's hearth.

Hammeg stared out in terror. Soldiers slaughtering villagers and villagers slaughtering soldiers. Villagers slaughtering each other! Who could tell who was on what side? Who could make sense of such madness?

But hold on. Hold on! There was a method. She could see that now. There was a horrible, awful system right before her eyes. Many of the villagers had ash across their faces, in a diagonal line, as if a sign! As if to signal they were on the same side. And she recognized them! She knew who these ash-villagers were. The war protestors! They were the war protestors, creating war on their front doorstep, slaughtering the soldiers in cold blood. The war carriage blew up in flames! A mammoth stood on its hind legs as spears sank into its belly. The great animal fell upon a burning building with a crash through all the land! It wailed in misery as it died.

The remaining beasts of war and soldiers retreated, a few counter-protestors fleeing with them. The protestors cheered as the remnants of the war procession fled the way they came, over the mounds and into the dark.

Amlota quieted into murmurs and the crackle of burning rubble. Hammeg's heart raced. Would they come free her? But she knew this would never come to pass as the ash-laden protestors entered her hut, their glares cutting into her like they had for weeks. Let them shame her! Dirty little things! Children with smeared faces like soot. She cried in pain as they sat her up.

"What have you done? What have you done?!" she screamed at them. One of the protestors smirked at her, she recognized him. The boy from the council meeting! The one Alcomer employed.

"Betson. It's Betson, right? Why? Why have you all done this? I thought Alcomer talked to you."

"I killed Alcomer," Betson said. Tears came to Hammeg's eyes but they were not tears of sorrow, only fear. She watched as another youth walked in. Her stomach dropped.

With an ashen line across her face, Estod stood in front of the old woman, spear in hand.

"But you ... you ..."

"Enough!" Estod slapped the ex-Matriarch hard. Hammeg spat blood and glared at the little girl through her tears.

Warmonger

"You naïve little thing," she said. "I was going to save you from the draft."

"I am thirty-three, you old crone. You never asked." She snarled at Hammeg with disgust, a disgust Hammeg recognized in herself for others. Estod had learned by watching. The little bitch had been biding her time. That was clear now. She had been no daughter of Mother Hammeg! This was what the Matriarch got for trusting anyone other than herself. How foolish she'd been.

"It'll never work. Your little play-pretend. It's not that simple. The army will come back and wipe you out," Hammeg smiled.

Estod shook her head. "This is our world. You could have listened. I wish you had listened."

"You are small."

"We are not. Only a fraction of the village left with the army. We will move from throughout the whole Fifth Province with our message, with talk of secession and independence against the Nation. Because you are right, Hammeg. We are stronger together, just not in the name of blood thirst."

Hammeg looked over at the dead General and laughed. "This is a mistake. We will lose the war now."

"The war has always been right here, Mother. You just never wanted to see it." Estod nodded to the others, and the little traitors left Hammeg on the floor, writhing about on her woven rugs. Hammeg coughed at the inhaled smoke as the children of a new world cheered her to sleep while her home grew bright.

And her old bones rested.

The Way Things Were

Janis left her phone with me while she ran up to the counter to order drinks. I hadn't been inside a café in years, and the cleanliness of the place unnerved me—not to mention the Downtown Guides who'd carded us on our way in. They'd looked me over with suspicious eyes (probably because they didn't often see brown folks around here), and I knew I was only here because I was Janis's plus one. A localized branch of the nation's Safety Alliance forces, members of the Portland Safety Alliance, always sported orange helmets and riot gear. The city of Portland had tried to put a fun spin on the concept, announcing that Downtown Guides were mostly there to help inform visitors about the fun and "weird" opportunities of downtown Portland with a little "Ask Me!" button pinned to each bulletproof vest. Janis assured me they were friendly, but I had heard otherwise. Now they'd shifted their attention to a homeless man outside. I looked away as they quietly escorted him from the neighborhood, and I tried to focus on the video Janis wanted me to watch. Though she had graduated college years ago, Janis's family still paid for her Premium Teal Package—a plan that included 15 GB of Google and Facebook services. The video on her phone took over a minute to buffer; after five commercials the video started.

SMAN with Paige Woods.

A woman in professional attire, award-winning broadcast journalist and news anchor Paige Woods, sits in the center of a modernist set. Large drifting cityscapes and graphic design elements float behind her. Introductory music dies down, and Woods gets right into it, speaking fast and to the point.

> Woods: Breaking news tonight as an unidentified ball of light appeared in downtown Austin, Texas, earlier this evening. Hello, good evening. I'm Paige Woods. The following footage was illegally uploaded to YouTube and has been trending on Twitter for the past four hours. We have obtained special permission to air this footage, as this is an SMAN exclusive.

The video opens in the center of a picketing crowd, part of a demonstration to protest the detention camps in Canada and Mexico. People cry out as an orb of blue appears the center of the crowd—it's massive, the size of a small house. Some take pictures with their phones.

Everyone gasps as three figures step out of the orb. They are bipedal, taller than any human, and shine brightly.

   The Way Things Were

The figures of blue light tower over the humans like great pillars. It is hard to tell if they're confused; they have no faces. There's a sequence of sounds, but it's jumbled and incomprehensible. It's as if the first figure is trying to speak.

"What's happening?!" someone cries, and the noise stops.

A hush sweeps over the crowd, then the figure begins again. "We would like to extend an invitation," a voice says, but it's drowned out by screams off camera. A truck speeds toward the three figures, but light has no physical form, so the truck just runs through and into the crowd. The audio blows out, and the camera flies to the ground.

The clip ends.

Janis came forward with our coffees. "Pretty wild, right?"

"Holy shit," I said, taking my drink. "That guy ran into all those people."

Janis sighed. "We don't know that yet. For all we know, it could be a deepfake."

But something told me computers hadn't made the video. "If it *was* real, that was horrific."

She took a sip of her latte then shook her head. "But those aliens, right?"

"What makes you think they're aliens?"

"I don't know, it's not that big of a stretch. Weird stuff's been happening all the time now. Remember the Simon incident at the square? Anyway it's all over the internet—haven't you seen?"

"I don't have a package, remember? And those things ... people got hurt because they arrived. What if they come here?" I asked.

Janis laughed. "Nick, we have enough weird things to worry about in Portland."

Shouts rang out from outside. We turned to see the homeless man running past the window, the Guides in pursuit. One Guide lifted her gun and shot the man with a stream of electricity. He hit the pavement, shouting every curse word he could think of while the other Guide handcuffed him.

"Oh geez," Janis said. "Like that guy." She chuckled and took a sip of her drink. I looked down at my lap, trying to ignore what was happening both outside and across the table from me.

My other partner, Dal, worked at the welding shop on Hawthorne with a bunch of white cishet men—which made it a bit awkward for Dal, who hated gender and used they/them pronouns. Inside the shop I found Dal alone amidst a light show of orange sparks. They saw me approach and immediately stopped, shoving their helmet up.

"You shouldn't be watching without eye protection," they said. Dal's welding mask hung over their forehead like a space helmet. If there were aliens in Texas, I figured, Dal could be their astronaut. "How was your trip to Janet-town?"

I made a face. "It's Janis, and she's fine."

"Hey, whoever you play heterosexual house with is fine by me," they chuckled.

We smiled at each other for seconds that felt like eons.

     The Way Things Were

"Hey, so did you hear about the, uh ... aliens?" I asked.

Dal's playful attitude dropped. "D'you mean the Texas shit? Saw it this morning. My neighbor Anita's got YouTube, so we rigged her phone up to the TV. That was so fucked up."

"So you think the video's real?"

"I mean, I bet there's wackier shit out there than aliens. It's the truck I'm interested in," they said. "If you pause the video, there's a white trillium on the side of the car. Seems like the people in it were gonna run into that crowd with or without the aliens, Nazi shitheads."

"Oh, yeah. Probably." I didn't want to encourage Dal on one of their Nazi rants.

"But hey. You still up for pizza and sex tonight?" They winked.

I smiled at them, thankful the terrors of the world could just melt away with one safe person.

"Sure."

Paige Woods sits in her chair once more, accompanied by a tired-looking, scruffy man with a bowtie.

> Woods: Hello and welcome back to our ongoing coverage of this breaking story. Early this morning another orb was sighted in Dubai at the newly opened United Nations headquarters. The following footage was uploaded by Singapore representative Reza Lim.

A blue orb appears in the center of the Third Committee. One tall figure of light steps out this time. The General Assembly members gasp and jump from their chairs.

"In the beginning," it says, "there was but one thought: the a priori of consciousness. This would not be the last, for the nature of thoughts is duplicative, and thoughts give rise to ideas, and ideas give rise to form. Soon forms began to differentiate from one another, and the phenomenal surface came into being. On every surface, there are junctions—forks in the paths of realities that lead into the vast multiplicities of the Manifold Aether. Some planes descend into darkness, while others rise into enlightenment; many do both.

"We are the Ouliponites, and we hail from such an intelligible surface. We come in peace. Our kind transcended our phenomenal forms eons ago in the age of posteriori cognitions, and we learned to ride the threads between surfaces. This plane of yours spirals exponentially into darkness, and we have heard the cries of your suffering.

"The Ouliponites offer salvation for the Used onto the next surface over—the surface of our noumenal world. Wickedness has spread throughout your reality. Our own realm knows no such suffering, only sublime existence and eternal life. On the next full moon, we shall descend once more unto this darkening surface, and those willing may transcend the threads with our own kind. The constraints of this place are but atoms to the Aether."

The clip ends.

> Woods: As you may know the earlier appearance of these beings in Texas has garnered the attention of several opposing groups, from the newly formed Saints of Muspelheim to Evangelical dioceses, and opposition from the President of the United States himself. With me tonight is Dr. Mathew Carthorn of Western Washington University. Dr. Carthorn

    The Way Things Were

specializes in philosophical literature and meta-physical theory, and he has informed us that he has some fascinating information on these aliens. Thank you for joining me tonight, Dr. Carthorn.

Carthorn: Pleasure to be here, but I would like to emphasize that I specialized in philosophical literature and metaphysical theory before the schools shut down.

Woods: Of course. Now, I understand that, if these clips are to be believed, this "first contact" may lead to global catastrophe. How much of a risk might these Ouliponites pose?

Carthorn: None at all, Miss Woods. While some people may have you believe the foundations of reality as we know it have unraveled in the past few days, I would propose that, if anything, the revelation of the Ouliponites has solidified several theories regarding the universe—or multiverse, I should say.

Woods: Are you saying you support these aliens? What theories are you talking about?

Carthorn: Well, I am no expert in quantum mechanics. That would be my wife. (Chuckles) But from what I understand, the Ouliponites may confirm our hypotheses about M-theory, or the big bad version of string theory.

Woods: Er … string theory? Can you explain that?

Carthorn: No. (Laughs) But I'll try. All matter in the universe is probably made from these hypothetical, one-dimensional vibrating filaments called "strings." There are two types of strings: closed strings and open strings. Think of a closed string as a hula-hoop and an open string as a jump rope. Hula-hoops can bounce around and do whatever they like. A jump rope, however, needs something to attach to, or it'll go flittering off into the cosmic void.

Woods blinks, not exactly sure where the professor is going with this.

> Carthorn: So! These open strings, or jump ropes, attach themselves to these physical objects called "branes," short for "membranes." Think of those as two schoolchildren on either end of the jump rope, skipping it. I'm horribly butchering and simplifying all of this, by the way!

> Woods: I'm sorry, professor, but what does this have to do with the Ouliponites?

> Carthorn: It has everything to do with them! Just everything. If we pay attention to the language the Ouliponites are using, it all lines up with string theory. "Threads" are strings, and "surfaces" are membranes. It's all the same stuff, just different jargon. Until now we did not know if strings or branes existed, but we have these other-worldly beings—vastly more intelligent than our best minds—with these interdimensional portals, the gateways, coming along affirming our theories. String theory has always predicted higher dimensions, and here we are!

> Woods: Is that what the aliens mean when they state they "ride the threads"?

> Carthorn: Yes! Until now we could not see these other branes because open strings are required to stay put with their branes. But a closed string, a hula-hoop, could possibly fly-off one brane to another, from one schoolboy to the next. It just all depends on the value of that hula-hoop's spin—something the Ouliponites must have harnessed somehow.

> Woods: (Adjusts earpiece) Hold a moment, professor. This just in. There are reports of orbs appearing at all state capitals … and the detention centers throughout the north and south. And … everywhere? We're being invaded! The orbs are impenetrable and

   The Way Things Were

are no longer blue but colorless. What does that
mean, colorless?

Carthorn: (Shrugs) Probably gray.

Woods: The president has declared a national state
of emergency. All orbs have been prohibited from the
public and are guarded by Safety Alliance troops.

Carthorn: Oh, those orange-headed fools.

Woods: Dr. Carthorn! You can't say that.

Carthorn: Come the next full moon next week, I think
I can say anything I want.

Carthorn laughs, while Woods stares frightened into the
camera.

Janis laughed along with Dr. Carthorn on her smart TV. We were
sprawled out on her living room floor with her friends, wine drunk
with large bowls of blue dye and gloves.

"I *love* that guy! He truly doesn't give a shit," Janis said. She
leaned back, spilling a glass of merlot on the white carpet. Keisha
and Hadley, childhood friends of hers, went rushing for paper
towels.

"Oh, don't worry about it!" Janis said. "By the time we're done
dyeing our pussy hats, this whole rug will be blue. A little wine will
only add more color!"

"Why are we dyeing these, anyway?" I asked. Janis had asked me
to come over with my vintage pink pussy hat. We were soaking
them in dye while watching the news.

"It's for solidarity," Keisha explained. "So the Oulipo know we're on their side."

"Get it?" Hadley said. "Cuz they're blue. Everyone's doing it. This is gonna be so fun! I haven't been to a protest for years."

"You know what's *not* fun, though? Buying dye for synthetic fibers. So expensive! Had to get a rush-drone to drop this stuff off this morning. No lattes for *me* next week!" Janis joked.

I shook my head. "'On their side' for what? You didn't tell me anything about this."

Janis rolled her eyes. "Sorry, I would've told you sooner, but you're always off with that guy, Dal."

"They're not a guy," I said.

"Anyway," she said and then put on her deep mock-serious voice: "It's for *Traverse Day*. When we storm the capital and let the people of Oregon leave if they wish."

I shook my head, unwilling to believe that Janis and her liberal friends would actually break the law. "Guys, the Safety Alliance's guarding the gateway, and all the capitals are already on lockdown."

"That's why it's important that we resist this." Janis leaned over, slapping her gloves onto my cheeks and dying my face, giggling.

"It's all over the web!" Keisha said.

"Again," I smiled, "I don't have a package."

"Oh my gosh! Here, lemme look it up for you." Hadley pulled out her iPhone XXIII and browsed the Huffington Post. Under the headline "Why We Need #TraverseDay Now More Than

 The Way Things Were

Ever" was the thumbnail of a video revealing a group of white men standing on a capital building's steps. An update in bold was below.

"Hold on, that's new," Hadley said. She swiped up, and the video airdropped onto the smart TV.

UPDATE: Saints of M Leaders Vow to Uphold President's Portal Ban in the Pacific Northwest.

Six members of the Saints of Muspelheim stand upon the steps of the Washington State Capitol in Olympia holding a press conference with a local TV station. Slicked-back undercuts, suave gray pea coats, and white, chiseled features: these men look more like the cover models of an H&M ad than a hate group. Each man has a white trillium pinned to his shirt. One of them speaks into the microphone.

"We, the Saints of Muspelheim, address the people of our nation with concern. Creatures from another world have crossed our borders and have called for mass immigration at an unprecedented scale, while also describing our country as 'wicked.' They have disrespected our nation, accusing us of 'spiraling' into a so-called 'darkness.' But darkness for who, exactly? Why isn't everyone invited to become enlightened? These so-called Ouliponites, illegal aliens in the most literal sense, have self-identified as enemies of the state and of Western culture. Their political agenda is not for us; it is for themselves and their affiliates, the 'suffering.' These free helicopter rides to another world are meant to distract us from the threats that may lie on the other side of their portal.

"These creatures have proved themselves to be more than technologically advanced, and a human extinction event looms before us. If we choose to stay behind as Earthlings, are we not doomed for decimation at their hands? To abandon your fellow human is cowardice. The Saints of Muspelheim, the 'wicked deplorables,' support the president's ban on gateway immigration to and from this reality, and any realities we may encounter in the future. We must make a stand. The Saints of Muspelheim will not give in. Come Traverse Day, the aliens will be met with confrontation against this radical form of mind-policing."

The room was quiet after that. It was difficult to process the jargon, but I remembered what Dal had told me about these men. The Saints of Muspelheim were not idealists. They were Nazis.

"It'll be fine," Janis said. She no longer slurred, as if the Nazis had sobered her up. "Remember what we vowed all those years ago? We're here to resist. Democracy dies in darkness."

Keisha chuckled. "It's already pretty dead. I haven't gone a day without some Downtown Guide ID-ing me while I was minding my own business."

"Oh my gosh," Hadley said. "I keep telling you not to worry. Those guys are just there to help. They're freakin' called the Portland Safety Alliance!"

"Easy for you to say; you're white. Personally, I don't feel safe," Keisha said. She pointed to the TV. "And I don't know if I want to fight one of those Saint guys."

"They're called Nazis," I added.

"They're actually just idiots." Janis downed the rest of her wine. "And we don't have to fight them. Violence doesn't solve anything. We'll challenge them and let them realize how stupid they sound. The Oulipo are a beacon of hope. Do you guys remember when 'hope' was our slogan?"

Hadley snorted a laugh. "I'm sorry, but how are these aliens a beacon of hope? They're literally offering us a way to run away."

     The Way Things Were

"This isn't about us," Janis said. "It's about the people who are suffering, who want to leave, who have no other option." She looked over at Keisha. "Who feel unsafe around our Downtown Guides."

"Thanks, I guess," Keisha said.

I spoke up. "But, babe, it's … dangerous."

Janis scoffed. "So? That anarchist you're fucking would go."

"That is just so cool, by the way," Hadley interjected. "I *love* poly people." She nodded in a sign of approval that made my skin crawl.

"What do *you* want to do, Nick?" Janis asked. They all stared at me, blue dye on their gloved hands. I looked around the room. Being the center of attention was not my forte.

"I don't know. I hate Nazis, but I don't know what to do about them. Maybe we shouldn't go. I'm not like Dal—and Janis, I'm sorry you hate them. I just don't want anyone to get hurt. Please."

Janis shook her head. "That's sweet, Nick, but I can't sit back. And I don't *hate* Dal; I just think he's one of those dogmatic punk-communist assholes. It's not my fault your boyfriend thinks I'm too privileged or whatever."

I tried not to show my discomfort. "I told you, babe, Dal uses they/them pronouns, and they just come from a different world than you."

Hadley giggled. "Is Dal one of the aliens?"

"Hadley, can you not?" Janis snapped.

Keisha pulled Hadley away, whispering, "Stay out of this."

My girlfriend sighed, losing steam. "And you're right. Me misgendering Dal is problematic, and I'm sorry. I just … it feels as if you like

Dal more than me sometimes." She looked around the room—at each of us, at the blue stains and one red stain on the ground. "This world is so fucked up. I think I'll go to bed." Janis dragged her feet on her way to the bedroom. She turned back. "Nick, will you come to bed with me?"

I winced. "Maybe I should go home."

Woods: Professor Carthorn, I've been asked that we stick to the subject matter of our possible endangerment from these alien terrorists. You mentioned off camera that these beings, the Ouliponites, have possibly visited us before?

Carthorn: They're perfectly safe! That's all the usual propaganda.

Woods: Professor, please—

Carthorn: Now, it's just speculation on my part, but it would make sense if we consider the works of Immanuel Kant and a radical literary French group from the 1960s.

Woods: What about the Ouliponites' technological weapons?

Carthorn: That's all nonsense. Back to what I was saying, "Oulipo" is not a new word to the human race. It's a shortened name for "Ouvroir de littérature potentielle." In 1960s France a group of writers and mathematicians formed a club of sorts where the object was to find new forms and patterns of writing to be utilized.

Woods: And did that help them defeat the alien threat back then?

The Way Things Were

Carthorn: Oh please, Miss Woods! There have been dozens of thought experiments originating from the Oulipo—the human Oulipo. Georges Perec, a favorite of mine, once wrote an entire novel without once using the letter e. Another method, the snowball technique, simply adds an extra word to each line, until the entire piece ends up looking a bit like a staircase! I love it!

Woods: What does this have to do with our interdimensional Ouliponites?

Carthorn: That's the big mystery, isn't it? The mission of the French Oulipo was to investigate alternative methods of writing with a playful attitude. Writing is always constrained by something, be it time, language, or what have you. The French Oulipo's solution wasn't to abolish these constraints but to recognize these constraints and creatively embrace them. Perhaps that is what these Ouliponites are doing with the fabric of reality. Did the Oulipo in France get these ideas from such visiting beings in the sixties? Or maybe the other way around? There's just so much to consider.

Woods: But again, you mentioned that even the 1960s may not have been the first time these beings visited.

Carthorn: It all has to do with the philosopher Kant, who lived in the 1700s. Kant describes an intelligible method, thought thinking itself. Such thought must come from what he described as an "intelligible realm" that doesn't require any visual stimulants, sensual impressions, or material forms. It's just pure mind-stuff.

Woods: Another realm?

Carthorn: Possibly! The universe we are observing right now is probably not the only universe—our Ouliponite friends are beginning to prove that. And even the universe we do observe might not really be the world within itself.

Woods: (Adjusts earpiece, eyes widen) Professor, we don't have much time.

Carthorn: I'll be short. We must look to the language of the Ouliponites. The phenomenal and noumenal world is something both the Ouliponites and Kant describe. "Phenomena" includes the things we are aware of, the world we create in our minds according to our sensations. This chair, that cameraperson, those notes you're holding. "Noumena" describes something more. Things we seem compelled to believe in but lack the actual evidence to know. Kant was trying to prove the existence of God when conducting these studies, but perhaps he found the inkling of something else. The ultimate a priori beings.

Woods: What did that mean, "priori"?

Carthorn: "From the earlier."

Woods: (Sees something offscreen) We are almost finished. Thank you again, Dr. Carthorn, for the fascinating take on the Ouliponites. I'm sorry we don't have more time.

Carthorn: (Grins) They're here, aren't they?

Two orange-uniformed Guides approach Carthorn and take him by the arms. Carthorn looks into the camera and shrugs.

Carthorn: Listen, tomorrow may represent a "never in a lifetime chance."

Guide: Come with us, Mr. Carthorn.

They walk off camera, but Carthorn's microphone is still attached.

Carthorn: To miss out, to not cross the divide to a utopia without the fear and violence we see all

        The Way Things Were

around us today, who would ever want to miss that
train?

Woods looks on as Carthorn is escorted from the building. She looks into the camera, helpless.

    Woods: I want to go, too.

Dal and I lay naked in bed, listening to the SMAN interview on
their FM transistor and staring at the water-stained ceiling of their
studio apartment.

"I haven't seen her on TV since that interview. Do you think she
quit?" I asked.

Dal took a drag from their cigarette. "Probably got shot along
with the professor by those orange pigs."

I hid my face in the crook of their neck and breathed in their
scent. No shooting. No violence. No burning world. Just Dal.

They drew back. "Hey, you're not going to this Traverse thing,
right?"

"Janis is set on going, on 'resisting hate,'" I said.

"Huh, didn't think she had it in her." They turned and looked at
me. "Don't go, though. Or at least, I'm asking you not to. You do
know there'll be a shit-ton of Nazis there, right?"

"I ... yeah, I do."

"These people get violent fast, Nick. We've been following them
for a few months, and—" Dal stopped themself.

I blinked. "Who's *we?*"

"Fuck," Dal muttered. "Just … some people I've been working with."

"The welders?"

"God no." They laughed. "They're all idiots." Dal's laughter died down. Some strange wall came up between us right there on that mattress. Dal and I shared everything with one another, or at least I thought we did. "C'mon," they said. "It can't be *that* surprising."

I cleared my throat, not sure what to ask. No, that was a lie. I knew what to ask. I just didn't want to say it.

"Dal, do you … hunt Nazis?" I asked.

They coughed. "I mean, *hunt's* a strong word. We just … track them down. Doxx them. Infiltrate their ranks and turn them against each other. It's important that they don't get a platform."

"Well, you obviously fucking failed at *that!*" I said. "What are you even gonna do tomorrow at the gateway?"

They sighed, looked over at me, and shot some queer arrow through my heart. "There will be so many people there. People who are looking for a way out of this shitty world. And those motherfuckers, those Nazis, fully intend to stop them so they can—what? Put everybody *left* in those camps up in Canada? We're not letting them show any strength. If people wanna get through, then they're fuckin' gonna get through. Fascists don't get to decide what's right and what's wrong."

"And you do?" I asked.

Dal scoffed. "Listen to yourself. Are you really gonna be on the side of pure fucking evil?"

   The Way Things Were

"Dal, you're running around with a group that goes around punching people."

Dal got up and started to wrangle on a pair of jeans. They sighed. "Nick, I love you, but that was some naïve shit right there."

I swallowed a bubbling argument. "I don't want you to get hurt. You know how I feel about violence."

Dal slid their pants over their ass and zipped them up. "I won't get hurt, and I don't want you to get hurt either."

"Why do *you* have to fight the stupid Nazis? Can't you let others take care of that?"

"Others aren't doing jack shit, and it's up to us to work together. Don't you think everyone should help as much as we can?"

Little tears of frustration formed in my eyes. "What can *I* do?" I yelled. "I'm just a dumb kid. I miss not being stressed out all the time about rising oceans and Internet Packages and the fucking Safety Alliance! I miss the way things were! I miss not knowing you *hunt* people!"

I started crying for real, right there and then. Dal and I didn't do this sort of shit. But they wrapped their arms around me, and I didn't push away. I just cried into their chest, mourning the death of the world I once knew.

I calmed down a little after a few minutes, and Dal took a deep breath.

"Okay, so when I was a kid I hung out with this group of boys. They were just nasty and hateful, and I was one of them. We beat the shit out of anyone who wasn't like us. But I was lying to myself, thinking that it was okay to do that to others, and I realized I really wasn't like the other boys anyway. I mean, c'mon! I wasn't even a boy," they chuckled. "So one day I just snapped. I fought back. Ever since then I haven't been able to put up with patriarchal or xenophobic bullshit."

They looked away for a moment. I held them tighter and could feel their heart beating faster.

"Don't tell the other punks this—I'll lose my street cred—but I actually don't *like* hurting people. But sometimes it's necessary. In a way, those Nazis are just that same group of boys from fifteen years ago. We can't let them get away with their shit. When the system wants you dead, the only option is to fight back."

Paige Woods reappears on SMAN days later. A number of people suspect it isn't really Miss Woods, but a deep-fake. She is cheerier than ever before.

> Woods: Breaking news as Interstate 5 is blocked from Ashland to the Canadian border. Millions of criminals appear to be flocking to their state's capital cities. The National Safety Alliance advises all civilians to stay indoors and at home until otherwise instructed. Do not approach any potential gateway or become involved with any activities that are related to the illegal event "Traverse Day."

I did not know Salem's capitol campus could harbor this many people, and it took me a while to realize they had come from

    The Way Things Were

all over Oregon. Keisha and Hadley never showed up, so it was just Janis and me. Over half the crowd sported blue pussy hats, blue particles swarming about within the whole, in contrast with the orange helmets of the Safety Alliance. A line of armed troops had formed around the orb and was warning people to stay back. The orb itself towered over the people like a great gray beast threatening to swallow up the capitol if it expanded any further, but the people flocked to it like it was their friend. I hadn't seen any Nazis yet.

People squished and fumbled over one another everywhere, some carrying signs and wearing blue hats, others carrying children and stuffed suitcases, and some apparently just there to watch what would happen. Janis and I held hands and tried to make our way into the crowd.

We walked past a group of people with crosses who shouted and spat at us and said we were willingly walking toward the realm of false gods and that Jesus was the only way to Heaven. We kept pushing through, Janis's hand painfully squeezing mine. Thousands upon thousands swarmed the capitol, looking up into this swirling, colorless, limitless sphere of light.

And then it turned blue.

The people screamed in delight, ecstasy, terror, joy, hatred. Two Ouliponites stepped out from the gateway, with Safety Alliance troops scrambling to get out of their way. We could see the aliens clearly, even as far back as we stood; they loomed over the crowd like awesome redwoods. The Ouliponites looked around as if assessing how many people—the "Used," as they called them— had showed up. One waved its arm, and the orange troops were gently moved to the side, screaming in protest. The great beings turned to one another and nodded. They raised their hands to the sky. Our ears almost blew out as the masses screamed. And to everyone's joy, to everyone's horror, they spoke.

"The full moon has arrived. As promised, the Ouliponites invite the Used of this realm to escape. We hear the turmoil of all planes: from the shores of Diix to the hills of Amlota. Darkness and authority rule this surface. As one wicked thought breeds another, thoughts gather to attract demons of all varieties. We invite the Used to ascend to the next surface. We provide refuge from the grave, the monstrous, and the ravenous. There is room for all who wish."

The people screamed praise and damnation and everything in between. I saw people sobbing all around. After all this time, after all their suffering, someone had heard them and was offering help.

I saw a small dark object fly through the sky.

Screams. Agonizing, painful screams rang out before I saw the explosion. Shrapnel and body parts flew away from the gateway's base, but the beings stood untouched. In the heart of the crowd, dozens of people had just been wiped out. People screeched as they fled for their lives, half of them heading away, the other for the gateway.

The Ouliponites ushered in those who ran toward it. *"Come, chil-dren of darkness. Come into the light. Your physical forms, no matter how wretched, will be transcended and forgotten."*

I could see people running in, disappearing forever behind that utopian wall of blue, including some orange-helmeted Alliance troops. Janis and I held each other's hands tightly as we tried not to get trampled.

 The Way Things Were

"Come on!" Janis yelled. "We have to help those people!" Others were dragging the wounded and dead into the orb with them, heeding the alien's words about "physical forms."

I stopped in my tracks, pulling her to a halt and shook my head. "There are others that can fix this! They'll make the fascists go away!"

"We're here, aren't we? We can help, too," she told me.

"I thought you just wanted to make a statement!" I yelled. "Dal was right. It was Nazis. They said they'd stop us from leaving, and we didn't listen!"

A gigantic truck with a white trillium emblazoned on the side ran through the crowd, people screaming underneath it. A few Safety Alliance troops cheered. Others trampled one another in a mad dash to flee.

Janis pulled us out of the way just as the truck sped past. A number of white men with white trilliums printed on their shirts—some of whom I recognized from the welding shop—jeered at us from the back as it sped to the gateway. Two more Nazi trucks followed and circled the gateway.

The first truck sat idly, and a Nazi in a gray pea coat climbed onto the truck's roof and shouted into a megaphone. "Do not listen to these aliens' false Zionism! They are enemies of the State and their promises of a multicultural utopia will only lead to our destruction! Any attempts to approach the portal will be met with force!"

The Nazi turned to the Ouliponites and shouted up at them, "And *you!* Blue cuck fuckers, you are an enemy of the United States and the white race! We will take back this country, and we will find ways to disassemble your pretentious bodies atom by fucking atom!"

The Ouliponites slowly shook their heads. *"We can do no harm, and harm may not be done to us. Your dark efforts are fruitless compared to the likes of noumena."*

The Nazi spat in their direction. "We'll see about that, faggot aliens!" He climbed back into the truck as it sped off to join the others in their testosterone-filled patrol of the orb.

I pulled Janis's sleeve. "I made a promise that I wouldn't get hurt today."

She shot me a glare. "Then go home. I'm staying."

A car honked behind us, and people moved out of the way as it drove forward. I recognized that car. It stopped next to us. It was packed full of people in black hoodies with bandanas hiding their faces. The driver rolled down the window and pulled off their hood.

"You okay?" Dal asked. My heart sank and swelled at the same time. They looked over to my girlfriend and nodded. "Janis."

"Dal," Janis said.

"The Nazis are here!" I cried.

"We know," said someone in the passenger seat. I recognized Anita's voice. "We didn't know about the missile, but we came prepared for the trucks." More honking, and a dozen more cars filled with punk fighters wove carefully through the crowd.

"We gotta go fight the Axis. Tell whoever's still here to help carry injured people into the gateway if they want to go. Physical injuries

     The Way Things Were

disappear on the other side, right? Some lives could be saved," Dal said. And then they drove off with the others toward the Nazis.

Janis yelled for help, and a dozen or so fellow blue hats ran toward the injured.

"Do you still want to go home?" she asked.

I paused, looking back at the partner I loved heading toward danger and to the partner I had been so apathetic toward about to do the same.

"No."

One of the punk cars swerved into the path of a truck. Two more cars followed, forming a blockade. Nazis poured out of the truck.

Janis and I found a trampled woman, barely conscious, amongst the still bodies. She moaned as we shook her awake.

"Help me get her up," Janis said.

I looked around. Trampled limbs. Crushed skulls. Blue hats and orange helmets and white flowers soaked in red. Red! So many hues and shades of red upon red upon red!

"*Help* me, Nick!" Janis yelled.

Shit.

More punk cars formed a barrier between the wounded and trucks, and I could see people fighting hand to hand in the distance. Gunfire rang throughout the campus. Other punk volunteers helped the blue hats escort the wounded and Used who wished to go through the gateway, while more punks kept the Nazis and Alliance troops at bay and the Ouliponites watched over everything from above. I helped Janis get the poor woman up. We supported her shoulders and began walking her to the gateway. We made it behind the line of cars and quickly rushed the injured woman toward the light.

The gateway hurt to look at. Behind the walls of the orb, I could see masses of energy swimming around and off into the next plane. The assortment of cyan shades and swirling hues seemed like that of the northern lights, and I found myself tearing up.

Janis held the injured woman's hand out to the light. The woman cried out in pain from the movement, and Janis soothed her as we slowly pushed her into the gateway. She dissolved into energy—becoming, presumably, one with another universe.

"You are true light," a voice said.

We looked up to see one of the Ouliponites watching over us, translucent blue. I felt like a child once more, looking up into the towering wonder of the celestial world. I saw no chaos within its astral form, only an aura of ethereal compassion as stars and nebula drifted about within. I dropped to my knees. Maybe this was Kant's God after all.

"You stupid fucking cucks!" someone called out.

A Nazi, the same one in the gray pea coat, ran at us with a gun in his hand. Before either of us could make a move, the sound of gunfire coincided with an explosion of red from Janis's stomach. She screamed.

"No! Fuck, Janis! No!" I cried. We dropped to the ground, and I tried pressing down on the bullet wound. Tears flowed down Janis's face. She clutched my arm so tight it broke the skin.

"Fuck," she said through gritted teeth.

The Way Things Were

A figure ran toward us. Dal.

Dal charged the Nazi and threw him to the ground, the gun flying off into the gateway. The Nazi looked up in surprise, just in time for Dal to punch him in the mouth. Teeth flew into the air.

The Nazi cried out in pain, his mouth and nose dripping with blood.

"Please don't hurt me!" he begged.

"Too fucking late!" Dal screamed in his face.

They jumped off the Nazi and kicked him in the chin. The Nazi kept crying as Dal dragged him by the pea coat toward the gateway. The Saints of Muspelheim leader squirmed and pleaded, trying to wriggle out of his coat.

"No! No stop! I can't go there! The aliens are going to kill Western culture! We are the majority minority!" he screamed.

Dal swung the Nazi inches from the portal and placed their foot on his side.

"The *actual* minorities want you to fuck off," they said.

Dal pushed forward with their foot and sent the writhing fascist through the gateway, where he dissolved into something inhuman like the rest.

"Darkness cannot survive the forces of Intelligence. His being will change into something better, something brighter," the figure of light said above.

Dal ran up to Janis and me. They helped press down on Janis's wound, and she winced in agony as Dal checked her pulse.

"Her pulse is fading," they said.

I cried, nose full of snot and tears dripping down onto Janis.

"Please don't go. Please, please, *please* don't go. I'm really, *really* sorry, Janis. For everything."

Janis smiled and touched my wet cheek. "It's too late," she said faintly. "But that's okay."

"Fuck!" I held onto her hand and kissed it.

Dal nudged me. "I need to get her up," they said. I wasn't much help as Dal carried her. I just kept crying.

"Didn't think I'd ... actually be going," she muttered. Janis was getting weaker by the second. I sobbed, holding her hand.

She smiled at me. "I loved you, y'know ... a lot." She turned to Dal. "Do it."

Dal sent her through the gateway, and she disappeared forever, off to become a peaceful being of divine intelligence.

"She will live on as pure light," the Ouliponite said.

Through my tears I saw the Nazis and Safety Alliance troops driving away with their trucks, the punks and blue hats cheering and helping the Used enter the next realm, and the Ouliponites looking on. I breathed in.

"It's not too late. You could leave this world for something better." Dal said.

I took their hand and kissed it.

"I think I'd like to fix this one."

 The Way Things Were

Snow Thing

Darren felt the joints of the world collectively ache as he pulled the bowstring back, the arrow aimed at the abomination in the white trees. Silence, concentration, and a steady shot. The branches cracked and rustled as the creature jumped through the forest, clumps of snow falling and hitting the ground in muffled thumps.

"That is my friend," a voice inside said, but he knew this was false. His friend had died back in the cave. That was no longer Jared.

It'd been his idea, venturing off into the mountains. Jared suggested the coast instead, or maybe Amlota, the neighboring village where they could meet nice girls: people their age they hadn't grown up with, so it didn't feel like incest. But Darren shot down these ideas and mocked Jared for wanting to stay so safe.

"Be a man for once in your life," he said. The mountains held pure wilderness, offering the chance for a boy to prove himself in the face of survival. Manhood awakening. This was at least what he told Jared, who had reddened in shame at the thought of being so sheepish. Girls could wait. The mountains called. Darren almost half-believed his sermon himself. Hunting with his best friend did sound more alluring than chasing girls, but for other, more selfish reasons.

The bowstring held tight, threatening to snap. If only Jared could keep still.

No, not Jared. The creature. The thing that did not belong. It jumped to another cedar too far away for Darren to make a confident shot. What was it thinking as it hopped tree to tree? Was anything from Jared's past life still in there? The creature bound deeper into the woods, and Darren followed.

Getting to the mountains took two days on horseback. There had been opportunities, of course, for Darren to take the risk. The first night proved colder than expected, the two of them huddled around the dwindling fire.

"We should get closer," Darren said. "For warmth." It was less than ideal, but Jared didn't seem as reluctant as Darren predicted. He could have chanced it there, probably should have. His arm could have wrapped around Jared as he brought their faces closer,

Snow Thing

barely touching, the sweet scent of Jared's breath as Darren inhaled, closer, closer, until lips finally met.

But that would've been too soon. Darren didn't dare, and he felt content with the proximity he'd obtained for the night. His time would come on this trip. He would tell Jared everything.

Tracking the monster in silence proved difficult, his feet crunching through the fresh snow with each step. Darren took it as a challenge. He'd wanted to go hunting, didn't he? The creature sat atop a pine, chewing on something in its hands. Or claws. Definitely claws, since this was not human, Darren reminded himself. He peered at the thing from the snow-covered ferns below. It held a chipmunk in its claws, decapitated and red, as the thing snarled and gnawed on its meal. A few drops of blood dripped down before him into the snow.

Despite its ungodly features, Darren could still see signs of the man he loved underneath it all: Jared's unkempt hair, the prince-like features of his face, the same scars on his arms he'd had all his life. Shame that these were obscured, how the very body that was once Jared now sported unnatural appendages, coats of mangled black fur, and two hollowed eyes. The eyes. That was how Darren knew Jared was no longer Jared. Green, kind eyes that had given Darren looks of worry in the past had turned milk white, refracting light in the back like the other forest animals' eyes. Darren watched the ghost eyes as they scoured the forest, not wanting to be disturbed as it tore the rodent apart.

Darren had killed a similar chipmunk on their first hunt. Jared had winced as Darren pierced its neck with a fishing hook and dangled it in the air with a grin.

"Bait." He smiled at Jared. His friend had turned pale at the sight of gore—which was ironic enough in this moment, under the pine tree. He couldn't name what had come over him to disgust Jared like that. Something about *wanting* Jared also made him want Jared to repulse him. If he could push Jared away, it wouldn't sting as much when his friend inevitably rejected him. His heart ached to have those moments again. They had waited near their trap, chipmunk hanging on its noose. Something had to come by, perhaps a curious bear or a starved smilodon enticed by the near impossible enigma of a floating rodent carcass. Hours passed, and nothing ever came.

"This is boring!" Darren whined. Jared nodded. They went back to their camp where the horses waited. Darren fumbled through his belongings until he drew his bow and a collection of arrows. Jared opted instead for a spear when he packed. Together they made a strange duo.

"Let's find our prey," Darren rejoiced. This was the part he'd been looking forward to. Together they would hunt, strengthening their bond, and Jared would realize how important Darren was to him. They had no need for girls; they had one another. Perhaps if things went well, they could stay here, live off the land, and support one another as real, genuine soul mates.

This was the dream that circled in Darren's mind as they prowled the forest. The mossy woods dripped and crackled alive just after a sudden rainfall, so their movement was unheard as they walked about the forest floor. Darren was hungry. They had consumed the last of their stores that morning, and he felt the urge to provide for the person he cared for most. A lust for blood, something that even he would never admit to, ran through his veins. Some simple opossum, or fox, or even better yet, a deer just needed to

Snow Thing

cross their path, and Darren would take aim and shoot the animal through the throat, and Jared would see Darren for the real man he was: a hunter, a caregiver, someone who would always ensure Jared's safety. Someone worthy of love.

That never happened, though, as the sky flashed and screamed a great thunder. The rains returned, frigid this time. Darren's hopes were dashed as they ran through the rain, their fur-lined shoes soaked through in the spashing puddles. The tintinnabulation of rain carried on, hitting the forest's wide leaves like drums. They turned corners, tripping into bushes and helping each other up, mud fully coating them within minutes.

Jared asked, screaming in the weather, where the camp was. Darren found himself shaking his head, for he didn't know. The forest looked all the same in the storm. They kept on. Darren saw a chance, grabbing Jared's hand and taking the lead.

"Don't let go!" he shouted, and he could swear he felt Jared squeeze his hand as they braved the storm. Winds picked up and mixed with rain, stinging their faces. Darren led them through the last of the trees, and they looked up not to see their camp, but one of the great mountains itself.

"Shit!" Darren exclaimed. Jared tried to pull him back into the trees, but there was something to the left. A dark gash had been ripped into the side of the mountain, forming a black opening. A cave. Darren's heart raced. They could take shelter within. Build a fire. Stay the night. The two of them, alone in peril, emotionally charged and equally vulnerable. When would such an opportunity ever arise again?

Jared tugged at Darren's hand. They should keep on. Perhaps the horses were spooked. It would not be hard to retrace their steps.

"Let's hurry!" Darren ignored him, running with him by the hand toward the dark abyss within. Jared had no choice. The cave's opening had been the blackest black Darren had ever seen.

Until now, for the creature's fur was even darker. The thing looked like a shadow perched in a tree. A shadow with lights for eyes. Darren's muscles strained, still pulling the bow back. He could feel his arms involuntarily shake. It was now or never. That wasn't Jared!

The arrow cut through the air, the bow reverberating as Darren freed it. The animal swerved to the side as the arrow just missed it by a hair. The weapon hit the pine branches behind, snow falling to the ground. The creature looked down at Darren; it could see him. It hissed.

Darren reached back for the next arrow in his bag. He looked back up just in time to see a row of sharp teeth rushing toward him.

The two boys leapt into the darkness. The cave proved stale and cold, but compared to the downpour outside it was a haven, and they decided to stay put. They could see the heavy rain turning to ice. Jared continued to fret about the horses, and Darren assured him they were capable animals.

"They can fend for themselves. Besides ..." he took Jared's hand, "you're always my first priority."

Jared drew back. The look of worry on his face assured Darren it wasn't from the risky action. Jared spoke, talked about how he didn't feel right in this place, how he wanted to leave. It was slimy inside, and dark. What if something lived deeper within? Darren persuaded him against it. They performed this elegant dance over the next hour—Jared trusting his instincts and Darren poking holes and workarounds into Jared's logic.

Snow Thing

"Just sit with me, please," he said. They sat together listening to the sleet pour. The cold crept into Darren's fingers and toes, and he wanted Jared's hands again. Jared's scent wafted around him, made him dizzy. How his heart swelled when he breathed in Jared's air, when the conversation carried on into the night, how after a lull Jared's head rested upon Darren's shoulder.

He awoke alone the next morning. The rain had turned to snow, and the light outside shone into the cave. He looked down to see something at his side. A black, stringy tar that juxtaposed itself with the white snow. Where Jared had slept, the tar had seemingly exploded and trailed off into a series of tracks and splatters that led deeper into the dark.

"Jared!" he called. He followed these tracks, the cave illuminated enough by the reflection of outside's snow. The trail was a horrific, bloody record of dark slime, veering off from left to right and concentrating in certain areas of further "explosions," as if Jared stumbled, fighting with his thoughts to clear the demons of his mind. The black ooze went deeper and deeper.

Darren came up to a figure in the dark. He cried out in shock. The figure gave no sounds of breathing, of shuffling or squirming or any indication that Jared needed help. Only silence. Darren stepped closer. Jared's face was to the cave wall. The last of the tar could be seen dripping down his legs, pooling at his feet. Darren could not see too many details in the cave's light, but something was un-Jared about Jared. He reached out for his friend's hand.

"Are you all right?" he asked. A cracking sound, and Darren witnessed a pair of eyes glowing in the darkness. He screamed. He hit it with his fists and felt the inhuman qualities that covered Jared's face. After so long of not touching! The creature screamed back. He had chased the damn thing out of the cave, grabbing his bow and arrows as he caught a glimpse of it fading into the snowy cedars. That was this morning.

They now wrestled in the snow. Darren held the monster back as it tore into him with its hind claws. Darren grasped the end of the arrow like a knife, aiming for his opponent's heart.

"Hold still, Jared!" he yelled.

The monster swiped, and Darren felt a sharp sting at his throat followed by a gush of warmth. The creature stepped back, as if amazed at what it'd done. Darren saw a look of worry, a hint of regret, within those eyes. The monster started crying.

Darren's muscles released, and he sank into the snow. He watched as the animal climbed the hillside and away through the winter forest, and he descended into darkness.

Snow Thing

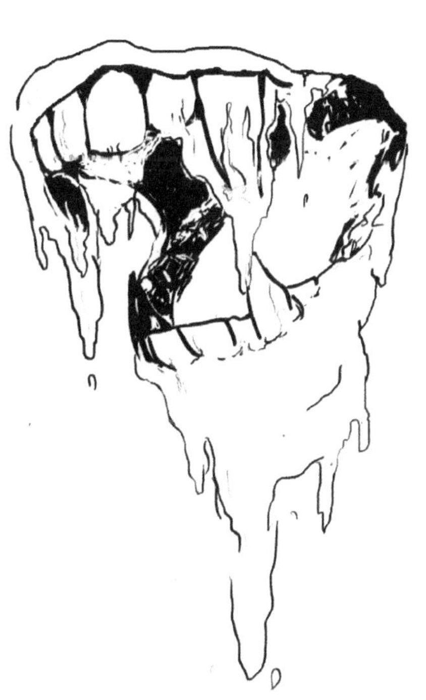

A Devil in Woman's Likeness

It is an odd thing, but everyone who disappears is said to be seen in San Francisco. It must be a delightful city, and possesses all the attractions of the next world.

— Oscar Wilde

Crimson glimmered in the nighttime waters of the red-light district, and Irving Craven inhaled tobacco, wishing he held something more powerful than the cigarettes he purchased at the drugstore on Grant Street. Of course, the Barbary Coast surely possessed more powerful sins to offer, but nothing there would ever match Irving's exotic tastes. Something that retained a sense of elegance while relieving the stress of reality, if only for a few hours. Opium or hashish perhaps, or if he was lucky, the nectar of the true decadents, absinthe herself. But Irving did not know where to purchase such goods, and he did not much feel like asking the locals, the low, despicable beings that scoured the streets with their obnoxious laughter and ridiculous music. A pelican swooped past, adding to the noise and sending a shiver down his back. Irving pulled his frock coat tighter around him. The poor thing, an antique at this point, was the only fine jacket he had left, and it stood between his self-proclaimed status as a dandy and his (depressingly real) status as no better than the bile that walked around him. Whores, criminals, drug lords, and pretty waiter girls; "the Paris of America" indeed! He exhaled into the night, allowing the salty air to whisk the smoke away. The briny sea breeze made him miss the Atlantic. But Boston was gone now, away and dead with the rest of his old life. The Pacific hardly proved a suitable substitute. The damp air was difficult to breathe in. From across the water, Alcatraz Citadel shimmered amidst the darkness, a tangerine light making its rounds from the top of the lighthouse. He could hear the barks of sea lions in the distance. The thought of such rancid creatures caused him to sneer in disgust. Foul things. Steam poured from his mouth with each breath. As he turned, his ankle gave out with a sharp pang.

"Blast the devil," he muttered while rolling the ankle in its socket before he continued, gait slightly adjusted. Irving had not found what he came for. Perhaps he never would. He kept on anyway, walking up Meigg's Wharf away from the sea and back up toward

   A Devil in Woman's Likeness

the all-encompassing chaos. The climb back up one of the many hills that plagued San Francisco only caused his ankle to ache more, and his calves burned with each step. The fact that he was already out of breath upset him. Passing the maddening lights and boisterous dance halls, Irving made his best attempts to avoid all eye contact up the garnet sidewalk while trying not to breathe too hard. Great structures of brick and wood towered over him at every side, set against a marmalade hue from the surrounding lanterns and ascending into obscurity within the onyx sky. The scent of sea salt wafted from the wharf up to the district, and Irving could not fathom how everyone else would go about their business as if the entire City didn't reek of ocean life.

He came up to a familiar saloon, the Dash. A pair of waiter girls stood at the entrance. Irving looked down. He had encountered this duo before. One girl nudged the other as he approached and curtsied.

"G'evening, my lord," she said in an English accent, a terrible mockery of the Anglo tongue, something to mock him and his last remaining jacket, the way he held himself. She had done this several times after an unfortunate encounter months prior. She had kicked him out of the saloon after a bash, and Irving figured it was because his old-world habits had offended her. If only he ceased to be so conspicuous and could fade into the shadows like so many others in this corner of Hell. But of course, part of this was his fault. Anecdotes of his odd mannerisms and obsessions were beginning to spread. Perhaps he deserved such mimicry.

Irving gave a hesitant nod. "Good day, madam," he replied.

The woman snickered with her friend and curtsied again as he walked past. "Oh, my lord! Young master dandy, sir! Would you not like to partake in a rousing glass of brandy at our fine establishment?" the waiter girl called in her fake accent. The other woman gave a small laugh, as if to humor her. Irving could never make out the other one so much as she always kept to the shadows. Her friend though, the first pretty waiter girl, was another matter.

She stepped out into the light. "There goes the fine dandy!" she mocked, not bothering with fake English anymore. "See how he walks! All's he's missin' is his cane!"

"Lilith, that's enough!" the second girl said. Something rang queer in her voice; it was a fraction too high, a smidgen too false. The first woman sneered and slipped back into the saloon. The remaining waiter girl turned to Irving, face still hidden in the shadows.

"I'm sorry about her," the girl said. "She just likes to play rough, that's all."

Irving said nothing, trying to think up something to say and utterly failing. He simply shook his head and turned to make his way back home.

It did not make much sense, mocking him for his fine tastes. He had only been in the City for three months and had already struck up a reputation as something to make fun of. The laughable dandy of the streets.

Awful San Francisco. Disgusting, abhorrent, putrid San Francisco. The eastern shore had quite a false reputation of the west. Land of creative opportunity. The seacoast of decadence. All falsehoods. The City's streets were always filthy, a number of the buildings had hardly been established since the last earthquake, and a sense of insanity set him on edge whenever he walked down the crowded Pacific Street, always ducking and running so as not to get hit by some horse or car. He made his way back through the

    A Devil in Woman's Likeness

night toward the great house he lived in, located in the heart of the Presidio Reservation's dark forests. His place of living served as an oasis from San Francisco. Irving thought of the granite architecture and the art contained within, but most of all whenever he thought of the Presidio Mansion, he thought of the greenery.

One would never believe plant life grew inside, but as soon as one stepped into the mansion's grand hall, they could see the entire ceiling was made of glass fantastically woven into colorful and exotic shapes to let in sunlight. When Irving first arrived, he had believed for a moment that he had stumbled upon some urban jungle, that the mansion he had heard rumors of was in fact long abandoned and nature had begun to reclaim her land. Irving heard the hushed whispers drifting about town that the building within the forest was ruled over by a witch. Some ex-convict from the Golden Years that staked her claim decades ago, back when resources were readily scattered about the Bay Area. One could do just about anything in the City fifty years back. A lawless western criminal setting her roots down and raising a mansion did not seem so out of the ordinary.

The Presidio Mansion was one of the few large structures that had survived the earthquakes of '38, '65, and '92, and the outdated architecture gave the house a certain grandeur that the other buildings of the City rarely bestowed. The marble and granite foundations and columns running across the exterior instantly differentiated the Presidio Mansion from its wooden peers as well. No other building was made of pure rock. Pure grandiosity. It was what attracted Irving to this prohibited place: the rumor of the only thing of opulence in this disgusting coastal city. Irving had packed up his camera, plates, and tripod one gray morning and set off for the house in the woods nestled in the heart of the Presidio military reservation. Rumor had it that the grounds were off limits even to the armed forces surrounding it.

Imagine Irving's astonishment at the array of chloroplasts that met his eyes as soon as he entered that mansion. No one had answered the door, so the young man let himself in. Nothing of the sort would had ever happened back in Boston, where footmen rightfully greeted all guests as they arrived. Little did he know he was being watched. The Presidio Mansion's doors opened to a colorless hallway. Irving set his photography case, this great lugging thing he had managed to drag up the hills, aside. Again, a footman absolutely should have been there to take it. Light poured in from the end of the hallway, and Irving stepped forward. That is where he met the vibrant hues of shamrock and pine, and that is where he met Euryale.

The ground was covered in dirt, or rather, it was *only* dirt. Vines, trees, and shrubs populated the space and grew over withered pieces of furniture. Irving looked up to see the glass ceiling, which was moulded into intricate shapes and patterns as if to form its own transparent Sistine Chapel. The expansive ceiling created a sense of awe, as if the architecture were about to swallow Irving whole. Plants crept their way upward toward the sunlight, and Irving grimaced as he noticed the vines snake their way around the Corinthian columns and arches that held up the glass ceiling. He would have felt greater disgust if the architecture were not so alluring. Light shimmered in the garden as Irving moved about, the sunlight glistening amongst interior trees and overgrown chairs. The witch of the Presidio Mansion must have left ages ago, leaving the walls to decay and the floors to crumble to the likes of trees and saplings. He noticed something else in the garden, however. Several things.

     A Devil in Woman's Likeness

A statue greeted him. Irving cried out in shock. It was a perfect sculpture of some long-perished chap, posed as if fleeing from something. He bent closer to inspect the granite man. Exquisite detail—the carved muscles, the almost hint of crafted stubble, the finely rasped surface creating the illusion of pores. The man stood there, frozen in time. There was something about that stillness, and Irving found himself wanting to create something similar to this statue. The capturing of pure refinement in a single moment. Irving had to meet the creator of such fine artistry. Then he noticed another one. And another.

That was eight weeks ago now. Irving continued down Pacific Street, past more concert saloons and cheap brothels. He was not the kind of fellow to go looking for trouble. He kept his head down as he walked along the dirty streets of the Barbary Coast. Despite his best efforts, his eccentricity was more than apparent, this pompous dandy in his nice old jacket strolling about like he had wealth to spare. In truth he had spent the last of the night's money on the drugstore cigarettes, but that wasn't something to get upset over—Euryale could conjure coins from the earth in a second. That didn't mean he would get more than his weekly allowance, however.

Irving strode by a dark alley, a group of men standing around its entrance. They snickered venomous laughs reminiscent of earlier gangs that ravaged the City back in the 1840s. San Francisco would always be a lawless town. The fall of mankind was starting, and its origin point would be the West Coast. Irving continued on. He heard scuffling feet behind him and the continued gruff laughter of the men, a little older than he. They were wiry beanpoles in worn, second-hand coats and derby hats that covered up their ratted hair. Irving quickened his pace, and the laughter behind died down. The footsteps grew louder—directly behind. Irving broke into a run.

He found himself pinned against a wall soon after. A knife pressed against his throat as he looked into the filthy face of a gangster.

"Where are you off to at this time of night, good sir?" the gangster asked. His brothers gathered around him, bloodthirsty for something to happen. Irving could have sworn he saw one of them lick his lips.

"Home," Irving said. "On the military reservation. The Presidio."

"The Presidio? You're not the sort to come from the Presidio."

Irving looked in the direction of his home. How safe he could have been if only his ankle hadn't been so stiff. One of the men's eyes widened.

"Hold on, Gilbert. I think he's telling the truth. You live in that house with that witch, don't you?" This man's voice betrayed his age. Irving couldn't fathom he was older than sixteen years.

The first gangster, Gilbert, smirked. "There's no witch. That's just a rumor made so idiots like you don't go trespassing."

"She's not a witch; she's something else entirely," Irving intervened. He felt smug as he peered closer at the attacker's face. A little fat in the cheeks with a crooked, unsightly nose; not exactly what he'd been looking for.

"What are you looking at?" Gilbert spat.

"He's not lying. There really *is* a nasty woman in that forest," the boy interrupted. "I've seen her. And her house is filled up with goat men, and people she's turned into stone." He couldn't seem to

    A Devil in Woman's Likeness

stop himself, in that adolescent sort of way when one had to prove they knew something. Irving remembered being that age back on the East Coast. Reading yellow books, photographing orchids, learning photography from his father; why had he moved out and away from all that, where his life was about to end?

"Quiet!" Gilbert snapped. He turned back to Irving. "A wise guy like you shouldn't be roaming around these streets at night looking this nice. Someone might come along and take everything you have." He pressed the knife harder against Irving's throat, smirking. "Why don't you give it to us so you'll be safe for the rest of the night?" he said with a slow twist of his wrist.

It was a shoe that saved Irving. He could not have predicted his savior, nor could have any of the dirty men. A hard-cobbled woman's shoe flew through air and struck Gilbert the gangster in the jaw. He let go of Irving as he cried out and staggered. Some of the men laughed nervously at the strangeness of it all, and others much more brazenly at their leader in pain.

From the street, they could make out the silhouette of a woman. Irving realized it was the pretty waiter girl from before, the nice one, as she walked forward.

"Get lost, you goops!" the girl yelled in a deep voice.

Gilbert scrambled to his feet and spat blood. "Or what?"

The waiter girl stood up to him, considerably taller and all the more terrifying in her evening dress. She jerked her knee up and hit him in the crotch. The man cried out in pain, dropping to the dirt like a brick. The others watched as their boss writhed in agony. Irving felt his hand being grabbed and yanked away, and he and the pretty waiter girl ran up the alley and away from the gang of men deeper into the eastern ward along the harbor. She pulled him down a back alley, and they kneeled over to catch their breath.

"Thank ... thank you, miss," Irving said, still breathing hard. He found himself dumbstruck, not knowing whether to be thankful.

"You're welcome," the waiter girl replied. "I saw those ruffians follow you down the street and thought I'd help out. I've seen what they do before. Damn bullies," she said. The girl looked at him as if there were more to say. "Sorry about earlier."

"No harm done," Irving said and stood upright. "I have never met a lady quite like yourself."

"Oh, about that ..." the girl said. She reached up for her scalp, and Irving watched her rip her hair right off her own head. Irving's savior had not been a pretty waiter girl. A pretty waiter *boy* stood right in front of him, illuminated by the nighttime lamps and wearing a dress. "Sorry about the confusion here, but my name's Otto."

Euryale looked through the morning paper in the luxurious, crumbling dining hall. The room's great windows gaped open on one side of the room, letting a cherry tree from outside sprout its blossoms into the mansion and fill the space with the scent of spring. The floor remained littered with an array of shattered glass and luscious petals. Artifice and natural forms tangled into one within the confines of the Presidio Mansion. Euryale's serpents turned the pages for her, with the headline "Victims of Vesuvius May Number 2,000: Fertile Country Converted into a Desert of Ashes and Sand" printed out on the front page. She barely noticed the horned footman setting her café au lait beside her on the ruined table.

Irving watched the gorgon's orange eyes—how those retinas must have stopped thousands of soldiers in their tracks, robbing families of good husbands and wives and petrifying armies with a single glance into the hallowed void. Euryale rolled them in annoyance.

The faux dandy knew better than to push the subject, but curiosity took the better of him.

"What is it?" Irving asked. The lady of the house shot a look up at him, and Irving could have sworn he felt an extra centimeter of granite creep up his leg.

"What do *you* care?" the gorgon snapped back. The rooted serpents collectively hissed.

Irving said nothing and looked back down at his eggs. The dining table felt too long for just the two of them. As much as he had grown up dreaming of such lavish, dark settings, he now felt uncertain of what to do with himself in these situations. He could never admit it, but living luxuriously bored him. His thoughts drifted to the previous night. The madness, thrill, and absolute sensation of it all! Irving had not felt such a rush in years.

After rescuing the misplaced dandy, Otto Flynn had taken him back to the Dash. Irving had only been in once before, after the disastrous and embarrassing encounter with the cruel waiter girl, Lilith.

"She told me about that," Otto said over whiskey. When offered, Irving had requested absinthe. The bartender gave him a look of disgust. "We don't serve such fine drinks here, doodad," he said.

Otto laughed at the insult and ordered a glass of wine for Irving instead. "No green drink for you, fancy boy. You'll have to settle for red."

Irving accepted the drink, apparently of no charge, and Otto winked at him while sliding the glass toward his hand.

"But don't worry about Lilith," he continued. "The word is she'd only let you in because she thought you were a disciple of Sappho. When she figured out she fell for a *male* dandy, she was mortified."

Occurrences began to fall into place for Irving. The waiter girl Lilith had only begun to show disdain for him once she established physical contact. The arm around his shoulders, the stroking of his chin. She likely felt the rough stubble of his face. Irving gasped at the realization. Otto chuckled.

"You're a lick of an androgyne, to be honest," he said. Irving sipped from his glass, saying nothing. He could feel the icy glare from Lilith from across the saloon. The pretty waiter boy downed the rest of his drink. Irving could feel himself being sized up. "But I think I like it," Otto said, chewing his cheek in contemplation.

Irving swallowed. Something about this man before him captivated his interest. The curls of his dark hair. The chiseled bone structure. The long eyelashes and brilliant eyes.

The ideal model.

He cleared his throat. "Darling Otto, why is it that you dress like a woman?" he asked.

Otto shrugged, motioning for the bartender to pour another glass. "It's part of what this place offers. A kind of refuge from the world outside where fellow inverts can escape. Plus, it's not a bad way of payin' rent," he said.

 A Devil in Woman's Likeness

Irving looked over at one of the booths lining the saloon walls. A young man led a much older gentleman by the hand into a booth and closed the curtain behind him. Irving swallowed. He looked back to see Otto sizing him up once more.

"Are you also a ... uh?" Otto said.

Irving shook his head. "I suppose I am a bit of an odd duck, but not in the ways such as these," he said. Otto smirked as if in disbelief. Irving continued, "But that isn't to say I abhor the concept."

Otto laughed, and Irving laughed with him. He strummed his fingers on the bar counter, trying to figure out how to ask Otto what he wanted from him.

"But my dear fellow," he began. "What do you do when you're not ... dressed up?"

Otto sipped his second drink and smiled at Irving. "I'm an artist," he said.

Euryale's voice pierced through the memory. "Excuse my aggression," she said. Irving snapped back into the present. "I am a tad on edge today. If you must know, we may be having company soon," she said.

"Whom?" he asked.

The gorgon gave him a small look of annoyance. "Just say 'Who.' And it's my sister." She held up the newspaper, pointing at the Vesuvius headline. "This is her doing."

Irving's eyes widened. "Do you mean ... ?" he started.

The gorgon snorted. "Oh! No. No not *her*, she's dead. And an idiot," Euryale said. "Probably still has her head stuck on that shield somewhere," she muttered.

The faun footman walked up to Irving carrying a tray of muffins. Irving kindly accepted one, which only garnered a smirk as the faun's response. It was difficult for Irving to get used to the fauns; they insisted on never wearing shirts. Sometimes in the shadows he would catch glimpses of their chiseled bodies moving around in the dark, usually with one another. They never took interest in Irving however, usually acknowledging him with an air of disdain and superiority.

Irving tried to not let the faun's smirk get to him, the same way he tried to keep their tightened bodies from letting him feel insecure about his own. The footman brought the tray over to Euryale, who bent her head over it, allowing the snakes to feast upon the remaining muffins as if they were rats. Irving winced. It seemed unnatural, reptiles eating baked goods. When they had their fill, she sat up.

"How are your pictures coming along?" she asked.

Irving picked at his muffin. "Terribly slow, but I may have a new muse soon."

"Besides me?" she asked. Her eyebrows shot up.

Irving shrugged. There were only so many photographs one could take of a gorgon. With the exception of himself, he found that mortals typically petrified when they viewed photographs where Euryale looked at the lens, which had resulted in a horrific gallery opening that he was forced to flee. He had yet to mention this to her.

"You will always be my first muse," he said, "but an artist must never create the same thing twice."

 A Devil in Woman's Likeness

Euryale scrunched her mouth. He couldn't tell if she was hurt or not. They finished their sweets, and the gorgon stood up.

"When you are done with your new muse, I will need you. Prepare yourself, Mr. Craven," Euryale said to him. "I need to pay a visit to Mr. Phelan."

The pretty waiter boy, who arrived without his dress that day, gasped in astonishment as he looked about the grand hall. Irving had snuck him in through the back, where the mansion truly began to crumble beyond repair and the scorch marks usually kept the fauns away. Anxiety riddled Irving's thoughts regardless. What if the fauns *did* come in and discover that he had snuck this man into the mansion for just the purpose of art? What if *Euryale* came in?

The space held the aura of an untamed jungle. White orchids exploded about the room and filled every which way with their scent to the point of nausea while trailing plants snaked their way up the walls and columns to create a wall of botanical flesh. But amongst the disgusting greenery sprouted the naked forms of various races, ages, and genders—all converted to a single muted color under Euryale's tangerine gaze. Otto Flynn mistook them for sculptures. Irving remained silently glad that he did not have to explain otherwise as he set up his camera and tripod across the humid room.

"I can barely tell that these were made with a chisel and hammer," Otto said. He stroked the cheek of a handsome chap, albeit not as muscular as Irving would have preferred. Otto ran his fingers over the granite shape of the soft, once-plump stomach. Irving winced.

Reality always proved more disappointing than the dreams of artists. It really was a shame clothing could not be converted as well.

"Did you make these?" Otto asked.

Irving winced, sliding his first plate carrier into the camera. "No. But Otto, I'm just about ready. Why don't you come over here and change into this?" He held up a toga of sorts—his bed sheet, but certain limitations would have to be worked with for the sake of l'art pour l'art.

Otto stopped, uncertain, hanging off the statue. "Will that really be necessary?"

"I doubt you haven't worn anything more elaborate, waiter girl," Irving said. "This 'toga' will aid us in recreating traditional classic portraiture. Think of Ancient Greece, or the great Romans before the collapse of the empire."

The waiter boy tilted his head and chewed thoughtfully at his cheek before a wicked smile and devilish light lit up his features. Irving took a step back as Otto rushed headfirst back into the jungle, leaving Irving holding the sheet.

"Otto!" Irving said in a harsh whisper. He looked around. No sight of any fauns or gorgons. But creatures of the Old World were stealthy. There was still the possibility of being ambushed.

"Otto, come back!" Irving whispered again. What was this erratic boy doing? He had ignored Irving's toga entirely. Irving tried not to imagine the various spiders and insects getting tangled up in Otto's clothes, how the leaves and dirt were probably scuffing up the waiter boy's perfect face. He was messing up everything. Or, worse than a spider or insect: a faun. Irving stamped his foot and cried out in pain as he forgot how heavy it was.

   A Devil in Woman's Likeness

"Are you all right?" Otto called from within the foliage.

Irving sucked air through his teeth. "Just marvelous," he called back sunnily.

"Well, wait just a moment. I have an idea you might like."

Sweat formed upon Irving's brow and the palms of his hands. What would Euryale do if they were discovered? He caught a statue staring at him and glared at its lifeless eyes. "Stop that," he told it.

Otto stepped out from the bushes, naked. A crown of leaves adorned his black curls. The pretty waiter boy had transformed into a full-blown living spectacle, a modern-day Adonis. Irving felt something stir within his lower half. This wasn't what he had envisioned at all, and yet ... Otto standing there in the humid interior garden, perfect body in its purest form—delightfully perverted, in a way, and yet what Irving felt was not so much a sense of vile sin than more of a ... classical righteousness, if one could call it that. Perhaps. Irving continued to stare at the phallus dangling mere feet away from him.

"Are you blushing?" Otto asked.

"No, I'm just a bit overheated. It's terribly hot in here. Can we get on with this?"

Despite his initial fears, Irving found Otto to be a glorious model. Otto Flynn posed graciously, showing off his natural form through the foliage and amongst the cracked columns. He patiently waited each time Irving had to flip or switch plates, and even suggested additional poses and photographs. The photographer's face continued to redden as he looked over Otto's firm chassis through the camera lens. This graceful yet muscular figure, posing stretched in the ruined gardens of Greece from so long ago—the way he bit his cheek while coming up with ideas, curls intermingling with leaves above a glistening brow wet from the ghastly temperature, and the lovely way in which his genitalia hung between his thighs as a result. Irving swallowed. Why was this making him so nervous? He had never felt like this with any of his previous models, such as Euryale. Yet his hands didn't tremble like this around them. He felt as if he were suffocating in Otto's presence. Every humid, hot breath he sucked in while gazing at the olive form leering back up at him was more provocative than the last. He felt his lungs were going to burn out his chest and leave his insides a steaming puddle. Irving pressed the shutter.

It would be just a moment before Otto could move as his nude image was immortalized along the plate, more sculpted than those in stone around them. Irving took the moment to stare. He pretended to look introspective as he planned the next shot, but in reality he was transfixed by a form more perfect than nature and all of man's planned architecture around them. His brain screamed a single incoherent note that was more of feeling than a sound, though not one he knew. Irving settled for beauty. He was not quite sure it was right, but he knew that it was certainly not wrong. Surely the forces who crafted the man before him had distilled artistry in an essence before shaping into the ideal of human. Taking loving care as they delicately chiseled every feature over the lean body, taking special care with the heavy lidded eyes and gently bowed lips so that the purity they founded could radiate outward.

Irving wanted to fall on his knees and praise those forces. His thoughts collapsed back into incoherency.

Otto frowned. "What's wrong?" Irving's moment was up.

 A Devil in Woman's Likeness

The photographer shook his head, quickly removing the loaded plate and trying to cram the next plate into his camera with unsteady hands. Something continued to catch on the end—this equipment took delicate care—and Irving swore. He looked up, horrified at the words he had just muttered in front of his guest. But the pretty waiter boy only laughed.

"You act as if you've never set eyes on a naked man before," Otto said.

Irving avoided his gaze, instead glancing over at the stone boy that had set things in motion. While Irving had never known him, he considered the statue a friend, his only friend in this odd circumstance he found himself in. One day, he and the statue would be the same, but he wanted to know one in the flesh, in the thriving, breathing reaches of reality. The result of this goal looked at him with a warm smile, some species of glance Irving could have never foreseen in a thousand years. How it ruptured something inside him! Ruined him! The waiter boy's very presence stirred something utterly alien inside of the photographer. The word *hope* drifted up in his mind, and Irving sat down in shock. Otto rushed next to him and put his arm around Irving, which helped nothing in the least.

"Are you feeling well?" Otto asked.

"Ghastly," Irving spat out. "I think our session is done for today. I must lie down."

Otto breathed out a laugh. "You talk in the strangest way, Irving Craven. As if you were an English prince without the accent."

The dandy was at a loss for words, having been utterly read by this crossdressing enigma within ten seconds. So what if he wasn't English? Decadence was a mindset, not a nationality.

"I was wondering," the waiter boy said, "If I come back tomorrow—fully clothed—would you mind showing me around the house? I've always wondered about it growing up."

Words could not escape Irving's throat; he wasn't fibbing when he said he needed to lie down. Irving nodded, if only to get the gorgeous boy out of his presence so he could think clearly again.

Otto smiled, making Irving want to faint. "Great, I'll come by in the afternoon. Give you some time to recover from ..." He gestured at his privates, as if they were nothing. "Well, *this*." Otto laughed. He got up, retreating into the bushes to dress.

Irving swallowed, brushing away beads of sweat upon his forehead. He didn't want to be alive right then. He didn't want to *exist*. Why was he so afraid of taking up space, for using what privileges he had rightfully bought? Because he was worthless, of course. What some may have called self-doubt Irving only referred to as rational thought.

The waiter boy stepped back out, thankfully clothed this time. "Sorry about my idea. I just wanted to make our art authentic. True ancient classical portraiture, you know?"

Irving swallowed. "Well, yes. I do agree. It was quite a grand idea, to say the least."

Otto smiled again. Lord above, if he could only leave. "I like you, Irving Craven. It was good makin' art with you today. Us bohemians gotta stick together."

They shook hands, and Irving let him out through the back. As he watched the retreating figure of Otto Flynn, he reflected on what the boy had said. His mind raced; it had been his first time seeing a (living) naked man. And what was a bohemian, and why had Otto

   A Devil in Woman's Likeness

referred to them as such? Irving looked over the City down below. The usual gray skies had lifted, replaced with unusual sunlight and a warm breeze over the San Francisco landscape. Along with the City, Irving began to see things more clearly.

The Grand Opera House of Mission Street rang abuzz that evening, with celebrities, politicians, and highly esteemed folk of the like flocking to the barnlike structure as if it lived up to its name. Euryale hung onto Irving's arm, wearing a brilliant gown colored in a deep maroon with a heavy veil over her head covering tightly coiled snakes. She had altered the material properties of Irving's coat as well, just for the night, embedding a pattern of crystals woven into the fibers. The two shone brightest in the midst of the elite San Francisco crowd, looking only slightly awkward as Euryale towered over her date like an Egyptian palm. Irving's condition had crept up to his knee at that point, so Euryale began her conversion process on the other foot's toes, in order that he could walk semi-normally for this public appearance.

"Be on your best behavior tonight, Irving," Euryale whispered.

"I always am," he said.

He could see her smile through her veil. The gorgon scanned the horizon of heads in search of a certain someone, Irving was sure. He just didn't know whom. Or *who*, as Euryale would have him say. The entrance hall of the opera house writhed with the likes of the upper class, and Irving caught glimpses of infamous locales such as Maynard Dixon and Arnold Genthe, an illustrator and photographer, respectfully. Irving had never admired Genthe's work, photographs with too much life contained within. He was secretly disappointed that Genthe had not been one of his gallery casualties, but of course the photographer had never even arrived to his show. Irving ducked his head in the hopes the fellow photographer would not speak to him.

"Oh, how I loathe these folk," Euryale said. "You should have seen the people of Greece. Much less ridiculous." She motioned toward an older woman encased in a silver wrap, a diamond tiara at the top of her head. "No one would have worn *that*, for instance," she said. Irving laughed. The woman looked over at them and glared before shuffling inside. Irving's face turned red with embarrassment.

Euryale let out a small gasp only audible to Irving beside her and pulled her date across the hall to a gaggle of men in fine suits. She focused on one man in particular, a rather short one. The man's eyebrows shot up for a second as he looked in horror at the lady in maroon stalking toward him. He recovered his composure and stroked his trimmed beard as the gorgon approached.

"Ah, Mrs. Ellon. A fine night for opera, wouldn't you agree?" he said.

Euryale smiled sweetly. "Dearest Jimmy, please. We are always on a first-name basis."

"Are we to make this fine lady's acquaintance?" one of the other men asked.

The short man nodded. "May I present Mrs. Florence Ellon, a dear old friend of mine."

"I knew his father well back in the fifties during the Gold Rush. You could call me his aunt of sorts," Euryale, or Florence Ellon,

    A Devil in Woman's Likeness

said. She slid her hand down the short man's arm slowly as she spoke. The man quickly jerked his arm away.

"And who might this young lad be?" he asked.

Florence Ellon looked over at Irving as if he was an afterthought. "Irving Ellon."

"A grandson?"

"Nephew. *Actual* nephew," she lied.

The short man extended his hand to Irving; his grasp bruised Irving's delicate bones. "James D. Phelan, former mayor. I'm certain you've heard of me. There isn't a soul in the City that doesn't know the Phelan name," he said.

Irving racked his mind, trying to remember if what Mr. Phelan said was even halfway true. "Of course. It's an honor to meet you," he lied.

"The other members of the Bohemian Club and I really must be going now," Mr. Phelan said. Irving licked his lips. That word again, *bohemian.*

"Jimmy dear, I was wondering if I could have a word with you." Florence Ellon glanced over at the other men. Through her veil, Irving could have sworn he saw the hint of a sneer in her face. The men in suits looked away as if they had seen a witch.

"*Alone,*" Florence Ellon said, and the men fled into the concert hall.

James D. Phelan watched his retreated acquaintances, as if longing to be one of them. "I would love to, darling Firenze, but tonight is not the best. I want to get in quickly with the others so I can find a good seat. Enrico Caruso is playing in *Carmen* tonight.

He came all the way from Italy; it would be a shame if I didn't see him up close," he said, almost nervously apologetic.

Euryale caught him by the shoulder. Irving saw her fingers momentarily turning to stone, and Mr. Phelan gave out a brief cry as the gorgon held him in place. Euryale's serpents hissed underneath her veil, several heads slithering out to flick their tongues at the politician. Irving's foot ached just watching.

Mr. Phelan swallowed. "Matters have ... complicated," he said.

"Then I'm certain we can have a nice discussion about it."

Mr. Phelan kept quiet and caught Irving's eye. A look of knowing passed between them as they recognized another captive in the woman's schemes, mortals in touch with the Mythical. But this was the price for such contact. Just as James D. Phelan's family had done years before, Irving had made a deal when he moved in. A chance to enter an alternative existence within the supernatural realm in the gradual exchange for his life. Of course things were going to get difficult. Irving shot the politician a look. Mr. Phelan sighed.

"Tomorrow night at the Phelan Building," Mr. Phelan said.

Euryale let go, and James D. Phelan scampered off into the darkness of the concert hall to meet with his companions, hand protectively over his damaged shoulder. The gorgon spun around and headed for the door.

"Are we not staying for the concert?" Irving asked.

"I loathe music."

     A Devil in Woman's Likeness

Irving stirred the ammonium citrate and ferricyanide together in a bowl as Otto painted the mixture onto paper. They stood in Irving's makeshift darkroom in silence. Neither of them had ever seen the room in complete light, and Irving tried not to think of what sinister things lurked in the corners of the mansion's deserted spaces. In spite of ill-fated imaginings of possibly horrid things, the room worked wonderfully as a processing lab. Irving guessed it had once served as a bedroom, perhaps for someone who lived here before Euryale came in half a century ago and converted the residents to marble.

"Aren't we supposed to dunk these in baths?" Otto asked, referring to the paper he was washing.

"Keep your voice down," Irving pleaded.

"Sorry!" Otto said.

Irving sighed. The fauns typically stayed out of these rooms, but they would come looking if they heard anything. "For regular prints, yes, they do go in chemical baths. But these are cyanotypes. They work a bit differently," Irving said.

"What develops them?"

"Sunlight."

Otto chuckled, bothering Irving a bit. Why was this so humorous to him?

"What is it?" Irving asked.

"Using the sun to make photographs. Even in the City, we always find our way back to nature."

Irving sneered in the dark. "I would hate to degrade myself in such a way."

"Isn't that why we've been taking these pictures? To make art in celebration of the natural form?"

Irving felt himself blush at the mention of "natural form," and found himself thankful for the darkness that concealed the two of them.

"Anything I create is greater than the natural world or anything of this existence could ever conspire," he said.

"But the natural world is where we come from."

"And I rise above it. I am disgusted by this miserable reality. All bad art originates from the return to life and nature, and I certainly won't be a part of that," Irving said.

"Then why are we even doing this?" the voice in the dark said.

"The natural world and civilization will fall to a crumble of collapse and ruin—as you perfectly know being from the coast—and I will delightfully ignore it until I crumble into dust myself. These portraits have nothing to do with nature."

"That didn't answer my question," Otto said.

Irving hesitated, uncomfortable with finally stating his ideals out in the open like this, albeit in the dark. It was easier back in Boston, where there were fellow decadents, fellow readers of dreadful books, where everyone simply understood what Irving was trying to achieve.

     A Devil in Woman's Likeness

"These images serve as windows to something alternative, someplace I would much rather be. Nature is a forest of symbols I pluck from, but I must never debase myself by becoming one with it," he muttered.

Nothing for a few moments. Perhaps he had been too forward in his explanation. His heart pounded, terrified that the beautiful man in the dark with him wouldn't understand, would leave. He realized that was the last thing he wanted. There was something about him, this bohemian, that set Irving off in ways he never wished for. As if the wretched vines of Euryale's garden wrapped their way around his heart and dragged him back down into the soil.

He heard Otto chuckle. "You sound like an art historian," Otto said.

Irving blushed in the dark, embarrassed. Anger welled up in his throat.

Otto continued. "So, Irving Craven, if you hate the natural world so much and everything in it, then why am I in your pictures?" Otto's voice asked.

"Because you confound me! You set me absolutely on edge, and I do not know how to act around you!" Irving yelled. He slapped his hands over his mouth as his voice echoed through the halls. Irving and Otto stood in silence.

"I didn't know I was such a *bother* to you," Otto said.

Irving listened intently: The sounds of hooves clacking up and down the halls. The murmurs of gossipy mythical beings. They would turn Otto over to the gorgon if they found him, but not before having their own fun first.

"I can paint the rest myself, dear Otto. You really must go now," Irving said.

"I was just on my way," Otto said. He turned to Irving. "You're wrong about the natural world, y'know. It's the source of all beauty."

"Beauty is manmade," Irving replied, but Otto had already left.

The cry of a distant seagull cut into Irving's musings of the evening. The thought of Otto consumed him—the eccentric, joyous person who challenged his very ideals of art and life. He watched the darkened City from the Phelan building. Traffic continued to writhe about as cars, horse carriages, and pedestrians swerved around one another in a chaotic fashion. Somewhere down there by the water, a pretty waiter boy stood outside a saloon dressed in a gown, beckoning older men inside in order to make good tips for the night. The fact that Otto did such things excited Irving. He wanted to know more about Otto, he wanted to talk to him again about art, and, he realized, he wanted to apologize.

"Stop looking out the window. Close the curtain," Euryale said.

Irving did so, stepping back into the room where they awaited James. Ornate wallpapers the color of blood surrounded the room. Irving looked around at the clean furniture, the unbroken vases, and a bronze sculpture in the corner: a mother and infant, the mother's arm thrown up in protection with one exposed breast, the same agonized expression on both faces. The room appeared to be what the Presidio Mansion once had been years before the gorgon's encroachment, and Irving couldn't help but feel a spark

  A Devil in Woman's Likeness

of jealousy for Mr. Phelan's comfortable arrangements. Euryale sat under a grand painting of a withering geranium.

"What were you thinking about?" she asked.

Irving looked away. "Absolutely nothing," he said.

Euryale said nothing for a moment, studying him. Irving tried his best not to show any emotion, any hint of Otto in his thoughts.

"You have nothing to worry about, you know. So long as you are with me," she said, and she lifted her veil to let her hair breathe. An array of hisses and cries burst forth as her serpents came into the bright light. The Phelan building was one of few that used electricity, and like many things in the building, it set Irving on edge. Irving kicked at the Turkish rug that lay under his feet and gestured to the bronze mother and child.

"Is that your work?" Irving asked.

Euryale chuckled and stood up beside him. She looked over the sculpture as if they were old acquaintances. Her hand traced over the mother's lips.

"They trespassed into my home years ago, much in the same way you did," she said. "Some new whore of a mother undoubtedly cast off from the Barbary Coast. I found them in the garden taking shelter. The mother was breastfeeding."

Irving could see a look of discomfort, perhaps jealousy, on her face as she said this. She looked more proud than remorseful.

"I couldn't help myself. That act of intimacy, comfort with another being, in my own mansion ..." she said. The gorgon looked over at Irving and squeezed his arm affectionately. "But now I have you." She smiled. Irving felt the stone creep further up his leg as she spoke.

The sound of footsteps echoed down the hallway, and James D. Phelan walked into the room. He retained an air of respectability as he entered, as the Victorian glow of sensibility hung about him like an aura. Irving assumed he was the sort that commanded attention wherever he walked, a man who never accepted the word *no*. But Euryale served as something far more ancient, far more respectable and knowledgeable than any sort of West Coast politician. She had never even heard of the word *no*. James's spirit visibly shrank at the sight of her.

"Firenze," he said. The politician seemed untroubled by the snakes.

"Dearest Jimmy."

"My apologies for not entertaining you more thoroughly last night. The Bohemian Club only has the opportunity to publicly support the arts every so often. Did you enjoy *Carmen*?"

"Opera is for flapdoodles," Euryale sighed. "I'm afraid, dear James, that the City may be expecting unwelcome company soon. I am not the only abnormal thing in this world; you must have come to that conclusion."

James said nothing but glanced over at Irving—the same look as the night before passed between them, ordinary souls caught up in an under-world of expansive proportions.

"There are certainly unseen things on this planet I have come to learn of, such as yourself, but the City will continue on in the way it always has. The crucial element of our survival depends on our collaboration with these unseen forces," he said.

     A Devil in Woman's Likeness

Euryale breathed a sigh of relief and took James's arm. "I am overjoyed to hear you say such a thing, Jimmy. I agree entirely. I came here tonight to make sure the agreement between us was still strong." She looked around the room in haste, catching Irving off guard as she grabbed hold and dragged him in front of Mr. Phelan.

"I have also brought my nephew Irving to offer up as additional collateral if need be. Granted he *is* a bit slow—I have converted part of his leg to stone—but I'm certain he could prove an excellent servant with a little training." She looked Irving up and down, sizing him up. "You could use him for whatever you wanted, like the others."

Mr. Phelan coughed, gently pushing Euryale back. "I thank you for the offer, Mrs. Ellon, but I really must decline," he said. Silence filled the room.

The gorgon took this in, her cheeks flushing a hot purple. "I hope my fears are not to be confirmed."

"You have no need to fear anything."

"Where is she?" Euryale asked.

"Not far," a voice said outside the door.

Irving turned to see a sun-kissed version of Euryale down the hall. She made her way toward them, a femme fatale on the move. A taller, darker, and sleeker woman with snakes black as night and eyes the crisp gold of an afternoon in Athens—she embodied every aspect of the traditional Beardsley figure.

Euryale spat on the Turkish rug. "Stheno," she said.

"Greetings, dear sister," the new gorgon said.

Euryale shot a glare at James, who gave a small jump as she did so. "You two are acquainted?"

James D. Phelan swallowed, trying to find words that so obviously failed him in the moment. He cleared his throat. "Stheno and I met many weeks back and have been discussing future options for San Francisco," he said.

"You mean you met her while scouring the Barbary Coast in secret like you always do, looking for the next hedge-creeper to further defile. Do not listen to this man, dear sister. He is more two-faced than amphisbaenae," Euryale said.

The darker gorgon chuckled. "I've had the opportunity to know James quite thoroughly, both inside and out. I am disappointed, sister, that you have not been more proactive in your business dealings," she said.

"I abandoned the Old World to be left in peace, not revisit old mistakes," Euryale said. She turned to Mr. Phelan. "My privacy for the exchange of the protection of the City—is that what we have not always agreed upon?"

Mr. Phelan looked down at the carpet and shut his eyes a moment as if gathering courage. "The City has not always been protected as you preach. Crime runs rampant in this part of the country, and where you once had the chance to right the wrongs of your criminal past, you have done nothing to stop this community from casting itself further into a life of sin. The earthquakes and fires in the previous century must beg the question as well: What *have* you done to protect the City?" he said.

Euryale looked around the room. "I cannot be responsible for your human crimes and arson," she said, dragging Irving to her side. "I take in drifting youths, help them start a life anew in the

    A Devil in Woman's Likeness

west. Irving's a photographer. We're the best of friends," she added, stroking his face.

Stheno smirked and shook her head. "I have spoken with the fauns in the mansion, dear sister," Stheno said. "You turn them all into stone. Up to your old habits again."

Irving heard Euryale mutter something under her breath about dehorning and punishment.

"Stheno has approached me with an offer I cannot refuse, dear Firenze. The City must engage in further urban reform or follow the ways of Rome," Mr. Phelan said.

"We have a plethora of crime lords and villainous scoundrels running about the coast. What perfect materials for building more robust infrastructure around town!" Stheno said. She smiled sweetly at her sister. "Of course, in order to modernize the entire City, outdated, hazardous infrastructure must be demolished."

Euryale's orange eyes widened. "You will not touch my abode, Stheno," she said.

"Oh, I think I will," Stheno said, wrapping her arm around Mr. Phelan.

"Dear Firenze, the mansion wasn't yours to begin with. My father told me the stories," Mr. Phelan said.

"Oh shut up, you old mumbling cove!" Euryale snapped.

"The Phelan family has provided you with refuge on that military reservation for long enough. We will no longer be tormented by you and your threats, Mrs. Ellon. The witch of Presidio will be no longer," Mr. Phelan said, growing red in the face.

"They believe you to be a witch?" Stheno laughed.

"Humans are abysmally stupid," Euryale said.

"But smart enough to listen to reason." Stheno stroked Mr. Phelan's back. "I think we should expand the First District, honestly," she murmured. "A great deal of deforestation may be in order." She chuckled. The air throughout the room felt tense, and Irving longed to escape.

Euryale breathed heavily. Her serpents hissed in unison. Without thought, she pushed Stheno away and grasped Phelan by the neck, lifting him off his feet. The man cried out as the gorgon plunged her hand down his trousers. The grinding sound of petrification filled the room, and Mr. Phelan screamed. Euryale's snakes hissed in his face, and the poor man turned pale white as she held him up in the air. Irving tripped over his stone limb in shock, terrified at the awesome power of the gorgon. The politician's screams almost ruptured his very eardrums.

Euryale yanked at the man's groin and flung Mr. Phelan aside. He hit the rug next to Irving and whined in a way that reminded Irving of a small, whimpering dog. Above them the gorgon held the stone remains of Mr. Phelans phallus and testes.

"Please!" Mr. Phelan screamed. "Firenze, have mercy!"

Euryale squeezed, and the stone genitals crumbled in her hand. She let the dust fall to the floor in front of the broken man. Mr. Phelan gave out a small whimper.

"I will not be excluded from further plans regarding the City. It is my City, and I intend to rule it however I see fit," Euryale said, her snakes writhing and coiling around her head, energetically hissing and snapping at one another.

"Shutting oneself away does not qualify as rulership. One must rule the mortals with power!" Stheno said impassively, her own snakes silent.

"What do you think I'm doing, dear sister?" Euryale smirked, wiping the last of the dust from her hands. "The last time you did such a thing, a volcano erupted. Not everyone is so dramatic," she said. She grabbed Irving's hand, and he winced at the dust between his fingers.

"Come, Irving. We have no more business here. Mr. Phelan needs space to grieve."

They left the room, Stheno looking on after them, and James crying into the Turkish carpet.

The sheets of cyanotype paper fit under the silver negatives perfectly, pressed between the two glass plates of the modified frames Irving had crafted months back. Otto's blue image began to form in the sunlight, and Irving sighed. The familiar photographic process did little to distract Irving from his putrid thoughts. The things he had seen. The horrid, foul things! The image of Mr. Phelan's crumbling member slipping between the gorgon's fingers. Irving shuddered at the recollection.

Sunlight poured through the broken glass ceiling of the secondary hall and streamed in through hazy beams of various colors. Irving had set only one frame down in the light when he heard a rustling in the foliage. He gave a cry at the sound, turning to see none other than the pretty waiter boy.

"It's only me," Otto said. He held his hands up as if not to scare Irving.

"Otto! You *must* stay away!" Irving exclaimed.

"I see you're still a bit mad," Otto said.

"Do not say such things. *Mad* is such a blunt, ugly word and doesn't at all express how I feel about you," Irving said. He set another frame in the sun, looking around as he did so. Why couldn't Otto just stay away, where it was safe?

"I guess I, well … missed you," Otto said.

Irving wiped his brow, wistfully exhaling into the air and looking above, past the orchids and vines and into Euryale's broken, stained-glass ceiling. Were they watching?

"I came here to escape, to relinquish all my responsibilities and descend into an underworld of vile corruption and madness," he glanced over at Otto, "but then you came into my life."

"What are you saying?"

"My dear fellow, you know exactly what I'm saying. The thoughts I dream around you should be repulsive and insolent, and yet all I feel with you is something … strong and good-natured. Purity."

Otto took a step forward and stroked Irving's face. The dandy held onto the bohemian's hand.

"I'm afraid it's far too late, however. I'm destined for a short life of ruin," he murmured into Otto's hand. A batch of plants moved just beyond them.

"I don't believe that," Otto said. "You don't owe that old crone anything. What's keeping you from going away with me?"

     A Devil in Woman's Likeness

Irving buried his hands in his face, appalled at what he knew he must reveal. He bent down to remove his shoes.

"I must show you something," he said.

Otto watched as Irving slowly began to undress his foot. A gasp escaped him as Irving removed his sock and a podiatric stone made of pure granite graced the interior garden with its dreadful presence. The foot in question remained completely still, and neither man could bear to look at it for long.

"Is it ... is it infected?" Otto asked.

"My dear, it's pure stone. I am being converted into a work of art," Irving said.

"How ... but how could this even be?!" Otto exclaimed.

"There is a whole separate world," Irving began, "a realm which none of us could have ever surmised given our limited experiences. Otto, my darling, I came to this mansion in search of the wickedly divine, and I came upon more than a lad could ever have hoped."

Otto winced, taking a step back. "What are you?" he asked.

"I am a mere witness to the grand forces of the Olden World. My time is limited, but in that span I have been allowed to create art. Such stunning, magnificent art. But when I met you—the *real* you—I saw that all that had come before was a mere fragment in comparison to your form. Your graceful, lean body. The method in which you chew your cheek as you think. The heavenly curls of your hair. Otto, you are what I had wished to become! The purest art that ever was! But I am doomed to exist for the rest of my remaining days as a decrepit, foul, lowly thing. I am a disgusting, worthless being of evil and rot. Worse than the vile slime that creeps along the coast. Art that can never be. Because when I see you, I return to life! I find joy and ... and delight in your presence, and it ruins me! All bad art, all of it in every form, comes from returning to life and nature. You are everything, Otto. And I am nothing."

The pretty waiter boy shook his head. Tears began to form at the corners of his eyes. "I wish you could hear yourself—how wrong you are," he said.

Irving motioned to his leg. "Look at me. Even when I am done, I will never be what you are now at this moment. This ailment is up to my knee, dearest Otto, and I don't believe I will live to see the coming year."

Otto shook his head and took Irving into his arms. Irving flushed at the abrupt motion. The male scent, the near proximity to the divine beauty that this man was. The physical touch of another soul.

"I see so much in you, Irving Craven," Otto said. He smiled, some tragic grin that would have broken the hearts of hundreds of Greek poets or Aphrodite herself. "Maybe I can make you see ..."

Irving felt his mouth touching Otto's own. Tears rolled down his cheeks as the two men embraced and fell into the emerald foliage, creating art amongst the flowers.

"Get up, Craven."

Irving awoke to the darkness of early morning, feeling the warmth of Otto's chest beneath him. A familiar silhouette loomed over both men. Irving heard the hisses and cries of Euryale's hair.

     A Devil in Woman's Likeness

"The fauns told me you were up to malfeasance, but I never would have suspected something of this," she glanced down at Otto's member, "volume."

The bare Otto scrambled back at the sight of the gorgon. Euryale reveled in the sight of the frightened man. Her hair screeched in warning.

"Do you like it here in my little garden?" Euryale asked and laughed. Otto tried to get up, but Euryale snatched the poor man by the ankle and held him upside down. Otto yelled.

"Contain yourself!" Euryale snapped, her serpents nipping at Otto. "I could easily kill you with one glance if I wanted. Is this your new little muse, Craven?"

"Euryale! Stop this at once!" he cried.

The gorgon sneered at Irving, snakes hissing at him. "We agreed, Irving Craven. No outsiders in the Presidio. No one but the two of us!"

"Put him down! You put him down *right now!*" Irving cried out. He desperately tried to pull on Euryale's arm.

"You wanted to be a part of this, Craven!" the gorgon shouted. "I remember taking you in, despite my misgivings. Did our friendship mean nothing to you? I guess not. I see you now for what you are: a misguided fool so self-deluded into believing he wants to take part in the underworld and the putrid actions of the Mythical, that he was led into half-baked beliefs by a series of yellow books and dead poets!"

Irving's nostrils flared, and he clenched his fists. "I *am* abhorrent! Absolutely decadent! I am lowly and frail! It is because of you I have turned into this unfortunate thing!" Irving shouted. He looked over at Otto, still dangling and kicking at the gorgon.

"Please, release him. He is innocent to your unnatural games. There's no need for him to be a part of this," Irving said.

The gorgon looked back at Otto and scoffed. "I hate romance."

"Oh dear, I do hope we're interrupting something," a woman called. At the entryway stood Stheno and Mr. Phelan. The politician's eyes widened as he bore witness to the great gorgon and two naked men, one of them with a leg made of stone and the other hanging upside down.

Otto lashed out with his free leg at Euryale's hand. The gorgon dropped him and hissed as he hit the ground and crawled over to Irving. The two held one another in the presence of false gods.

"Leave be, Stheno!" Euryale called.

The other gorgon chuckled. Irving felt the blood leave his face as she stepped closer, nearer and nearer, like a predator ready to pounce. The hungry sounds of snakes filled the hall.

"We've come to make amends," Stheno said.

"Silence, gibface," Euryale snapped. Irving could hear a low growl emanating from her voice.

"I do mean it, dearest sister. It was your darling Jimmy who convinced me otherwise."

James D. Phelan cowered under Euryale's glare. "Oh, he can do more than shiver and drool?" she asked.

"Now, sister, play nice. I have been thinking since our last encounter. Why separate ourselves when we are stronger

 A Devil in Woman's Likeness

together?" Stheno said, threading her arm around Euryale's. Irving was surprised Euryale let her do so.

"What do you propose?" Euryale asked.

Her sister smirked. "Imagine, dear one: our own country. An authoritarian state without criminal action or nefarious deeds, made up of delinquents of the past. With Jimmy's political ties, your army of fauns, and my devices, we could reign as queens once again," she said. Stheno glanced over at Irving and Otto, and Irving felt Otto's hand tighten around his own. "We can start with these two boys right here," she said.

Euryale remained silent; Stheno gave a wink in their direction. Otto let out a gasp. Irving turned to see Otto's shoulder slowly transforming into a familiar gray. He held himself in anguish.

"Stop! Stop this at once!" Irving yelled, but Stheno only laughed.

Otto screamed, crumbling onto the ground in pain, utterly breaking Irving's heart with his cries. Mr. Phelan simply diverted his glance away from the unfortunate action. Irving glanced around the hall for something, anything, he could perhaps hit Stheno with. Otto's screams grew louder. The conversion of stone quickly spread down his arm. Irving rushed about, frantically search-ing through foliage and bramble. The sounds of Otto's pain only intensified his search.

"It will be over soon, dearest. I think I'll use your head as a nice bust for Jimmy's desk." Stheno laughed.

Irving tore through vines, his fingers bleeding. What could stop a monster? He ripped plants from their roots in his desperate search. There, in the foliage, sat one of the cyanotype frames. Surely a simple frame could do no harm to a gorgon.

But the glass plates. The reflective surface.

Tears ran down Otto's face as he sobbed, watching the palm of his hand transform to granite. "Please!" Otto cried.

Stheno laughed. "This whole City belongs to us now!"

Mr. Phelan turned to his original ally. "Firenze, please. This … this is madness!" he said.

Euryale turned to the politician, a look of disgust on her face. Something changed within her—Irving could see it in those sunset eyes as they turned the color of blood.

"This is not madness, dearest Jimmy. Madness is having lived this life of solitude."

Mr. Phelan took a step back. "What do you mean?"

"I have had the finger of scorn pointed at me all these years in protecting you while you posed before the world as a good and lovable man," she said. Her hair hissed.

James D. Phelan's face turned white, and the gorgon took hold of his throat. "My sister is correct. It is time we change our ways," she said.

The politician joined Otto in his screams, and both sisters gave out terrible laughs, inhuman sounds from an underworld unknown.

Otto watched as the tips of his fingers turned to stone. "Stop!" he choked out through tears.

"Hasten your conversion, sister. I cannot take much more of this one's cries," Euryale said.

"You are always one to cut my fun short," Stheno said. Her glare increased.

   A Devil in Woman's Likeness

A third cry shot out through the botanical hall.

Irving Craven ran toward the gaze of the gorgon, cyanotype plate in hand. The failed dandy held up the reflective surface to Stheno's face in a flash of bravery. The gorgon had hardly time to react. Her gaze met itself in an instant, and her eyes turned to stone, quickly followed by the rest of the body. The counter-conversion only took a matter of seconds before a statue of Stheno stood before them.

"Sister!" Euryale screamed. She rushed over to the new statue, shaking it. "Stheno! Dearest, no!" she cried.

Her sister never responded, sharing the same fate as her thousands of victims. Centuries' worth of pain bubbled up in Euryale's eyes, and lava tears cascaded down her face. Her snakes cried out.

"Why!" she screamed. Irving squeezed Otto's hand—whether to assure Otto or himself he was not certain.

"Another of the greats lost!" Euryale cried. She knelt before her dead sister. The gorgon's sobs echoed throughout the mansion. "You have destroyed my own blood," she said. She looked up at the three men, molten tears in her eyes.

The sight of a mourning gorgon flooded Irving with guilt. He watched Euryale with a strange mixture of pity, anger, and admiration. The light of dawn crept through the broken windows and onto Euryale's pathetic face. She looked into Irving's eyes.

"I only wished to be left alone, but then you came along, and then with my sister ... I believed ..." She cut herself off, looking back to her lost sibling. "I'm not sure." She turned back to Irving. "What have you done?"

The great Florence Ellon, Euryale of old, never spoke after that.

A soft rumbling emanated from below ground, deep within the earth. Otto squeezed Irving's hand as the dirt floor began to shake. The hall surrounding them began to tremble and shiver as the master of geological forces shifted the ground to her will. Around them the great Presidio Mansion shook with immense force. The remaining pillars began to fall.

"Best make haste, boys!" Mr. Phelan yelled as he ran out.

Irving felt Otto's hand tug at him. He looked over at the bohemian and on his cheek felt the touch of stone fingers.

"We need to go," Otto said.

The dandy looked back at his broken master surrounded by crumbling walls, cooling lava pooling on the ground. The last fragment of the underworld.

"The Mythical ..." he whispered.

A tug at his shoulders brought Irving face to face with the pretty waiter boy, who looked into his eyes and smiled.

"You are better than any fantasy, dearest," Otto said, and he covered Irving's mouth with his own in a kiss.

Irving imagined not immense gardens, not lavish mansions of gold and orchids or enticing drops of green absinthe, but pleasant rooms, warm fireplaces, and comfortable libraries, bed sheets in the early morning, laugher in the late nights.

Otto drew back; Irving could only smile. A pillar crashed to the ground right beside them.

"Follow me!" Irving Craven shouted, and he led Otto Flynn through the ruined halls as the ground continued to shake. He looked back once more to see the glass shattering above, fauns

     A Devil in Woman's Likeness

running for their lives, and massive stones crashing around the gorgon as she cried out in grief. The ancient woman's sorrow spread out from the forest and ran through the City's streets with a thunderous charge: buildings toppling over one another, the cries of civilians ringing throughout the land, and fires igniting the sky like Vesuvius before. The seacoast of decadence collapsed in a destructive finale, Irving could only smile as he ran, holding the stone hand of the man he had undoubtedly fallen in love with.

Afterword

To this day I cannot get the order of these ten (now eleven!) stories right. I've tried listing them out without double-checking myself numerous times, but there's always one or two that get misplaced in my mind. They always manage to get shuffled in my brain.

Like the threads the Ouliponites ride across realities in "The Way Things Were," the stories in this collection are interconnected if you take a closer look. Characters pop up in unexpected places, forcing you to return to stories (only to find they have been joined at the hip from the start). Sometimes returning characters aren't the same as you last encountered them; this is a book about the multiverse, after all.

In this afterward, I want to give you a little bit of insight into each story. Growing up, I always watched the "bonus content" DVDs to see the "making of" featurettes. I wanted to learn how movies worked behind the scenes. This is like that, in a sense. Enjoy these featurettes …

Bubbler Man

Everyone loves this story. I wrote it in fifteen minutes. Maddening! I've talked with a number of artist friends and we all seem to have that one piece of work that just came to us in no time at all, like Shirley Jackson when she wrote "The Lottery." Everyone just raves about it.

I wrote this story in 2015, after completing another short story called "Alder Underground" for Gigi Little's *City of Weird* anthology (in this collection it's titled "Lowline"). Several test-readers told me they didn't like "Alder," that it wasn't any good and that Portlanders wouldn't like hearing about their city in such a negative light. So in a panic, I wrote "Bubbler Man," and I ended up submitting "Alder Underground" anyway. I'm glad "Bubbler Man" found a home in *Moss-Covered Claws*. Whenever I'm doing a reading and I read something dark ("Hole Wall" for example) I try to end things on a lighter note, with the whimsical, optimistic tale of an oxidized-bronze man named Simon (named after the philanthropist who had the real-life bubblers installed, Simon Benson).

Boggy

Most kids have an imaginary friend. I, however, had an imaginary cryptid. I hesitate to call it a "monster" because I had those too, but those were different. A childhood spent reading-up on cryptozoological lore led to a lifelong fear of lakes, and before I knew it, I had convinced myself that a prehistoric creature, the *Tanystropheus conspicuus*, for all you paleo-nerds out there, was living in the peat bog near my house.

Like "Nessie" and "Ogopogo," I decided to give my creature its own adorable name. "Boggy" seemed obvious. The story itself is a love-letter to those golden afternoons of my childhood picking blackberries and getting lost in the brambles. In 2021, my creative team and I teamed up with local puppet troupe String and Shadow to perform a single-night event. During the event, actors Alice Rosewater and Mandy Ryle acted out this story alongside a life-sized Boggy puppet helmed by Luz Gaxiola.

Moss-Covered Claws came out one year after Covid first hit the U.S., and because of that, I never really got to hold a big, in-person launch event to celebrate (although the virtual one Tina threw me was just darling, I have to say). This puppet event, "*Moss-Covered Claws: Live From a Pond*," was my first public, in-person event for my book. And might I just say, it was an absolute splash! Watch the "Boggy" recording at: youtu.be/D9U9o_sTmZY

Acts of Violence

From age seven to thirteen I attended a Catholic school, despite being an unbaptized heathen. I was bullied for this in fourth grade—with kids saying over and over, "Jonah's going to

Hell! Jonah's going to Hell!" In retrospect, what a compliment! But at the time I was mortified to be different from the others. None of us ever beat each other up, though. A few friends have told me the level of violence in the story is pretty accurate to that of their own schools.

The internalized-homophobia I experienced in middle school isn't the only thing going on in "Acts." One of the main jumping points from this story was my own harrowing experience with sleep paralysis. Most folks who live through this terrifying experience—waking up before having any control over your body—report strange figures, little sleep paralysis demons and night hags who sit on your stomach, staring at the victim while they can do nothing but stare back. My sleep paralysis demon was hidden from me—I sleep on my stomach.

Imagine waking up and feeling something on your back. It studies you, sniffing you over, deciding what to do with you ... I thought I'd work this into a story a few years ago.

The conversation the "Fairy Godmother" and Dal have was heavily inspired by a series of Alan Watts lectures I was listening to at the time. I could fall asleep to Alan Watts; his voice is so comforting. His words, though, hit different when an eight-foot arthropod creature is speaking them into my ear, against my will.

Lowline

This was the first story of mine to ever get physically published in a book. "Lowline" appeared in 2016's *City of Weird*, hand-picked by the editor, Gigi Little, herself. I spent months on the initial draft. When I submitted the story, I secretly expected it to get rejected.

     Moss-Covered Claws

Fate, and Gigi, had other plans. A version of this story was included under the title "Alder Underground."

"Lowline" mostly draws inspiration from the daycations to Portland I went on while growing up (and continue to go on, honestly). But this story is also based on an experiment in New York called the Lowline Project. The Lowline Project was an initiative to convert an abandoned trolley system into a lush underground park using solar technology, which was completely hypothetical when I wrote the story. Since *City of Weird*, the Lowline Project opened a "test run" in an abandoned supermarket. It was called the Lowline Lab. While the Lowline Lab was successful and gained support, it closed down in 2017. Funding for a much bigger trolley project also fell short in February 2020.

In case you can't tell, "Lowline" reads like a transcription of posts from a Tumblr blog. (Are you at all surprised I was a Tumblr kid?) A lot of weird fiction from the early days was written in the epistolary format, usually in the form of "found journals." The modern-day version (or at least the 2015 version) seemed like it would be something akin to liveblogging. Maybe today Danny would be livestreaming on TikTok. Everything's!! Going!! Too fast!!

Hole Wall

This is based on something that really happened. No, I did not kill a pelican. Samantha Breaux, the illustrator of this collection and also my best friend, did get stuck in an empty internet port. We were staying with our friend Cecelia Meade near Astoria, Oregon. We had been drinking and late-night discussing God-knows-what, when finally, as we were ready to turn in, Sam spoke up and said: "Um, so … I need help, actually, everyone." She had absent-mindedly fingered this hole in the wall—because she's a gigantic lesbian—and had been trying to discreetly wriggle her way out the entire time (She was under a blanket, hence why we didn't notice.)

The next half-hour involved us pulling, twisting, and lubricating her finger with peanut butter, trying to wedge it out with a kitchen knife. We finally destroyed the plastic casing with some heavy-duty cutters. I made sure to document the whole situation all on Snapchat, like any good best friend would. Sam survived the ordeal unscathed, except for her pride.

Regarding the pelican scenes, because everyone comments on them after they read the story: I wanted to describe something terrible. This was me taking an intrusive thought a little further. It's a difficult process to imagine hurting another being, especially one so obviously innocent. I had to take a long break after writing that scene. The pelican's death draws from Coleridge's "The Rime of the Ancient Mariner," and if you look closely, you can see where I've scattered a few lines and elements from the poem throughout the story. There's also a draugr ship.

The Sea Cottage

This was the first story I wrote, back in 2011, when I was a senior in high school. I'd never written a short story before, at least not one I was proud of. I remember scrolling through Tumblr saving pictures I wanted to use for inspiration for this story. I still have that folder. There are seagulls and atriums and dinosaur skeletons and blue dresses and Ben Wishaw and even an illustration of a sea witch performing a spell on the beach. What more directly inspired this story was Ruby Beach off the Washington Coast, the

     Moss-Covered Claws

location where we filmed part of the book trailer for *Moss-Covered Claws*. Watch the book trailer at: youtu.be/xiPK-Vyru-I

The initial draft of this story has a happy ending, and upon rewriting it for this collection, I found myself ending things on a more somber, realistic note. The boy in the story (who turns out to be Jaime Craven from "Acts of Violence") originally left the sea witch with a heart full of optimism, confident he could take on whatever challenge life threw at him in the future. I like how the story ends now ten times better than before. Jaime's problems are not instantly fixed, and he doesn't know what's going to happen. He can only start to do the work of healing and hope for the best, which I think is a much truer reflection of the healing process.

Stripes

I wrote this story in the midst of a toxic relationship. I used to cling to someone who didn't know how to love other people, or at least claimed not to know. The distance they put between us drove my anxiety up the wall, and I would text them over and over again in hopes they'd respond so I could get a small hit of serotonin from their words. Yikes.

The original ending included Megan actually saving Sil from the demon. My beta-readers disliked this ending. "She needs to kill the monster herself," they said. "Not have her crappy girlfriend come in at the last minute and save the day." Alas, the relationship ended, and I saw that my beta readers were right.

As an aside, the demon in this tale (who terrorizes Syl) doesn't have a name in the story. But, she's none other than a character from my feature film, *Booger*. Her name is Jerusha Pachad and in *Booger*, her character is portrayed by the fantastic Kaitlyn Orchard.

Jerusha is one of my favorite characters I've ever written. I have a feeling we aren't done with each other. Watch the *Booger* feature at: youtu.be/bzjRt8sogoY

Warmonger

I consider "Warmonger" and "The Way Things Were" to be my "political" stories. I wanted to try writing high fantasy—a world completely separate from our own. I found writing a high-fantasy setting much easier to get political in. If I got something wrong about how the governmental system works, then guess what? It couldn't be wrong! I made it all up, baby!

I wrote this story during the 2020 quarantine, when tensions were still high about the upcoming election. I channeled my frustration into this story, trying to see things from a neoliberal point of view, as someone who just wanted things to "return to normal" though our dying world has so obviously signified, time and time again, that "normal" never actually worked anyway.

This was also the last story I wrote for the collection. "Low-line" was going to be in the first edition of *Moss-Covered Claws*, but I happily sacrificed it. "Warmonger" took its spot. My poor, poor publisher had to deal with this dick move I pulled. "I know we're deep into the developmental editing stage … but what if we swapped out one story for this new one I just wrote?"

The Way Things Were

One of my early readers, Karielle Jackson, told me this story seemed "very LeGuin-y" to her. I had no idea what she was talking about. I initially wrote it for an antifascist anthology, but it didn't

     Moss-Covered Claws

make the cut. A year later, when Susan DeFreitas was putting together her Ursula K. Le Guin tribute anthology, *Dispatches From Anarres*, I thought I might submit on a whim, especially after remembering what Karielle had said. This time, the story did make the cut. Today, I'm still so honored to be part of a volume of work that honors my favorite author.

The version of "The Way Things Were" included in this collection is an expanded version, with added segments of news interviews with Paige Woods and Dr. Carthorn. And, years after I wrote this story, when I read Le Guin's *The Dispossessed,* I had the weirdest sense of déjà vu with a scene involving intense violence at a public event and a helicopter. (I think it was a helicopter. It's been a few years.) Le Guin's scene felt like my climactic scene from "The Way Things Were"! But I had never read *The Dispossessed* before. How did this happen?! My hero and I both drew from the same lake of thought, and I am honored.

Snow Thing

This takes place in the same high-fantasy world as "Warmonger," although it shares more similarities with "Acts of Violence," really. It's secretly about the same time in my life, when I was in love with my male best friend and constantly tried to invent new ways to get closer to him. My efforts were borderline obsessive. But really, who hasn't stared at their sleeping unrequited love in the dark while "Here (In Your Arms)" by Hellogoodbye plays in your head? No? Just me?

A Devil in Woman's Likeness

I had such a wonderful time researching this story. From the gorgons of Greek mythology to the San Francisco earthquake of 1906. I learned of the Decadent writers and artists who came before me. Not just Oscar Wilde, but Aubrey Beardsley, Arthur Symons, Lord Alfred Douglas, and the other scribes of *The Yellow Book* of the 1890's that dabbled in the delicious sins of queer pleasure. ("A Devil in Woman's Likeness" is the name of an artwork by Beardsley, believe it or not. I almost didn't go with it as a title.)

Florence Ellon and James D. Phelan were real people, and I hope their ghosts don't mind that I've borrowed their identities for this work of fiction. They knew each other in real life, those two. Mrs. Ellon was Phelan's mistress of forty-two years, and he really was the (former) mayor of San Fran when the great earthquake hit. It wasn't always candy and rainbows with these scandalous lovers, as I pulled a quote from the real Florence Ellon and put it right into Euryale's mouth: "I have had the finger of scorn pointed at me all these years in protecting you while you posed before the world and a good and lovable man." Poor Florence. I wonder if she'd find solace knowing that over a hundred years later, she has power in a story where she is a fierce, complex force of nature who castrates ol' Jimmy.

I dedicated this book to two people: my husband and my best friend. But Florence can be the third. I'm dedicating the final story to you, dear Firenze. May your spirit grow in power each time a gorgon is mentioned.

     Moss-Covered Claws

Now, it is late as I write this, but I wanted to share one final thing. On the night before this book's virtual launch (it was peak quarantine times, after all) I was having a hard time figuring out the right way to say, "Thank you," to everyone who supported me during the creation of *Moss-Covered Claws*. This suddenly poured out, prompted by a childhood dream. The whole virtual book launch the following day was wonderful. I wore a pair of antlers and about thirty people came to celebrate my debut book with me. I read the following words at the very end of the launch. And I swear, although maybe they'd deny it today, my publisher Christina Vega cried a little during my reading. The following is not great or anything, but it's a nice little raw treat. There are hints of "Bubbler Man" and "Boggy" in there, as well, if you squint hard enough. You'll see. Here we go.

Something More Personal

I remember a boy who turned out not to be a boy, who at age four drew tales of hairy little monsters skulking around in trees. They blended in with young saplings, alders with sharp horns on their heads and sharper teeth in their mouths. The boy watched the alders as they drove past each day, swearing he saw them through the trees. They stared out at him. I remember pictures of these monsters, these nameless things, drawn in ballpoint. I remember not telling anyone.

How do you say "thank you" when those words sound so puny in comparison to what's inside? How do you convey your thoughts when you're not used to talking?

Jonah Barnett

"You deflect," Tina says. We stand in their cold office going over the outline of the someday book. No one knows what a virus is. "You think these characters are you and you're holding back. I want to see more of yourself in these fictional people."

But how do you put more of yourself in when you don't know if you even like who you are?

"That's another thing I noticed," they cut in. "The theme is depression."

You need to get this stuff out. It's foggy in the alders. The air is that certain color your publisher told you to find other words for. ("Why do you use the word 'white' all the time, homey?") Maybe if you move slowly the monsters won't see you, but you know that's shit. Everyone is watching.

God, just scream. Yell out thanks and gratitude and get it over with. But you cannot. You want to convey it in the right way. It never comes out right when you say it. They poke their heads out from behind the trees, inching closer. Eyes are pure void, or maybe it's creepier if they have pupils. It's always scary when the thing hunting you has a personality.

If you don't shout it out now you never will. Maybe you can send follow-up emails that say dumb shit like, "Thanks for believing in me <3," but they're not the same.

The monsters loom over you at this point.

"Just scream it out, baby!" Publisher Mama says, their words echo through the woods, cuz why not.

So you finally say

    Not in a scream

     Moss-Covered Claws

Not in a whisper

Just regular talking

Something like

"I can't believe it. I just cannot believe it. I mean I can. But barely. I mean … No, I can't believe it. I can't fathom how so many people reached up to support me, me, when I asked for help. I don't know how it's possible that there are people in this world with such love, such kindness, that they help me create a book of my own. That they ask for, and purchase, a book of my own. That they log-on as the world burns for a whole year just to celebrate me, as if they're making a small candle flicker in this deep deadly dark. I can't believe I did all this. Writing. Filmmaking. Cover design. Preorder perks. Letterpress printing. Marketing. Goddamn distribution. Live puppetry. Audio recordings. Zoom events. The works. Every last second of one and a half years leading to this moment of … I can't believe it."

I remember looking up at the things with horns. They just stand there now, arms outreached.

"I can't believe it. Thank you."

And they wrap their arms around me, pick me up, and carry me off into the gray mist.

(Thanks everyone.)

Acknowledgments

I am the absolute hugest believer in collaboration; ask any of the dozens of folks I've roped onto my film sets. I don't believe writing is as solitary as people say either. Really, if it weren't for the following people these stories would just be scribbles in a notebook.

First off, like obviously, a BIG thank you to Christina Vega: the most badass human I have ever met. You're the dearest friend who always supports me and gives the best hugs. You're one of the best parts of my life, and I hope we get to make art together in all forms until the end of time. Tina, you are literally the motherfucking best.

I want to thank my best friend Samantha Breaux. You always bring my stories to life with your artwork, as proven by the cover. Thanks for being my soulmate in this sad little world, you gay-ass nerd.

Dear Austin, my Number One Fan and half of my heart. You have no idea how loved I feel when your face lights up as you read my work. I have never felt more supported. I love you with my entire being. Live on a farm with me already, we'll get pigs.

Thank you to Genevieve Glassy, my creator and origin of all my best parts, who taught me what it means to be creative. You get the biggest thanks. One-thousand adores. (I'm sorry I don't write nice stories, though!)

Cecilia Meade, thanks for weathering the "we don't have MFA's" storm with me and guiding me through the twists and turns of creating a story. You're always down for anything, with that oh-so-rare "What's next??" attitude.

Karielle Jackson, my first and dearest editor, my TROPHY WIFE. You taught me how to analyze prose and I always turn to you when I need the most thoughtful feedback. Your story notes could be published into essays they're so fun to read. Okay, maybe not essays but they're still fun.

Thank you SO MUCH to Laura Stanfill and Gigi Little: the Forest Avenue Press dream team. What started as a simple selection of "Alder Underground" blossomed into years of coffee talks, on-camera interviews, endorsing and forwarding my work, and so much love and mentorship from both of you. I would like to especially thank you for helping us get this new edition of *Moss-Covered Claws* out into the world. It feels really good to have a wonderful team of people behind you. I love you guys.

Thank you Jackie Casella, for choosing my short story "Shell of a Mom" and publishing it on Creative Colloquy back in 2014. I was still in college then, freshly dumped, and I needed something to pull me back up. Getting published for the first time certainly did the trick. Thank you for all your support and love over the years (and for being on *Wordsmiths* too!).

To Kelsey Smith, you're the person who started it all. No, really. If you hadn't posted that ad for *City of Weird*'s call for submissions I would have never met Gigi and I would have never met Laura and I never would have met Valerie and I would have never adsjfhasdjkfhasdljkfhl … You have no idea how much of a secret impact you've made upon this writer's life. Thank you, Library Mama.

A huge thanks to the fantastic team behind the book trailer/film we made for this: Cody Castillo, Fiona Vogel, Genevieve (again!), Christian Carpenter, and Mae Deetz. Y'all really brought it for this one. I really have the best gang.

Thank you to Kristen Hall for surviving my 1,000 unnecessary commas and making me laugh as we cleaned these stories up.

Adrienne Rustwood! Thank you for helping us put the final polish on things, and teaching me about which species of orchids should go in Euryale's garden.

To Kate Threat: you deserve a huge-ass trophy for putting up with me during the pre order campaign. Plus, we put on that great fundraiser! Thank you thank you!!

My fundraiser readers (and performers!): Logan Fenner, Daniel Wolfert, Cecelia Meade (again!), and Alissa Tu—that was such a fun-ass event we put on. I think it was the one time I actually enjoyed a Zoom call.

Sam Tait: You designed such a gorgeous initial cover with the art my Sam gave you. The *Moss-Covered Claws* cover, created by Sam and Sam. Chef's kiss.

Knic Pfost: Thank you for doing the layout on this! And thank you for being flexible with my last minute additions (including these very acknowledgements).

Thank you so much to the wonderful authors who blurbed and endorsed my book! I still get butterflies when I think about the cool people who said "Yes" to endorsing this thing.

I also want to thank these rad peeps, who were my readers and editors and survey-takers over the years: Wyatt Gaer, Jacob Earl, Hilary Helton/Averil Dean, Bry Troyer, Susan Defrietas, Beth Cook, Daniel Valdez, Ian Rust, Indy Prince, Amber Sayman, Tanya Tran, Rachel Millena Saul, Jameson Doane, Nicholas Price, Zoe Wright, Marck Wilder, Sam Snoek Brown, and probably someone I am forgetting.

Thank you a million to my awesome team behind the *Moss-Covered Claws: Live From a Pond* show. We fuckin' killed it and made a magical night in this dark timeline: Alice Rosewater, Mandy Ryle, Austin Barnett (again!), Luz Gaxiola, Donald Palardy III, Emily McHugh, and Jessica, Scott, and Gwynn Babcock!

And oh gosh, thank you to everyone who pre ordered this book in November 2020. Doing a Kickstarter during election season in the midst of a pandemic and still reaching our $4,000 goal? It's magic, that's all there is. As soon as we made it I got into the car with Sam Breaux, drove through Taco Bell, and screamed relief into the Pacific Ocean while eating my burrito.

     Moss-Covered Claws

tinyurl.com/mossyclaws

READERS' GUIDE

1. Did you actually read this book? Kidding! Okay not really. Oftentimes, we don't finish a book before showing up to reading groups to talk about them. If you didn't finish the book, why not? If you did, did you consider stopping before finishing it? Why? And what made you decide to change your mind?

2. How uncomfortable were you while reading this book? If you weren't uncomfortable, what aspects resonated with you?

3. In case you didn't notice, there's a bit of comedy in each of these tales. Some might even call Jonah's humor to be a coping mechanism. What purpose (if any) do you think humor serves in these stories?

4. What rating would you give this book on Letterboxd.com? If you don't know what that is, it's okay, neither do we (Jonah is cackling in the corner as I type this). What rating would you give this book on Goodreads?

5. If you were a monster, what kind of monster would you be (your perceived self)? What kind of monster might your friends see you as (your real self)?

6. Do you even have friends? Joking. Okay we're not. You see, we don't have any friends. So, you know, add me on Snap.

7. Who was your last disaster gay-crush? What went wrong? What if a monster (besides you!) had been thrown into the mix? How might that have changed your relationship?

8. Some people categorize this book as horror, while others feel it's science fiction, fantasy, or LGBTQ+. ("It's good,

   Moss-Covered Claws

but it's not really scary …" someone said to Jonah at a party once.) How would you categorize this book?

9. If you answered the last question with "horror," tell us, does a story have to be scary to be categorized as horror, or are there other emotions involved in the reader's experience?

10. What purpose do stories set in alternate realities serve in our (human) world (planet earth)? We hate to be total brats, but we still have to know: is setting a story in a fictional reality the literary equivalent of burying our heads in the sand? How so?

11. The monsters in this book are mostly metaphors. Kind of … Either way, choose a story and explain what you think the monster in the story is a metaphor for.

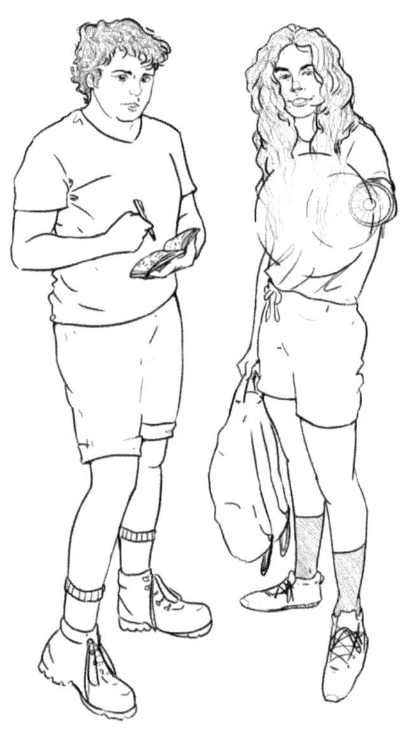

Step into the digital swamps of *Moss-Covered Claws* at bluecactuspress.com. The MCC book pages include a playlist, short film, and more behind-the-scenes extravaganzas.

About the Creators

Jonah Barnett is a filmmaker, writer, and multimedia artist. They have been published in the Forest Avenue Press collections *Dispatches From Anarres* and *City of Weird*. Jonah has directed and written three feature films, a dozen-ish short films, and four web series—with their film work being presented at the Olympia Film Society, Northwest Film Forum, and Trans Stellar Film Festival. They usually find themself exploring old haunted buildings or overgrown swamps with Samantha.

LinkTree: linktr.ee/JonahBarnett

Insta: @maliciouswallydrags

Facebook: @wallydrags

Youtube: @lazyeyesinc

Samantha Breaux is a German-Panamanian artist with degrees in microbiology and pharmaceutical sciences. She incorporates her passion for animals and nature into her work, oftentimes with a dark, cheeky twist. Her free time is often spent playing video games, creating her own computer, and exploring hidden coves or ruined power plants with Jonah.

Insta: @heckboi

About the Press

Blue Cactus Press is an independent and hybrid publisher. Our mission is to craft books that serve as community resources and tools, written and made by people from historically marginalized groups.

We envision a world in which books empower & celebrate communities we walk in. We strive to implement equitable business models that center collective liberation as the rule, not the exception, and offer makers dignity, autonomy, and creative voice in our practices. We work toward a future in which our planet is prioritized over profit and publishing practices are accessible and gate-free.

We seek creatively satisfying, financially viable, and relationally resonant work. We value curiosity, craftsmanship, and relational responsibility among humans, our environment, and other living organisms.

To support the press, please request our books at libraries, become a member at patreon.com/bluecactuspress, and/or purchase our books at bluecactuspress.com.

Hello, Dear Reader,

Welcome to the back of the book. You are a devout reader, indeed, if you've made it this far and are willing to indulge me by reading this note. I'd like to take a moment to say thank you, so very much, for purchasing this delightfully monstrous little book by Jonah Barnett, and for supporting independent publishing.

Moss-Covered Claws would not have been possible without the wide and continuous backing of readers and writers like you, who heard Blue Cactus Press' call for support as we launched a Kickstarter campaign to fund this book amid a worldwide pandemic, political and civil unrest on a national level, and a forever-quarantine in Washington state. To each and every one of you: thank you for supporting the press and the publication of this book. More importantly, thank you for showing your support for our tender, devious, and anxiety-riddled author, Jonah Barnett. Jonah is a phenomenal writer and an even better friend, and we are so excited to be on this literary journey with them (and you).

We hope you enjoyed each story in *Moss-Covered Claws*. If you didn't, you probably have no soul or sense of humor and we invite you to burn this book for vindication as you crouch over a camp-fire, lost and wet, somewhere deep in the dreary woods of western Washington. May monsters visit your campsite while you sleep.

If you did enjoy the book, please let us know! We'd love to connect with you on social media @BlueCactusPress or on our website at bluecactuspress.com. We can't wait to hear your story.

Christina Vega,
Publisher | Blue Cactus Press

9 798987 335246